GW01451740

WU LOU

A NOVEL

LU XINHUA

TRANSLATED FROM THE CHINESE *by* CAPELLA CAO

This book is a work of fiction. Any references to historical events, people, or places are used ficti-tiously. Other names, characters, places, and events are products of the author's imagination, and any resemblance to actual persons, places or events is entirely coincidental.

Pine Bush Publishing, Inc.
Copyright © 2024 by Lu Xinhua
English translation copyright © 2024 by Capella Cao

All rights reserved. This book or any portion thereof may not be reproduced or used in any form or by any means whatsoever without prior written permission from the publisher except for the use of brief quotations in a book review.

Paperback ISBN: 978-1-960172-08-2
eBook ISBN: 978-1-960172-09-9
Library of Congress Control Number: 2024942113

Cover design by Richard Ljoenes
Interior design by KUHN Design Group | kuhndesigngroup.com

Printed in the United States of America
First Printing

Pine Bush Publishing, Inc.
350 Northern Blvd, Ste 324
Albany, NY 12204

https://www.pinebushbooks.com/

OPENING

Deep in the dense forest, the gloomy daylight and the whirling tree shadows were all over the place.

The cicadas on the cottonwood trees were endlessly raucous, the mountain streams were rambling unhurriedly, and the small temple hidden under the tall banyan tree was serene, peaceful, and uncontested with the world.

As small as the temple was, it had a tiny, square courtyard with a potholed brick pavement, so mossy and slippery that people often fell on their backs if they were not careful.

However, no one expected that one day someone would fall on his back in the Buddha Hall behind the courtyard while embracing a jade Buddha statue, which was a head taller than a real person.

That was exactly the scene at the moment: Tutu was covered in blood, her hands and her face bloodstained. Frightenedly, she opened her bloodshot eyes, which slightly distorted her persimmon-like plump face. What the hell just happened? Her fiancé, a young officer of the Khmer Rouge, who was so vivid and handsome, bold, and determined, who spoke in a tone as unflinching as the mountains, was suddenly smashed to death without any warning, without even having time to leave her a single word.

She turned around and saw Master Wu Lou, whom she had always treated as her own brother, standing behind her.

"How did this happen? How?" She raised her hand to rub her eyes, again and again, opening and closing them, unable to believe that what she saw was real. The man she had known so well was now lying in front of her on the ground, his body covered with blood, his head cracked open by the Buddha statue. The Buddha statue, which she had spent so much time with, revealed its true white jade inside after its head was peeled off its clay exterior under the massive force.

"Brother, what—what's going on here? Are we in a dream?" She opened her arms as if to pull away the nightmare chained around her neck or to catch the indistinct past; yet, in the end, all she could grasp was her brother's flimsy clothes and thin shoulders.

"Brother—" she cried again before she went blank and passed out in his arms.

She was soon awakened by the caws of several crows in the banyan tree, just as their cawing had presaged a bloodbath before.

She opened her eyes and saw Wu Lou, whom she affectionately called "Brother" due to their shared upbringing after he and his master had taken her in as an orphan. Now the sole head monk of the small temple and her savior, the man she had hoped to be with forever appeared lost and despondent. He held her shoulders and body with one hand and stroked her head with the other. His body was trembling uncontrollably, and his lips wriggled, but he could not utter a word. Since the old master passed away, this was the first time Tutu had seen her omnipotent brother as panicked as she was, frightened, confused, and helpless ...

He must have felt deep disappointment and remorse in that help-lessness, for he had, after all, committed a "killing"—albeit uninten-tionally. This was a great sin for a monk who normally wouldn't even swat ants, flies, or mosquitoes. Moreover, what he aimed to practice was Anāsrava, the "dharma of non-leakage," hoping to achieve "eter-nal freedom from all leaks," a state of being free from defilements that bind beings to suffering. But now, as far as she knew about Buddhism, he seemed to have not only leaked but also broken the precepts...

"Brother, I'm scared," she said, as she tightened her arms around his waist and buried her head deeper into his chest, not bearing to take another look at the man from China lying on the ground, the man she had already committed herself to in the heat of her passion. Nor did she dare to meet the eyes of Wu Lou, the man she admired and adored, for whom her feelings had grown beyond the bounds of their upbringing together. She once believed they would have been the most beautiful couple in the world if he hadn't been so determined to walk the path of cultivation and seeking. But then, miraculously, Wu Huaiyu, a boy from Guangxi, China, appeared in her life. She was originally willing to interact with him out of the impulse to protect her brother. They had no one to turn to. Many monks were dispersed, and some were even arrested, so to know someone from the Khmer Rouge, especially an officer, of course, would help them more or less; at the very least, in case they got into trouble, there was someone who could put in a couple of good words for them. Of course, she was being petty as well. Since Wu Lou was determined not to marry her, she wanted to upset him. But who would have known? She slowly became fond of this guy from China. She thought that although he bore little resemblance to Wu Lou, with much fairer skin, in many other respects they were similar; both were ambitious and idealistic, fully dedicating themselves to their chosen paths, unswayable once their minds were set. Gradually, she found herself discomposed.

But now, his dexterous hands, his well-defined lips, his eyes that "talked" to you, and his ever-cheerful and uplifting voice and smile, all these had been mercilessly shattered and brutally crushed, leaving only memories that were no longer true in retrospect and the bloody reality in front of her eyes...

"What to do? What to do?" she thought, and finally broke out of his arms, turned around, took a few steps forward, bent down, and pressed her hand against the Buddha's head, as if trying to lift it off. But it was futile; the statue didn't budge. Now, up close, she clearly saw his unrecognizable face and the large pool of blood on the ground. Suddenly, the nightmarish memories of her parents lying in a pool of blood revived in her mind like a flash of lightning; she couldn't bear it and let out a scream, fainting once again.

Seeing this, Wu Lou hurriedly took a step forward and caught her.

· · ·

Later, in a daze, she heard the wind outside, howling faster and faster, and soon turned into the trampling steps of an army.

"No!" She awoke abruptly, fiercely broke out of his embrace, and shrieked at her brother Wu Lou, "Why are you so foolish? Why don't you run yet?"

"Run? Why should I run? It's not like I have—"

"Don't be naive. No one will believe you. I know these people; they have been looking for an excuse to get at you! It's not like you don't know how many people have died for no reason since they took power."

He began to panic a bit. "But it's their world now. Even if I wanted to run away, where could I go?"

"First to Thailand, then to the United States. I've heard that they accept Cambodian refugees. You have relatives who worked in the Lon Nol government."

"What about—what about you?"

"I have to stay."

"Not an option. If we leave, we leave together. Otherwise—"

"Otherwise what? Don't worry about me. I'm young; they won't do anything to me. Their battalion commander likes me too, and I'll explain everything clearly to them."

"But..." Wu Lou didn't know what else to say.

"Hurry up and leave. Once their troopers come, you won't be able to get away."

"You..." He still hesitated.

"Stop shilly-shallying. Listen to me, I'll be fine. After I take care of everything, I'll find a way to go to the United States to find you."

* * *

She looked around nervously for a while before sending him off through the temple gate, then ran towards him again and hugged and kissed him goodbye under the banyan tree in front of the door.

He finally left, walking away with frequent lingering looks back at her.

Grayish-white kasaya, long pants, straw sandals, towering kapok trees.

In the sunset, the trees were red, the leaves were red, and the fallen petals were also red.

There were no other paths through the woods; the narrow trail stretching into the distance was like a red carpet spreading toward the horizon, or like a winding stream flowing with blood. He walked on the scarlet, like a staggering bird with broken wings or a fish desperately struggling out of the bloodied water.

Redness, a never-ending redness stretching far into the distance.

Life emerges from redness, and it seemed that, inevitably, life must return to it in the end.

CHAPTER 1

This is a thrilling scene that took place in the Cambodian jungle many years ago.

Nearly half a century later, it began to frequently appear in my mind and dreams. Although the fine details often blur, the intense stench of blood at the scene remains the same.

Perhaps humans do indeed have past and future lives, reincarnating across different countries and species.

Master Wu Lou, later known as Miller, might be such a presence for me.

But recently, I often find myself pondering: "Why did I come to know Miller or Wu Lou? What is the significance of our acquaintance?"

Through the years, having experienced many betrayals and deceits, I've often been pessimistic about history and reality, and at times, I've been deeply disappointed or even despairing about human nature.

But Miller was different; it was a special experience with him, so much so that I often dream of him now.

The feelings he gives me in my dreams are also unique; sometimes, he appears as a crystal-clear ice sculpture dripping with water, and sometimes he runs barefoot through the jungle, or sits at a casino card table, laughing.

We first encountered each other at the Commerce Casino in Los Angeles. At that time, I was a card dealer, and he was a player at my table. I flicked numerous cards to him, and he tipped me generously.

Years after I left the casino, we ran into each other again at the Cypress Flea Market. But our roles had reversed by then: he was a vendor in the market, and I was his customer. He sold me green bamboo, iron begonias, and manuka bush, among other things, and I paid him cash.

It is often said that it takes a hundred years of practicing virtuous deeds for people to share a boat crossing.

I sometimes wonder if the reincarnating encounters between the two of us could span at least three hundred years.

While the past, like water, is submerging my heart, I can vaguely see him wobbling and shivering in an ice-cold stream, his round, chubby face, dark, spongy hands, and the mutilated little finger on his left hand.

I ran into him five years ago when my wife and I visited a flea market about thirty kilometers from home.

We had just bought a three-story villa on a hillside. The house felt a bit dated, with old-fashioned steel-framed windows and concrete stairs covered with a thin layer of carpet that was tough on the feet. Black, yellow, and even dark red were visible on the edges and corners of the freshly but carelessly painted walls. On the other hand, the backyard was huge, nearly half an acre in size and perfectly rectangular—ideal except for the sloping hillside that made holding water impossible;

only indescribable wild grasses that looked like edible vegetables grew there. We initially thought they were mustard greens and were thrilled at the prospect of having free ingredients for our mustard green wontons right from our backyard. But in no time, the greens shot up to waist height, with furry little thorns all over. Disappointed, my wife wondered whether it could be rapeseed. I shook my head. "No, impossible. Rapeseed plants bloom with yellow flowers, and I've seen them before." Turning to her with a wink, I teased, "Didn't you stay at the Heilongjiang Corps farm? Haven't you seen rapeseed before?"

"No, I couldn't tell," she said, smiling. But then, in a sudden turn of mood, she sneered, "Of course, I'm not as worldly and wise as you—who can 'help the shoots grow by pulling them upward.'"

As quick-witted as I am, I was tongue-tied, only managing to shrug in self-ridicule and say, "How embarrassing!"

The following is a true anecdote from my adolescence.

At the end of 1968, we, the Red Guards—who were once predominant and unrivaled during the Cultural Revolution, following Mao's call to fight wherever we went in the hope of "smashing an old world and establishing a brand new red world" overnight—heard the great leader's latest supreme directive on the radio: "It is necessary for the educated youth to go to the countryside and be re-educated by the poor peasants."

As the son of a military cadre with an urban household registration, I was naturally among those required to "settle in the countryside to do farm work." At that time, there were three options for assignment: one was to go to the frontier, the second was to remain local, and the third was to return to one's rural hometown.

I was still young then, only fifteen years old. After much consideration, my parents finally decided to send me back to my ancestral home and asked my uncle from the countryside to come to the military unit to pick me up. To this day, in my hometown, whenever the era of my rural settlement was brought up, everyone there, whether it be the elderly who have aged or children who never met me, would tease my "pulling stems upwards to help crops grow" while giggling, as if recounting a legend. But back then, I was indeed serious. I was filled with a revolutionary enthusiasm that dared to think, speak, and act as advocated by our leader, aspiring to achieve great deeds in my hometown. My scientific experiment project was quite simple: to pull the stem upwards about a half-inch or one centimeter just before the wheat began to head. I hoped that by doing this, I could shorten the growth period of wheat seedlings while making the wheat ears grow thicker, breaking the local yield record of 500 kg per mu.

I planned to first experiment with the wheat seedlings along both sides of the ridge, and if successful, I would then apply the technique to the larger fields. Who would have known that when I went to the fields the next morning, those wheat stalks that I had pulled up not only failed to maintain their upward growth but were drooping their heads as if hit by frost. They looked even more like rows or groups of "class enemies" being criticized at a struggle session, bending over and bowing their heads to accept criticism and torture from the masses.

I realized that I made a grave mistake.

Had the leadership not cut me some slack because my father was an army cadre, I would have been labeled as an example of sabotaging the leader's directive of "grasping revolution and promoting production" and been sent to the ranks of "class enemies."

On the day we moved into our new home, I was still walking

around in the yard under the starlit sky until very late, sometimes squatting down to touch the grass and the moist soil beneath it.

How do I put it? I felt more exhilarated than peasants who, after the revolution, received the landlords' tiled houses and unearned wealth. I also felt profoundly secure, free from fears of sudden dispossession by former landowners. I earned wealth through diligent labor: dealing cards and pedaling pedicabs. Now I could do what I wished on my land—dig a pit or a trench and build a wall; I could pursue the most beautiful picture of the yard imaginable: vegetable garden, orchard garden, flower bed, and lawn.

It's somewhat regrettable that, over time, what I say at home carries less weight, and my wife has the final say on almost everything. The reality is that our family relies almost entirely on my wife for food and other household needs. In her eyes, I am just an "idiot" who can only write and knows nothing about daily life, and it is natural that I am led by her and tolerate her occasional reproaches and complaints. Nevertheless, within the scope of my responsibilities as a yard architect, a role assigned by my wife, I still maximized my imagination as a writer and demonstrated the spirit of the legendary Foolish Old Man Who Moved the Mountains. With only a spade, a pickaxe, and a small rubber-wheeled cart, I flattened the hillside at the front door and built a solid retaining wall in less than three years.

As I placed the final large brick on the retaining wall, feeling the triumph of finally "winning the battle with the heavens and earth," I gently caressed the eight hard calluses on my hands, which I wore like medals made from flesh. I could not help kissing them, my heart filled with a winner's pride and joy that were beyond words.

Although the land had been leveled, my naive aspiration of turning it into a vegetable garden, orchard, and grassland, and the hope of frequently enjoying fresh corn, broad beans, and sweet potatoes, all vanished into thin air when my wife, dutiful yet increasingly bossy, shouted, "No way!" with a decisive slashing gesture.

"Haven't you had enough of being a farmer?" she asked in a sarcastic tone, one hand on her hip and the other pointing at my nose.

All I could do was adjust my mentality accordingly and compromise, which turned out to be the right approach. Whenever I gave in, my wife would no longer be combative and might even reciprocate. She then said, "Alright, didn't you always want to plant bamboo? I can agree to that."

However, to buy this type of green bamboo — which is cherished solely by Asian residents, particularly those well-versed in Chinese culture — turned out to be an ordeal requiring considerable effort. I visited nearly every nursery within a twenty- kilometer radius of my home, yet I couldn't find the bamboo I was looking for.

Then one day, I thought of the large flea market near Artesia city where I had previously lived. I remembered seeing bonsai and green bamboo there, so I decided to go and check it out.

To call it a flea market was a bit of a misnomer. It was more like a massive supermarket or a bazaar, with as many counterfeits as genuine goods, as well as a blend of new and used items. It used to be a parking lot for Cypress College that was only open to registered and pre-booked vendors on Saturdays and Sundays, with a fee, I suppose.

We parked the car by the roadside. I put on a straw hat, the kind commonly worn by western cowboys and garden workers. My wife, holding an umbrella, joined me as we braved the scorching sun, walking from stall to stall at the market. Unfortunately, we did not find any green bamboo. I let out a deep sigh: Americans have meat to mouth but no bamboos to house—what a disappointment and sadness in life.

"Honey, look!" my wife suddenly exclaimed.

I quickly looked in the direction she was pointing and saw the tips of some slender, tall green bamboos swaying about a hundred meters away.

Fearing someone else might buy the bamboo before I could, I rushed to the vendor, leaving my wife behind.

"How much for one pot?" I asked, panting, as I glanced at the three pots of bamboo.

The stall owner, who had his head down as he repotted an azalea, looked up: "Forty-five."

When our eyes met, we both froze.

"You are—Miller? Yes, Buda!" I blurted out. "Remember me?"

Miller gazed at me for a moment before bursting out with a hearty laugh. He raised his arms to chest level, his left palm facing up in a card-holding gesture, and then quickly flicked his right hand, imitating the way I used to deal cards at the poker tables.

"Do you still remember my name?" I said, laughing and eagerly shaking his muddy hand, which was soft yet firm, with rough skin and hard knuckles.

He raised his other hand to his head, squinting and thinking for a moment, but shook his head regretfully, saying, "Sorry, I can't recall."

"Terry," I said.

"Yes, yes. Terry," he said, gripping my hands tighter, and asked, "Are you still working at the casino?"

"No, I left a long time ago."

"Yeah? I also stopped going there a long time ago."

Meanwhile, my wife, a neatnik, hurried over, and her face fell as soon as she saw me holding his muddy hands.

I hastily let go of his hands and turned to her. "This is Miller," I said, trying to explain it to her in the simplest way possible, "a friend of mine, and more than a friend. Whenever I think back to my days as a card dealer, Miller is the first one who comes to mind."

My wife looked doubtfully at Miller, who stood before her with his body slightly hunched, rubbing his hands together in front of his chest. He wore a black sweatshirt, his face was tanned to a bronze hue, and his lips curled upwards into a crescent-shaped smile.

I had to quickly explain to her in Chinese, "He was the most generous tipper I ever met, bar none. Honestly, my book *Wealth Flows Like Water* was also inspired by him."

My wife still looked skeptical, and I could clearly read in her eyes and hear her silently muttering: "Yeah, right. Save that for the ghosts. Aren't you just trying to cozy up to him to get a better price?" She then turned her attention to the bamboo plants, extending her hand to feel the leaves quivering in the wind and the bamboo staff.

"How much is a pot?" she asked.

"Forty-five."

"How much are you going to cut the price down to?" she whispered in Chinese.

"None," I replied, my voice soft but my tone firm and unquestionable.

"What? Say that again?"

"Not only will I not cut any, but I will also pay him fifty dollars per pot," I added.

"Have you gone mad with fever?" said my wife, extending her hand to touch my forehead.

I dodged and mumbled, "Yes, I've gone mad. I am paying him fifty per pot, and the difference will come from my allowance."

My words and my uncharacteristic stubbornness almost convinced my wife that I had truly lost my mind. She stood there, mouth agape, looking at me and then at the trembling bamboo leaves beside her, as if they reflected my trembling heart.

For the first time, she did not argue with me and listened to what I said.

We paid, said goodbye to Miller, and loaded our car. On our way home, she finally could not contain her urge to warn me, "Do not shake hands with strangers in the future."

"Miller is not a stranger."

"The rule applies to acquaintances as well. Do you know how many germs are on a person's hands? And his hands are so dirty."

"But he is a good person," I quibbled intentionally, while thinking to myself, "Fortunately, you did not become a doctor as you wished. Otherwise, I would have to wear a gas mask to leave the house."

"It doesn't matter if he is a good person. Remember, when you get home, the first thing you need to do is to wash your hands." In the unquestionable tone commanders often use on the battlefield, she added, "Thirty seconds won't do; you need to use more dish soap and scrub for one minute, including brushing under your nails with a used toothbrush. I won't stand for one second less."

"Yes, ma'am," I agreed, nodding almost obsequiously but thinking to myself, "Hmm, you won't be there to watch me..."

But then I heard her ask, seemingly unsure, "Is Miller really your friend? How come I've never heard you mention him?"

"Well..." I hesitated and said ambiguously, "It's a long story. I'll tell you when we get home."

"No, tell me now, so you won't doze off while driving."

I glanced at her and said, "Only if you don't settle a score after we get home."

Uncharacteristically, she readily and generously agreed. "Fine," she said. "I promise. It's just fifteen bucks more, and I'm not that stingy."

CHAPTER 2

I first met Miller when I was a novice card dealer.

It was in the mid-1990s, and the casino business was thriving. All other industries were desolate, and the casino was the only flower blossoming in a bleak landscape.

Players swarmed in, their names crowding the registration board like tadpoles. The boss then utilized the wide corridors around the gambling pool, setting up additional card tables, instantly adding more than a dozen. However, since those were extra tables and the space was cramped after leaving a walkway for the passersby, only low-betting games were played on them, mostly catering to workers from construction sites, restaurants, and garment factories. There were also some retired elderly who, despite their advanced years, still had an undiminished passion for gambling, among them seniors in their eighties or nineties, physically challenged and confined to wheelchairs.

The action in the casino usually peaked on Friday nights. From a distance, the dozen or so card tables lined up in the corridor looked like dining tables, seats full, steam rising, smoke swirling (smoking wasn't prohibited back then). Players looked like they were gathered around a stove, savoring Korean BBQ. The cards leisurely dealt by the dealers were like pieces of pancakes stuffed with meat or vegetables. Of course, some were still being seared in the middle of the table.

In short, with each hand of cards dealt, there were usually calls and shouts in various accents and tones from around the world: "Ace, ace! Heart, heart! Club, club!" Soon after, there would be a mix of cheers and curses rising and falling: "Good! Wonderful!" or "Damn, such bad luck," "Bad dealer." Then someone would start booing, "New dealer! New dealer!" It was indeed one smiling family, but many frowning ones.

Every day when I went to work, as soon as I drove into the vast, seemingly endless parking lot and saw the wide variety of gamblers' cars—brand new Mercedes and BMWs, slightly older Nissans and Mazdas, Japanese pickup trucks with crooked bumpers, and clunky Fords with their trunks and taillights wrapped up in plastic sealing tape like casualties —streaming in from all directions, a melody, like a never-fading radio wave, would sound in my ears, except that the lyrics were transformed by me: "Pigs and sheep, where are they heading to? They are heading to the casino owner to be skinned."

It was on such a night, in the resplendent glowing lights, that I entered the casino through the western main entrance with its gilded doorframe, passed through the staff passageway guarded by tall and study security personnel, swiped my card, went up to the second floor, and entered the dealers' exclusive locker room. Then I was thrown into the same daily routine: I changed into a white shirt with pleats at the front, tied a black bow tie, slipped on a soft blue satin vest, picked up my essential—a beggar-bowl-like chip bowl—and finally returned to the dealers' lounge to listen to the supervisor loudly call the roll and read aloud the day's schedule.

That night, I started off at a Texas Hold'em table at the far end of the eastern corridor. Glancing at my watch and seeing that I had five minutes left before my shift, I quickly walked downstairs, replenished my chips at the cashier window open only to in-house staff, and then hurriedly headed to my workstation, where my pocketbook would bulge, and a lucky few would get rich, while most others would be bled of their chips like animals in a slaughterhouse.

The job of a dealer was quite different from many other professions that received a fixed biweekly or monthly salary. Casino owners usually only paid dealers the mandated minimum base salary, and the main income for dealers came from tips on the card tables. Normally, after a hand was dealt, the winners would tip based on the amount they won, sometimes throwing you a yellow chip (50 cents), sometimes a blue chip (one dollar), or even pushing several blue chips towards you. However, this is a general rule and not always the case. Tips were inherently low at tables with lower betting limits. On the other hand, high-limit tables were often reserved for VIPs — savvy gamblers dwelling in the casino all year long. Even if they didn't win, these players still had to pay fees based on time or a commission per hand. Therefore, they tended to be frugal with their tips, avoiding them whenever possible.

We typically made money at the Texas Hold'em tables with 3–6 or 4–8 limits. When the tables were full, the pile of chips in the middle of the table after each hand was quite substantial, so players were more casual in tipping. However, there were exceptions — such as when we encountered one or even several stiffers, those who were stingy with tips and happened to win every hand. In such cases, we just had to accept our bad luck.

Of course, the scheduling route arranged by the supervisor was also crucial. Which tables would feed you a fortune and which ones would feed you frustration was largely determined by the assigned route. But ultimately, the key to a good night's income depended on whether or not you dealt the right cards to the right people.

In the eyes of the gamblers, the hands of the dealers were the hands of fate, or of God, the determining factor in their wins or losses, happiness or sorrow, excitement or frustration. Hence, some of them, especially when they were on the brink of winning but suddenly lost due to a demon card from the dealer, felt as though they had been ascending to celestial heights, only to have the ladder yanked away at the last minute. They became so angry that their faces turned blue, their lips began to tremble, and their eyes turned bloody red. In such cases, the dealers often bore the brunt of their anger. They cursed incessantly, and though I did not understand Korean or speak Vietnamese, over time I came to realize that the Korean "Seo Bulnong" and the Vietnamese "Lo Ma" were not good words. However, casinos had rules: employees should always remain silent and submissive and were not allowed to stand up to customers, regardless of their harsh words, insults, or abuse. Here, the customer is God, and there are no human rights or democracy to speak of.

As with every gambler, a dealer's ability to earn tips after getting on the table depended on luck. Usually, according to our own situations, like the Chinese proverb "Eight immortals crossing the sea, each showing their magical powers." Pretty, sweet girls who ingratiated themselves with players naturally earned more substantial tips. Without these advantages, I could only triumph by my speed and accuracy in dealing cards, reading cards, and calculating the chips on the tables. A round lasted half an hour, and while others could deal at most twelve decks of cards, I could deal more than fourteen.

Assuming an extra two dollars in tips per table if I handled twelve tables a night, I could make an additional twenty-some dollars each night.

Sometimes I found myself distracted and absent-minded, my thoughts straying away from the poker tables for no apparent reason. For instance, each solid chip might turn into a droplet of water, each stack of the chips a puddle, and the green, velvet-covered card tables into lotus ponds of wealth. The winners and losers swapped in and out like a merry-go-round of spinning paper lanterns, but what struck me most was the constant flow of chips across the table. Of course, occasionally, when young, pretty women took a seat at my table, I could not resist the temptation to steal a glance at them. Consequently, due to my distraction, there were indeed occasions where I dealt the wrong cards or mistakenly pushed the winner's chips to the losing players.

It is worth noting that pretty girls don't always bring the enjoyment of beauty. Most are spoiled by men and have bad tempers. They often throw cards in anger more casually than they would slap a man after losing money. I once saw a Mexican girl who, whenever she played cards, had several boys standing by and watching from a distance. Her face was fair, her facial features well-proportioned, like a doll. But once, after losing a big hand at my table, for the first time she did not slam the cards down but rather stared at me angrily for more than ten minutes without moving her eyes. I panicked, so much so that my hands trembled and dealing cards became a struggle. Later, when I saw her stand up from the table, her figure was so bulky that I couldn't help a slight feeling of schadenfreude. It made me think, What's the use of just having a pretty face? A good figure and a beautiful soul are important too.

The players sometimes seemed distressed when at my table. The complaints I heard the most were, usually in a pathetic, begging tone, "Hey, Terry, slow down, slow down. Even if we die, let us die slowly if we must, alright?"

Well, that was another story.

That night, I took over the shift from a girl of Vietnamese descent. She was petite, with big sparkling eyes that seemed able to seize any opportunity and adapt quickly. When I lightly tapped her on the shoulder, a customary signal among dealers for a shift change, she turned around, nodded with a smile, and then turned back to collect the cards and chips on the table. As she picked up the chip bowl and stood up from the swirling seat reserved for dealers, she suddenly leaned in close and whispered in my ear, "Number six, great tipper."

I nodded and winked at her in thanks, but couldn't help thinking to myself, "I'm no god; how can I let whoever I want win?"

Yes, as I took my seat at the table, trying to appear calm and composed, I couldn't resist a glance at the customer in seat number six and sent him a friendly smile.

It was Miller. I learned his name from other players later. By then, he had won a lot, with chips piled up in front of him. He stacked them up bit by bit with his chubby, clumsy-looking hands. Upon seeing me smile at him, his already beaming face grew even more festive. The corners of his mouth curved slightly upwards, extending outward like a crack in the sky and revealing two rows of straight, snow-white teeth. His chin, reminiscent of an inverted plateau, also lifted slightly, causing his dark, round face to bend as a whole, like the vault of heaven. The fine beads of sweat dotting his forehead shimmered like stars.

I was a little mystified for a moment. He looked familiar, but I could not remember where I had seen him.

Then I heard someone at the table call him Buda. It dawned on me—it wasn't actually him I had seen, but the Maitreya Buddha who is found in many temples across China, usually seated at the first main hall at the mountain gate to welcome worshippers from all over with a big jolly smile.

His open-hearted laughter was identical to that of the Maitreya Buddha. It reminded me of a couplet at the entrance of Lingyin Temple in Hangzhou. This temple, situated near the legendary Fei-lai peak—a massive limestone cliff said to have flown from a distant land—is adorned with many Buddhist sculptures. The couplet, which flashed into my mind like the Feilai peak, reads "Buddha's teachings are boundless, behold me with bare chest and belly, ultimately all return to one smile; from where did the peak fly in? May people humble their hearts and universally liberate all sentient beings."

At this moment, I found it somewhat absurd and ironic that this person, whose appearance, manner, and speech resembled that of Maitreya Buddha, and even shared a similar name with him—Miller, sounding almost like Mi Le (Maitreya) in Chinese—had openly violated Buddhist precepts and become a gambler who now sat at my poker table.

But I had to admit, that night the atmosphere at the card table seemed out of the norm because of him, much more harmonious and friendly than usual.

I looked at him in between dealing cards. The more I observed him, the more he seemed to resemble Maitreya Buddha. I could not help recalling the words of an eminent monk of XiLai Temple whom I was once close to: "Give people confidence, give people joy, give people hope, and give people convenience."

Though Miller at the gambling table might not necessarily give people confidence, hope, or convenience, I can testify from personal experience that his presence, at least, always gave people joy.

He won several hands and lost a few at my table, but he seemed indifferent to winning or losing, never taking gains or losses to heart, and always laughing cheerfully with "a state of mind that is free from any attachment."

I came to respect him in a way, for his comfortable state of constant eternity, joy, true self, and peace. This had nothing to do with him throwing me tips in the teens that night. In my years of life experience, I had learned that the great path often lies in a low and dirty place, and noble men are rarely in positions of honor.

Then again, I was not immune to cliche. When I finished the "kill" at this table without a drop of blood, instead with peace and even joy, and was about to move to another "slaughter table," I gently reminded Miller, who had moved to sit right beside me at seat number nine, "You'd better call it a day while you are ahead."

"What's the 'better?'" he asked, looking up at me with an intense smile.

He was so close to me that I could clearly see the fine hairs on his face and the tiny, oil-glistening beads of sweat twinkling among them. I could even feel a rare beam of light emanating from the pea-sized bright spot in his pupil.

Momentarily stunned, sensing deeper meaning in his words, I pondered a response. He suddenly said, "Thanks for the reminder. But," he added, "I'm not here to gamble." Then he winked at me.

"If you're not at the table to gamble, then what brings you here?" I said, looking at him with a puzzled expression.

Later, as I dealt cards at the adjacent table, I was still thinking about what he had said earlier. He was so mysterious, truly an enigma.

Involuntarily, my gaze wandered over the heads of the gamblers, all with their different complexions, some happy, some sad, to catch another glimpse of him.

Earlier, when he sat close to me, I had noticed a few inconspicuous scars hidden among the roots of the sparse black hair on his scalp. But now his head was shaved, showing no trace of those dark roots. Instead, I saw a faint, oval halo surrounding the top of his head.

Stunned, I rubbed my eyes, thinking I was seeing things.

But each time I looked, that reddish halo seemed to persistently hover over his head.

He must be someone with a lot of history. An Easterner? Or a Mexican? A native Indian? As I dealt cards, my mind wandered more and more, my attention increasingly drifting. In my life, I had encountered many strange things and people, but none like Miller.

In any case, he must be a great master of something, I later concluded.

CHAPTER 3

People working in the casinos often had dual identities — they were both employees and customers. Especially for us dealers, who work hard dealing cards for modest tips, it felt deeply unfair to watch players quickly amass huge piles of chips. Moving among the tables while carrying trays of chips felt like holding a begging bowl. Although the chips tossed by customers were plastic and landed softly on the green velvet tablecloths, they somehow rang like coins or copper dollars falling into a worn bowl.

It was of utmost importance that we remain submissive and cheerful at all times with our guests. We had to suck it up and show no reaction when they threw cards or cursed at us after losing a hand. Naturally, after dealing cards for a long time, many of us, especially those like me with a strong interest in and addiction to gambling, often played a few hands or for a few hours at the poker tables after work or on our days off, enjoying the feeling of sitting at poker tables amongst the "God." Although we usually lost more than we won, we never grew tired of it.

If it weren't for my wife's nagging and the various restrictions she imposed, I might be better known today for my gambling than my writing; you never know how the cards may fall.

On one day off, my wife wanted to go shopping at the outlet near the casino, so I hesitantly suggested going to the casino to play for a while. She knew that I had never liked going to the malls and that it was sometimes annoying how I followed her around and constantly rushed her home. Sparing us both, she graciously permitted me to go to the casino on the condition that I could not lose more than fifty dollars.

I arrived at the casino in high spirits. After settling down, just as I finished my first hand, I noticed that a middle-aged man, unshaven, in clothes splattered with white paint, had lost all his chips. He fumbled in his pockets until he was convinced that there was no more money to be found hiding in any of them. He rubbed his scalp before he got up and left, clearly yearning for more.

The dealer, a Taiwanese girl, saw him leaving and raised her hand to signal to the floorman, calling out, "Seat open."

The seat was filled immediately by someone who came from behind and sat down next to me.

I turned and saw, to my surprise, it was Miller. I greeted him with a quick fist bump.

"Day off?" Miller asked with a smile as he settled in.

I nodded and asked, "You just got here?"

"Been here for a while, just in the hallway," he replied. He tossed a few chips onto the table, pulled three crumpled $20 bills out of his pocket, and handed them to the dealer, saying, "Deal me in."

Playing cards so close to Miller, I could just turn my head and see the fine hairs on his face, damp with sweat, and the deep wrinkles at the corners of his eyes, developed from years of prolonged smiles and laughter. It felt surreal. If not for the little finger on his left hand, which seemed to have been truncated a bit, I would have believed that I was playing cards with Maitreya Buddha himself.

Feeling my eyes on him, he turned to me with a heartfelt smile.

I suddenly remembered seeing a halo over his head once, so I started squinting and opening my eyes wide to search for it. Unfortunately, I did not see it again. But I made a new discovery: he bore a striking resemblance to the gilded God of Wealth statue that had recently been placed at the entrance of the Asian card games section.

The Asian card games section was primarily developed to attract customers from China, Korea, and Southeast Asia. The main poker games on offer included Pai Gow, Three Public Six Cards, and Asian Stud, among others. Considering the target audience of Asian tourists, the casino specially crafted a splendidly gilded God of Wealth statue to cater to the Asian cultural desire to get rich and placed him in the most conspicuous spot—right past the entrance to the Asian section. The God of Wealth carried a large bag over his shoulder, with the words "Gold Bag" on it in large characters. When ordinary people saw it, they easily got the wrong impression that he was there to spread the wealth and hand out red packets. Thus, passersby felt compelled to touch his kind, smiling face and the "Gold Bag" on his shoulder, hoping some of his happiness or wealth might rub off on them. Only those players and dealers who had been immersed in casinos for a long time understood that the God of Wealth was not there to "spread wealth" but to "collect wealth," and the "Gold Bag" was not for "giving out money" but for "collecting money."

I had heard that Guanyin Bodhisattva could show thirty-two manifestations. Maitreya Buddha, a Buddha, could certainly manifest in even more forms, one of which was probably the God of Wealth.

Sure enough, I had won three hands in a row since Miller sat down beside me, and now I had chips piled up in front of me.

"You'd better call it a day," Miller said with a grin.

This was what I advised him last time, and he returned it to me lightheartedly.

But winning this way was rare. I was hoping that with the help of the God of Wealth, I would be able to "chase the fleeing foes with the remaining courage and strength," so I said without looking up, "Ah, I just got here; my chair is not warm yet."

"Oh. But … is it good if the chair gets warm?" said Miller, staring at me and clearly implying something.

"Good is the end, and the end is good," I said. The song "All Will Be Gone" from *A Dream of the Red Chamber* popped up in my head, and I blurted it out, but I immediately felt something was off and said nothing further.

He smiled at me again, somewhat mysteriously, and winked.

I disregarded it and focused solely on the card games, wholeheartedly believing that today was my lucky day and a fortune would soon be rolling in. I had to seize it, seize it tightly and never let it slip through my fingers. My goal was not only to win, win, win, but also to recoup all the money I had lost in the past! Thus, for some time, I almost forgot about his presence. When I turned my attention back to him, he seemed uninterested in the card games and was more focused on the female dealer, often letting his gaze linger on her face and hands for long periods.

She was a new hire, baby-faced, with fair skin, big eyes, and chubby cheeks. Thanks to her resemblance to the famous Taiwanese singer Teresa Teng, we naturally called her Little Teresa Teng.

"Did you graduate from high school?" Miller abruptly asked, jokingly, while Little Teresa was shuffling the cards.

"Excuse me?" Little Teresa blushed, embarrassed.

"You look like child labor to me," Miller said, chuckling again. "You're from Cambodia, right?"

"No, Taiwan."

"Uh." Miller seemed somewhat disappointed and let out a soft sigh.

It seemed like something had touched his heart. He did not say a word for a long time after that, often discarding the face-down cards in front of him without even a glance, but his eyes still occasionally lingered on Little Teresa, causing her to blush a little.

"What's the matter? Does she look like your first love?" I whispered in his ear jokingly.

Slightly startled but not offended, he look at me calmly and said, "No, my sister."

"Sister?" I glanced at Little Teresa. "You two don't look much alike. You're always smiling, but she is known as a cold beauty. Almost no one here has ever seen her smile."

"Is that so?" he said, gazing at Little Teresa again as he murmured, "My sister was like that for a while too. But my sister never looked this pale."

"Your sister is that much younger than you?" I asked again, my curiosity piqued by his words.

"Oh, that's an impression from a long time ago," he said, his smile disappearing swiftly from his face.

"She is not with you?"

"I lost her. Many years ago," he said somberly. Not only was his smile gone, but now a trace of sadness struck his round, jovial face.

Then, as if to hide some inner secrets, he started to rub the shortened finger on his left hand with his right hand. The finger, without a nail, had a blunt, flat tip, reddened and whitened, and had developed a thick layer of calluses.

This was the Miller that I had never seen before.

He seemed to have realized his lapse in composure and noticed that I was observing his fingers. He turned back to me with a slight smile and said, "People can easily lose themselves. To lose others is also to lose oneself." After this, he no longer appeared interested in playing more. He gathered up his chips, rose to his feet, and dropped them tenderly into Little Teresa's chip bowl. He then added, "I don't want to lose to anyone else tonight, so I'll lose to you, my little sister," and left.

Little Teresa was momentarily astonished, as were the others at the table.

An elderly white man mumbled, "That's him. He is always like this."

"What's — always like this?" someone asked.

"I've lived a long time and only saw it once. That time he won the jackpot and insisted on giving away half of his winnings to us at the table, saying something about 'luck arise from the karma,' claiming that we all contributed to his win."

The old man's words were both unexpected and expected.

And then I recalled what he had just said: "People can easily lose themselves. To lose others is also to lose oneself."

Shortly after Miller left, I started to lose, and the chips I had won quickly flowed back out, along with my original stake. It was true to the old saying, "Easy come, easy go."

Although I lost the money, I felt quite happy inside, even feeling a sense of gain amidst the loss — although I wasn't clear yet about what exactly I had gained.

"Little sister? Didn't I once have a lovely and adorable little sister too?" On my way from the casino to the parking lot to get my car, the images of Miller's sister, the girl I considered as a sister, and Little Teresa, suddenly overlapped and alternated in my mind...

CHAPTER 4

A few days later, during a break, I quietly read a copy of *Vajrayana Paramita Sutra* while sitting on a single couch near the west entrance. I had gradually developed this habit of reading during breaks since I became a casino dealer.

We usually had a half-hour break after working two or three tables. So, in a night, I'd have about two hours of free time at my disposal. During these breaks, most of my colleagues would be in the staff lounge watching TV (as cell phones were not yet common back then), chatting, or dropping a few coins into the game machines in the game room to race a car or fish for teddy bears. However, I found these moments ideal for reading. I would typically bring an English novel or a Chinese book on various topics to work. I kept the thicker books in my locker and carried the thinner ones in my pants pocket for easy access.

As I was engrossed in reading, I was startled to feel someone gently patting me on the shoulder.

I turned around quickly, only to find Miller standing behind me with a joking grin, tee-heeing. He was much shorter than I had imagined, probably just a little over 1.6 meters tall. I realized that his short stature was due to his relatively short legs, which I hadn't noticed before since he was usually seated at the card table.

"How unusual for someone to read amidst the pandemonium of a casino!" he said and then asked me curiously, "What book?"

"A book about Buddha," I responded with an insinuating smile, referring to his nickname.

"Buddha?" He froze for a minute, glancing at the book in my hand again. "Is it in Chinese?"

I nodded but couldn't help asking him, "Have you ever read Buddhist scriptures?"

"Well, maybe. I'm not quite sure," he said, then smiled at me. "Even you call me Buda. What kind of Buda reads his own sutras and his own book?"

"Ah, so that's it." I laughed too and asked, "Then, have you read the Bible?"

He laughed out loud. "There is no such thing as Sutras or Bible. They are only called Sutras and Bible."

His way of speaking reminded me of what I had read in the *Diamond Sutra*, quite common in fact. For instance, it reads: "Subhuti, the so-called sentient beings are not sentient beings; therefore, they are called sentient beings in name." Another passage reads: "Subhuti, the so-called good dharmas are not good dharmas; therefore, they are called good dharmas." From this, I could roughly infer that he not only had read Buddhist scriptures but also had an extraordinary comprehension of it.

I asked again, "Have you ever studied Buddhism?"

"No, no, I do not study Buddhism. How could…"

Knowing that I had asked the wrong question again, I apologized. "Sorry."

But he did not seem to mind and said with a giggling smile, "Buddha, how could one truly learn him?" he said, pointing to the book in my hand, half as a conclusion and half as speculation. "This book, it doesn't seem to have the Buddha in it, does it?"

"Where are you from?" I asked, unable to contain my curiosity.

"Ah, I often ask myself that," he said with a chuckle, his eyes squinting into thin lines. Then he made a face and shrugged.

"You're not here to see your pretty sister, are you?" I said, joking back at him.

"Pretty sister?" He was momentarily taken aback but then laughed again. "I lost her long ago, but why do you still keep her in mind?"

I was stuck for a moment.

I knew he wasn't going to engage with me on the same level of thought and answer my worldly concerns at this moment. Catching a glimpse of the digital clock on the wall, flashing a set of red numbers indicating two or three minutes remained before I needed to be at the table, I quickly stood up. Half talking to myself but also to him, I said, "It's time to push."

"Hmm. This is a nice job you have; not only can you read books but you can also read cards and chips," he said with a sly smile. Then he waved at me and said, "See you at the tables in a bit."

The next table I was to push was a 3–6 limit Texas Hold'em. That was usually a table where tips were quite good, but as I stood behind the dealer I was about to replace and tapped his shoulder to take over, I caught sight of the guy in seat number eight who every dealer dreaded. He was a young Caucasian with chestnut-colored hair, well-proportioned features, and a straight nose, looking much like a college student in his twenties. He was a regular at our casino and a notorious stiffer. Fortunately, his poker luck wasn't very good today, and his chips were nearly gone. It would only take a little extra effort from me to knock him out of the game. Then I could sweep his remaining chips away, kill his will to continue the fight, and send him on his way.

As I was plotting his demise, he abruptly looked up from the card table and our eyes collided in the air. His face, which had already turned dead from losing, was now fired up and full of energy, as if after having seen a savior. Straightening up, he blurted, "Good, very good!" He then shouted at the dealer, who we jokingly called Sleepy-head or Filipino Dad, as he was dealing the last hand, "Change dealer! Change dealer!"

It wasn't only his shouting that gave me goose bumps but also his inexplicable trust in me, the kind of trust that a desperately ill person would have for the first doctor they find, inadvertently adding immense psychological pressure on me. Honestly, the odds of him winning were relatively high whenever I dealt at the table. In other words, as long as he was there, I would probably "kill" customers who tipped well, giving him a better chance to win — you know, like the more you walk at night, the more likely you are to bump into a ghost. To resist this psychological fear, I couldn't help but press the *Diamond Sutra* in my pants pocket and silently prayed, "Buddha, Bodhisattva, please help me, and do not let this thing come back to life in my hand."

What is feared is what comes. The first hand of hole cards I dealt him contained two aces, which I learned after the hand was over. Then, among the three community cards that followed, there was another ace, giving him a set of three aces, a strong hand. So, he raised first. Seeing this, the other five players, each holding cards of their own, followed suit. Next, I dealt the turn card (the fourth card), which was a heart. With the two hearts already on the table, there were now three hearts showing. Experienced players knew that someone might have two hole cards of hearts, making a flush — a hand of five cards of the same suit, which would certainly beat three of a kind. Sure enough, when it was the turn of the Korean uncle sitting in seat number one, he raised the bet without hesitation. The two young men in seats two and seven, fellow Chinese, had their eyes fixed on the Korean uncle for a while, seemingly unconvinced that he had made a straight flush but rather a bluff, so they exchanged glances and decided to continue to call the bet.

Speaking of these two fellow Chinese, in fact, they were not only fellow Chinese but also fellow Shanghainese. The one with small eyes was known as Mung Bean Eyes, and the other, who was fair-skinned and handsome, was often referred to as the Soy Milk Seller. At first, I really thought he worked at some kind of Chinese flatbread and Youtiao (Chinese deep-fried twisted doughnut sticks) shop. It was only after a while that I realized that wasn't the case. Whenever his face turned pale or he occasionally rubbed his back as he walked, Mung Bean Eyes would tease him. "What's the matter?" he'd say. "Sold too much soy milk last night? Take it easy." Then he would raise one eyebrow and wink at those of us who knew him. Since they knew that I was from the same hometown as them and that I had gained some sort of fame as a writer before I left the country, they were usually nice to me. The tips they gave weren't great, but at least they tipped.

But once, they spoke Shanghainese at the table to plot a cheat, so I had to remind them "English only" as required by the casino's rules. Unexpectedly, this offended the two of them. After I left the table, Mung Bean Eyes came looking for me to express his strong dissatisfaction. "You help us, OK? Why do you always turn your elbow outwards? Aren't you embarrassed?"

"The casino has rules," I said in my defense. As soon as these words came out of my mouth, Mung Bean Eyes cut me off and retorted, "What kind of damn rules are these? Americans like to set bullshit rules all over the world. In fact, they can only fool dum-dums. As long as there is a will, those rules are all just papier mâché, full of loopholes to exploit. Not just us, people from all walks of life exploit more loopholes than we do. Have you been to Huating Road? All brand names are sold there, from high-quality knockoffs to lower-quality imitations and everything else. Think about this, how can we develop without exploiting loopholes? How can our country develop? Huh? Next time you see us doing this—understand? Just turn a blind eye." I was speechless, but I could only shrug and smile.

I thought to myself that these two usually played prudently; for them to call the bet, they likely had either two pairs, a higher number heart, or three of a kind, and were hoping for another heart to appear on the table, or any card that would complete one of their pairs. That way, they could turn defeat into victory with a higher flush or a full house, a combination of three of a kind plus a pair.

Seven cards are dealt in Texas Hold'em, including two hole cards and five community cards, yet players aim to form the best five-card hand possible by combining their two hole cards with the community cards. Despite the seven-card restriction, the game offers numerous combinations, especially the last community card, which is the key and is as magical as flipping a hand to change clouds to rain, transforming princes into beggars, or ugly ducklings into princesses.

The young Caucasian man hesitated upon seeing this. Although he already had three aces, if the last river card was dealt and no pair appeared on the table, his fate would be no different from holding the three worst cards. He first glanced at me and my dealing hands, then lowered his head to look at his chips. Counting them by hand, he saw that he had only eleven left. Seemingly steeling himself for one last bet, he said, "All in!" and then pushed all of his chips forward.

What a demon, to make his wish come true! The last card dealt from my hand, believe it or not, made a pair of twos appear on the table, making him the ultimate winner of the hand with a full house. The Korean uncle, who had already made a flush, smacked his cards down on the table and jumped up from his seat, cursing "Seo Bulnong" over and over. My two Shanghainese fellows glared at me; Mung Bean Eyes shook his king of hearts and babbled bitterly in Shanghai dialect, "Look at this, look at this…" The Soy Milk Seller kept shaking his head, saying, "It's bewitched, bewitched! Your bewitched hand! You got me beaten!"

The only one beaming at the moment was the young dude, happily collecting a large pile of chips like a farmer reaping a bountiful harvest. Although I kept glancing at him, he kept his head down, pretending not to see me. In the end, he didn't throw me a single penny, nor did he even offer the customary "thank you" that winners usually say.

I could only blame my bad luck, my own hands, for letting me down.

The Korean uncle in seat number one grumbled for a while, and despite his frustration, he finally patted his behind as if to shake off the bad luck that this table — especially me, the dealer — had brought him, and left in a huff.

I quickly notified the floorman of the empty seat that needed to be filled and started dealing the next deck of cards.

Just as I dealt the first card, I heard a familiar voice coming from seven or eight steps away: "Deal me in."

Following the sound, I saw Miller.

Then my gloomy mood lifted like sunshine breaking through overcast skies, as if someone drowning in the bearish sea of stocks suddenly heard the sound of a Spanish bull stampeding—the kind of bullish surge I once hoped to catch in the market. I couldn't help thinking that with a laughing Buddha like Miller at the table, my chance of making money tonight shouldn't be too bad. As long as he won two or three hands, I could recoup my losses from inside the embankment with gains from the outside.

Strangely, for the next twenty minutes or so, each hand of cards I dealt, as different as they were, only made one winner: the white dude, who, to be fair, was quite good-looking. Think about it; for almost eleven hands in a row, he had won every single hand. Even when he got two hole cards that were totally rubbish, worthless, small, or non-consecutive to any other cards, I would make them form the only straight, pair, or flush on the table, so often that in the end, almost all the chips on the table, like frenzied fans, rushed towards him one after another and were then stacked by busy hands into a long, tall, and thick Great Wall of Chips.

Imagine the hatred in my heart. I tried many ways, including shuffling the cards more, or cutting the deck deeper or shallower to start, hoping to change my rotten luck and his bonanza. Even to the degree that later on, when dealing cards to him, I cursed him bitterly in my heart: "Die, die, just die."

Even after I had exhausted every trick in the book, I couldn't change his unbelievable stroke of luck, luck as prosperous as cooking oil over a blazing fire or as embellishing as a pennant banner with flowers.

I swept the chips from most of those seated at the table and pushed them towards the one person who refused to tip me. In doing so, I managed to offend almost everyone at the table, some of whom scowled at me while others looked as if their eyeballs were about to pop out.

What a dark night it was; I was in utter despair, almost on the verge of collapse! Why did heaven arrange such an absurd game of cards to make me endure torture and agony that seemed even more painful than the torments of hell? I frequently glared hatefully at my own hands — these disheartening traitors and betrayers that did things that pained alliance yet pleased the enemies. Especially seeing Miller right beside me, yet unable to make him win a single hand, and me sweeping away almost all of his remaining chips, I really wished I could chop off these hands of mine, which refused to obey my mind.

Somehow Miller still wore a smile on his face. It seemed he didn't come here to gamble but to watch the unfolding drama of the gambling table. That smile would soon grow fainter, like autumn dew drying up in the sun.

Suddenly he straightened up, resting his wrist on the edge of the table, his right hand gently tugging, rubbing, and squeezing the shortened finger of his left hand. Gazing intently at the young man, he said, calmly but firmly, "Hey, young man, you should tip. They depend on that to make a living and support their families."

The young man must have heard him but played dumb, keeping his head down and continuing to hide behind the wall of "wealth." Miller then reminded him again with a smile, "Young man, even if you don't tip, you can't keep those chips forever. They may seem solid, but they are like water, always flowing in and out."

The young man finally looked up at Miller. He stubbornly shook his head and said, "No. Tipping will bring me bad luck."

Now it was Miller's turn to shake his head. "Alas, you just don't get it and can't let it go." With that, he turned to me abruptly and asked, "Dealer, where's your book?"

These words were spoken so softly that probably no one else heard them clearly, but to me they were like thunder piercing my ears. Reflexively, I reached for my pants pocket and found that the bulging *Diamond Sutra* was still there.

But I had totally forgotten about it in the past twenty-some minutes.

Dealing cards, I realized, paid quite well compared with many other jobs. Making a living was no problem at all, and as a senior dealer I had saved a considerable amount of money. My bank balance had been steadily climbing. So why did I allow a non-tipping customer to upset me to the point of mania?

I nodded at him, saying, "It's still here." Then, with a deep sigh of relief, carefully untangling my twisted emotions, I retained my composure and was ready to deal the final hand at this table.

Out of nowhere, Miller said, "Deal me out." With a smile that felt like a spring breeze, he then pushed all of the remaining twenty or thirty dollars' worth of chips into my chip tray, stood up, stretched his arms to relieve his back, and said, "I'm a bit tired today. Not playing anymore." With that, he walked away from the table.

Dumbfounded, I looked at the nearly one hour's worth of chips he had left for me in the tray, and then I watched him depart. I was at a loss for words, and I almost forgot to deal the cards I was holding…

CHAPTER 5

That night turned out to be one of my life's turning points.

I realized that my mental state at that time had strayed further and further from my original intention when I chose to work at the casino as a dealer.

It all started one day when I was on a break at my job in finance and became captivated by a coworker's deft, professional card-dealing skills.

We were taking our daily lunch break, and this coworker came over and noticed a deck of cards on a desk next to me. He casually snatched it up and started to deal. He was extremely fast; each card seemed to be shot out, flying away then drifting down like a scattering of flower petals that eventually landing neatly in one place, forming a tidy pile. I watched dumbfounded. Later I learned that he had worked as a dealer in a casino, but eventually he had to give up the job because he was a compulsive gambler, and his earnings were never enough to cover his losses.

I was reminded of the old Chinese saying, "Choose your son-in-law at the gambling table," and the idea of becoming a casino dealer intrigued me. On the one hand, I heard that the tips were quite good, comparable to an annual salary of \$70,000 to \$80,000, even exceeding \$100,000 for the highly skilled. At that time, I had incurred significant losses in futures and stocks, and my wife had given birth to our second and third child. I was looking for a "quick and dirty" way to earn money for the family. Additionally, I thought that observing people at the gambling tables—watching how they rise or fall in the battle for money, their moments of joy and despair, the soaring highs and plummeting lows, and the moments when fortunes roll in and wealth scatters away—would be a wonderful opportunity for someone like me, who was passionate about writing novels, to understand the richness and complexity of human nature.

I never thought that, once I was immersed in it and became fully invested, I would slowly become enthralled by the flow of money and wealth on the gambling table. Tips, tips, and more tips…this became what drew me forward every day. I hadn't kept a journal for a long time, but I diligently recorded my daily tips without missing a single day and compiled a tally each month.

This was probably similar to how my former classmates, whether as journalists or editors at newspapers or as professors at universities, approached their work in China. While writing articles or conducting academic research was one thing, figuring out how to make more money became a top priority in their lives. Most of them had a "gray income" on the side, writing ad copy or penning flattering reviews for painters, writers, singers, dancers, or sports stars. In order to keep their iron rice bowl, earn promotion, and make more money, they emulated the Eight Immortals crossing the ocean, each using their magic powers, often saying things against their conscience without blushing or feeling any guilt, or doing things that went against their hearts with a straight face or worse, some even engaging in despicable acts or kowtowing to power.

I was seized with the feeling that I had almost become a monkey dancing to the incessant clang of gongs to maintain a constant flow of bananas from my master. A large part of my original intention to leave the country was to escape from my original environment, to break free from the shackles of power and the false, big, and hollow discourse system, to think freely and critically without having to look at anyone's face or obey anyone's commands. Now I realized that the essence of freedom also lies in the ease and detachment of one's heart. When one's heart is not at ease or is detached, all external freedoms are nothing but self-deception. At best, one would be free to walk from one cage into another. For example, although I had tried not to be a slave to power, I had inadvertently become a slave to money.

In my mind, I flashed back to the first day I reported to the newspaper office. A young female editor surnamed Han pointed to the desk in front of her and said to me and another newcomer, half-seriously and half-jokingly, "Treat these desks well. They will be with us for a lifetime, watching us slowly age." I finally left that desk where I had to keep my head down daily, writing articles that were written one day and discarded the next. I traded it for a gambling table. Every day, I'm up close with decks of playing cards, piles of chips, faces of the sleep-deprived, and eyes swollen and bloodshot from being immersed in the sea of happiness, anger, sorrow, and joy.

But this wasn't what I truly wanted. Initially I just wanted to make enough money to return to my original path: to pick up the pen and write again. But I hadn't realized that making money was like climbing a mountain—always eyeing the next peak, never feeling it's enough. Moreover, even if mountains of gold and silver were to pile before me one day, allowing me to have whatever I wanted, would I still have the ability to think? Throughout history, numerous heroes have failed to see through this, only to fall down when they tried to go one step further in the pursuit of wealth, fame, and other desires, and they did not end well.

Recalling what Miller said to the young white man — "These chips might look hard, but in fact, they are like water, always flowing in and out" — I suddenly realized that "wealth is like water; it can carry a boat, but it can also capsize it."

I even had a dream about Miller. He had won a lot of money at my card table, and as he was leaving, he came around behind me, slipped something into my pocket, and told me to look at it when I got home. As soon as I left the table, I went to a secluded place and hurriedly fished it out. It was an envelope that I thought was filled with money, but it was just a blank sheet of paper. I unfolded the paper only to find large characters written in imitation Song typeface with a brush: "Letting go leads to liberation; turning back reaches the shore." These words struck me like a loud gong in my ears, making my scalp tingle and awakening me as if from a dream.

For this reason, I resolutely bid farewell to the casino when the dawn of the new century shone into its newly built, brightly lit hotel.

Since then, I have become a true freelance writer, frequently traveling between China and the United States, writing, lecturing, and also engaging in charity work. Not only did I stay away from casinos, I also managed to avoid all of my memories of that world.

Five or six years had passed since the last time I had run into Miller at the flea market, shopping for green bamboo.

It had been sixteen or seventeen years since I left the casino.

At this point, the entire world, as far as I could see, seemed to be under the control and restriction of the coronavirus. People were unable to travel or visit friends and relatives at will, nor breathe as freely as before. Every face was hidden behind a medical mask, like a veil of shame, rendering them unrecognizable.

One day, wanting to get some fresh air, I went to the Cypress Flea Market and once again met Miller.

Miller was familiar with the newly adapted norms of the pandemic. His round face was covered by a soft, rectangular blue mask that concealed his always-smiling, crescent-shaped mouth.

He was moving a bag of soil for planting flowers and grass down from a deep blue Dodge van. Seeing me, he hurriedly climbed down the ladder, placed the plastic bag on the ground, and offered a fist bump as a greeting.

He had aged considerably in the several years since I'd last seen him. Not only had his hair turned almost entirely gray, but the lines at the corners of his eyes and on his forehead had grown noticeably more abundant. Still, his eyes remained bright, and despite the mask, one could still feel his genuine, unpretentious smile. The gaze of those eyes was kind and full of wisdom.

"How is your business?" I asked.

"Ah, ah, it's so-so. But I enjoy tinkering with flowers and trees, just like you used to enjoy dealing cards," he said with a smile. He then let out a cough that was forceful enough to nearly dislodge the mask from his face. When he reached to hold it in place, the soil on his hands dirtied the mask. He simply took it off, used it to wipe his hands, threw it away, and pulled out a new one from a pocket and put it on. He then said to me with a meaningful look, "Haha, today a single-layered mask, tomorrow a double-layered one, and the day after—wait and see, we might as well be wearing gas masks."

"When do you think this pandemic will be over?" I asked.

"What pandemic?"

"Is there any other pandemic? Coronavirus"

"Pandemic have always been around; we just didn't pay attention. If you mean coronavirus, hasn't there been a new Delta variant? It will continue to mutate. Virus is also not virus; therefore, it is called virus. In this boundless universe, due to causes and conditions, things come together and fall apart, and everything is constantly mutating. This is true for the color realm as well as the colorless realm. The same goes for religion. Otherwise, Buddhism wouldn't have diversified into so many sects and paths, and it is the beginning of the dharma-ending times."

"Dharma-ending times?" I froze and was about to ask what the "end time" was when he continued.

"Now some people think online shopping is convenient, so they can sit at home and buy whatever they want without leaving home. Haha, in the future, they will surely miss the good old days when they could walk around freely and shop at flea markets. In the end, this virus is also our humanity's opportunity to grow by encountering difficulties, a Bodhisattva's way of helping us adjust our pace of life. Haha, we have been moving too fast."

He rarely spoke so much at once, and these were words that I had hardly ever heard from anyone else, especially not from a flea market vendor.

Out of a writer's professional habits, I observed him carefully and noticed that he seemed much darker than before—his face, his arms, and even his feet in black plastic slippers were dark. He had lost two or three of his upper front teeth, and the remaining ones were not as white as they used to be; they had a yellowish tint, as if stained from excessive tea drinking.

"How old are you?" asked my wife, who was by my side.

People say that when a husband and wife are young, they are lovers, but when they are old, they become companions. Since the pandemic, we had been together almost everywhere we went, like shadows following each other.

"Seventy-three," Miller responded.

"Well, as the Chinese saying goes," my wife blurted out, "at seventy-three or eighty-four, if Yama doesn't call you, you will report to him by yourself. You'd better be careful!"

I glared at her. "Now, why would you say something like that? Indeed a crow's mouth."

She glared right back at me and said, "What did I say wrong? Nothing wrong with what I just said. Chairman Mao even said that you literati always like to nitpick."

Miller, reading what was going on from our tone and attitude, smiled and said, "Yama is my brother, and I can say hello to him. Even if I go, that's because he misses me too much and is eager to reunite with me. Don't worry about it; really don't. But still, I want to thank you!" he said with a smile and bowed to my wife with his palms pressed together.

My wife smiled back at him and said earnestly and sincerely, "You look just like a laughing Maitreya Buddha. I love Maitreya Buddha the most. I heard from the monks at the temple that Maitreya Buddha is the Buddha of the future. The pendants my husband bought me, jade or gold, are all Maitreya Buddhas. We even have a white jade-carved Maitreya Buddha in our cabinet. There is no way the power of Yama is greater than that of Maitreya Buddha. I bet he is counting on you to take him under your wing!" Miller burst into laughter at the remark.

"But I don't quite understand, why do you always seem so happy?" my wife asked, childlike in her curiosity.

"Well ..." Miller paused for a moment, then lowered his head to touch his watermelon-like belly and laughed. "Maybe it's because my stomach can't hold onto unhappy things."

A somewhat mischievous thought occurred to me out of nowhere, which I promptly acted upon by asking him, "So, do you still have worries now?"

I felt slightly smug posing this question because it was a trap. Someone without any practice would not be able to answer it. If he said yes, he was still a mere mortal; if he answered no, it would be even more wrong, as Huineng, the Sixth Patriarch of Zen Buddhism, said in the *Platform Sutra* that "worries are Bodhi. Without them, how can people become enlightened?"

But Miller didn't even think about it before immediately responding, "Yes, but they come and go."

"Wow, wonderfully said, truly brilliant." I clapped my hands in amazement.

"Where are you from?" asked my wife.

I had asked Miller this question several times before, but he had never directly answered me, as if it were an inconvenient or difficult topic for him to address.

But this time, he appeared not to want to hurt my wife's feelings, so he replied in a serious tone, "I can't clearly say where I am from. Because causality, you see, is something that has no beginning or end, and it disappears as it appears. If I must say, I can only tell you that in this life, I have spent time in Thailand, France, Greece, Italy, and Spain, and I can speak seven languages. My birthplace was Cambodia, but I also have Chinese ancestry going back three generations."

"In this life? Have you lived any more lives?" my wife asked with surprise, her eyes widening.

"Of course, and so have you." Miller laughed and added, "Everyone has lived through many lifetimes, but it's just we can't remember them all at once."

My wife looked somewhat bewildered.

I then opened my mouth, trying to explain something to her, but she turned away impatiently, saying, "I don't want to hear it from you."

Alas, it was indeed "A monk from afar recites the sutras better." I could only shake my head and turn my gaze elsewhere.

My wife did have more questions for Miller, but when she saw a customer approaching him to ask about the price of some discs on a side table, she had to let it go.

"Nowadays, everyone watches movies online," she said, turning to me. "Who would buy these discs?"

Thinking she was addressing Miller, I didn't answer and instead said, "He is busy doing business; don't get in his way. Let's look at the plants first." I pulled her along, and we wandered back and forth browsing among the pots and jars. Eventually, I took a liking to a beautiful pot of Iron Begonia. My wife wanted to ask the price, but upon seeing Miller talking to a seemingly well-acquainted customer, she had to drop the question.

Seeing this, I took my wife's hand and we went for a walk around Miller's dark blue Dodge van and took a few pictures.

The van was very old, definitely manufactured in the previous century, as indicated by the first digit of the license plate number starting with 2. The roof must have been modified, encircled by welded steel pipes with an assortment of flower pots placed in the middle; among them, a pot of cactus and two pots of onion lilies were blowing in the wind. The rear door of the van was open, revealing a cargo space filled with iron pipes likely used for setting up stands, as well as variously sized and shaped flower pots and flat black plastic containers that could be used to mix the soil. The driver's and passenger's doors were both half-open. Under the mottled steering wheel, next to the accelerator and brakes, was a large car battery. It looked new, but I didn't know what it was for. As I almost completed the circle around the van and came back towards the passenger side, I peered through the half-open rear seat door and saw that the interior was even more cluttered, filled with clothes, blankets, and other miscellaneous items, leaving just enough space for one person to sit.

As we approached Miller, he turned and asked with a smile, "Were you touring my home?"

The man who bought the disc had just left. Miller's left hand cupped a few one-dollar bills. Before he could stow them away, I caught a glimpse of his deformed little finger, which now looked black, as if it had been charred.

"Do you have a family? How many people in the family?" my wife asked.

"Haha, how could I have a family? I have long had no attachments."

"You're divorced? What about—what about the children? How many sons and daughters do you have?"

Miller laughed even louder, and after his laughter subsided, he said to my wife in a very serious tone, "You confused me. I don't really know what 'family' even means, or whether I have one or not."

My ears were tuned into their conversation, but my eyes remained fixed on the back seat of his Dodge. The empty seat, big enough for just one person, reminded me of an old monk in China I once visited. He slept upright every night. His room, only six square meters in size, contained a wooden bed just over three feet long and two feet wide, where he had sat at night for decades without lying down.

I pointed to the space in the back seat and asked Miller, "You sleep here?"

He nodded.

Right then, I seemed to understand something. But my wife was greatly surprised, and her sympathy was immediately aroused.

"Sleep here? In such a palm-sized space? You can't even lie flat," she said.

"Does one need to lie flat to sleep?" Miller said, again with a laugh, which seemed to confuse my wife even further.

Her train of thought having seemingly jumped in another direction, she asked Miller with great concern, "Aren't you seventy-three, well into retirement age? Why don't you apply for social security benefits? If your income is low, you can even apply for the California White Card, which allows free doctor visits without paying a penny!"

Miller curbed his smile, which was rare for him. "Isn't it more fulfilling and fortunate to be able to earn a living with one's own hands?"

His remark stirred something in my heart. I felt he had unintentionally touched something deep within me.

After I had gained some literary fame years ago, I had what many considered a bright future ahead, even holding a high-ranking official position equivalent to a department head. The teacher in charge of job placements earnestly tried to persuade me three times to take the job, but I thought better of it and politely declined.

My best friend and classmate, who was once the editorial director of one of the top Chinese literary journals, now spends his days doing home renovations and repairing appliances, and he thoroughly enjoys it. Additionally, there are two remarkable masters, Hanshan and Shide, both famous poetic monks in Buddhist history. One lived in the grotto, and the other was responsible for washing dishes at the Guo-qing Temple on Mount Tiantai. I had seen some portraits of Shide, who was short and slightly hunchbacked, always laughing and joking, with a playfully cynical demeanor. It's said that Hanshan once asked Shide, "If someone in the world slanders me, bullies me, insults me, mocks me, despises me, loathes me, or deceives me for no reason, what should I do?" Shide threw back his head in laughter, saying, "You might as well endure it, yield to him, let him be, avoid him, be patient with him, respect him, ignore him, and see what happens in a few years." When I took a closer look at Miller and thought about what he had just said, I felt he also had some of the Shide in him.

Some of the things that everyone desires in this world may not really suit you.

True happiness in life is actually quite simple, that is, not to be governed by external factors and to live freely according to your inner self.

I bought the iron begonia that I couldn't take my eyes off. When I got home, I planted it in the most prominent spot in the yard, and diligently fertilized and watered it, often finding myself lingering around it.

The rose-red petals of the begonia are so delicate and beautiful, but the thorns are incredibly hard. "Why would nature create it with such a mix of delicacy and strength, softness amidst toughness?" I often wondered while looking at it.

CHAPTER 6

During the intense period of the pandemic when the number of infected people was skyrocketing, we rarely went out except to the supermarkets to buy groceries and essential living supplies. Our most frequented one was Costco, often referred to as the "bulk packaging store."

That day, as my wife and I were placing a freshly roasted chicken from the deli cabinet into our cart, someone behind us called out, "Hi, Lily!" We turned around and saw Tutu, the real estate agent who had helped us buy our house five or six years ago. Originally from Cambodia, she lived on the hilltop adjacent to ours. We used to run into her on walks, where she was always being dragged, panting, by her large Australian shepherd, barely able to stop, but we had not seen her since the pandemic began. She is a cheerful and eloquent woman, fluent in Chinese with a southern accent.

As per the pandemic protocols, people had to stay six feet apart in addition to wearing masks. Tutu, probably worried that we wouldn't be able to hear her, raised her voice a little. "Hey, you know what? Your house has gone up by $200,000! How about that? Would you like me to sell it for you?"

I laughed, exchanging a glance with my wife, and replied, "We've finally got the house ready; we are not selling it. Besides, where would we live if we sold it?"

"Don't worry about that. I'll help you find another one! Over $200,000 is no small amount."

"Forget it, we don't want to put ourselves through all that hassle again; we plan to grow old and spend our last days in this house. Besides, if the selling price of houses has gone up, buying a new one won't be cheap either," my wife chimed in.

"That's true. But if any of your friends or family are looking to buy or sell a house, let me know. I'll offer the lowest commission and give you a rebate," she said, and when I nodded, Tutu turned to my wife and asked, "Is your backyard ready? Hey, your house, with its already beautiful view, must look even more stunning now after a tasteful couple like you have done it up."

This compliment pleased my wife, who quickly took out her phone, scrolled through her gallery, and showed Tutu some photos of our backyard that she had taken a few days ago.

"Wow, fantastic! Look at the fountain and the gazebo! The bamboo is also beautiful, blocking the view of the house below like a screen. Their flat roof is really ugly! Ah, this pier has such a unique design!" She continued lavishing praise, then suddenly stopped, her eyes widening. She lowered her head and yanked the phone so close to her face that it nearly touched her eyes. She continued staring at the phone as if no one else was around her until she looked up with an astonished expression. "Do you know this person? Where did you see him?" she asked desperately, pointing at one of the photos.

My wife leaned in for a closer look and saw that Tutu was pointing to a frontal photo of Miller taken the last time we saw him. He was seated on a square stool, with the lower half of his face covered by a lake-blue mask. His thick, black hands were palm-down on the knees, his back slightly hunched. He wore a black round-neck T-shirt with the Levi's logo and a pair of soft blue denim jeans. His face was round as a full moon, his eyes bright as morning stars. Even though half of his face was obscured, you could still sense that he was laughing heartily by his lowered, pale eyebrows and narrowed eyes.

"You know him?" my wife asked suspiciously.

"Hmm, he looks a bit familiar. But..." Acting out of character, Tutu hesitated and started rubbing her eyes.

Seeing this, I briefly explained to her how I came to know Miller.

But it seemed she wasn't really listening to me as she continued scrutinizing Miller's photo, her lips parted as if she had forgotten to close them.

Finally, after letting out a long sigh, she eagerly asked, "What did you just say? Where did you recently see him?"

"A flea market, over twenty miles away. Just take freeway 5 all the way south, about a thirty-minute drive," I responded.

"Can you forward this photo to me?" she asked, handing the phone back to my wife.

My wife was about to agree readily, but then she managed to hold her tongue and instead said, "This—might not be quite appropriate." After a moment of thought, she asked, "What do you plan to use it for? Are you thinking of using him for real estate advertising? That's actually a great idea. Really, Miller looks so much like Maitreya Buddha. If you dress him in a monk's robe and have him sit in the temple hall, people offering incense would truly believe it's Maitreya Buddha reincarnated. Ah, dear, you could even help come up with a few advertising lines!" she said, winking at me gently.

I immediately understood her intention and went along with her eagerness to seize a business opportunity, so I said, "No need to come up with ad lines; it's all ready-made. Just use 'Bring you joy, bring you hope, bring you confidence, and bring you a future.'"

"Wow, great, fantastic!" my wife exclaimed, clapping her hands in approval.

"Oh. No, no, it's not like that; that's not what I mean. I don't want it for advertising," Tutu said, shaking her head briskly.

"Then what do you want his photo for?" my wife asked, looking somewhat doubtful. "You have been in America for many years and perhaps are even more aware than us. America is a law-abiding society. If we give you Miller's photo without his permission and you use it for business purposes, that would infringe on his portrait rights. He could sue us."

"No, no, it's not that. This ... in a few words, I can't make it clear ..." Tutu, normally articulate and quick-witted, tripped over her words, mixing English with Chinese and appearing awkward and tongue-tied.

I couldn't help but break in to ask, "Do you know Miller? He seems to be Cambodian as well."

"Um, this ..." Unsure of what to say, she pursed her lips and thought for a while before responding. "Well, I might, it seems, it's just that many years have passed, and I could be mistaking him for someone else."

"That's no problem," my wife said. "We can arrange a time to visit the flea market together and that will clear things up, right? But how do you know Miller? Is he a celebrity in Cambodia too?" she asked quickly and directly, flicking her eyes to me as if to say, "Weren't you once a celebrity? But humph—you still have to listen to me at home!"

"Celebrity? Well, you could say that too." Tutu became even more hesitant but seemed to approve of the statement. She added, "Actually, strictly speaking, many people in Cambodia know his story, or know of him, so to speak. His photos were in the newspaper and were posted almost everywhere..."

"Wow, a real celebrity then! What's the story? Tell us about it." My wife's curiosity was immediately aroused.

"This, this is a long story," Tutu said. Right then, her cell phone started ringing and she quickly retrieved it from her bag. After the call, trying to regain her usual composure, she said apologetically, "Sorry, a client called wanting see a house, so I have to leave now." With that, she began pushing her cart towards the checkout counter, but after only a few steps she stopped and turned back to my wife and asked, "Lily, are you free tomorrow?"

My wife nodded yes.

"I'd like to come over and see your beautiful yard," Tutu said, pausing briefly before turning to me. "And to hear more about Miller — that's what you call him now, right?"

"Yes," said my wife, quickly nodding. "Of course, you are always welcome," she added. "After all, you were the one who helped us buy this house."

CHAPTER 7

Unexpectedly, as soon as we returned home from Costco, having barely stepped through the door, Tutu followed right in behind us. Before we even had a chance to greet her, she, out of breath, eagerly requested to take another look at Miller's photo on our phone.

My wife promptly took out her phone from the small leather pouch she carried, flipped to the page with Miller's photo, and handed it to her. Tutu took the phone and stretched the screen as large as possible, zeroing in on Miller's truncated finger before muttering to herself, "It's him, definitely him. But he's also aged." She then looked at us with red eyes and said, "Didn't you always ask me how I speak Chinese so well? I used to say I learned it after coming to America. There were too many Chinese officials and rich businesspeople immigrating to the United States, driving up housing prices in Los Angeles to an absurd level, often buying houses in cash. I wanted their business. But I want to be honest with you today—though what I said was also true, the main reason I can speak Chinese is because my first boyfriend was a Chinese. And, um ... I never expected you to know my brother ... that's incredible! Of course, he was not my boyfriend; he was my ... brother. Really, it's unbelievable! You never would have thought that I am, in fact, what you now call Miller's sister, although we are not blood-related."

"Sister?" I suddenly remembered my former Taiwanese colleague "Little Teresa Teng," whom Miller had once said resembled his sister. Intrigued, I took a few more glances at Tutu. Though she was now over sixty, between her eyebrows, eyes, and slightly puffed cheeks, there was a young Teresa Teng in her. But the ravages and torments of time had left their mark. Despite carefully maintaining her skin with skin-care products, the sagging flesh on her cheeks and the criss-crossing wrinkles at the corners of her eyes were clearly visible and her cheeks were far from being plump and rounded. Her skin was very much like that of an over-ripe persimmon: still appearing full but somewhat dry and cracked due to the lack of moisture.

"Ah, really? Is that true?" I blurted out, and then exchanged a glance with my wife, who was equally astonished. "What a coincidence!"

"Um, there's no mistake. I have held him in my heart and thought about him all these years, and almost every year, I sketch a portrait of him in my mind, so that if we ever crossed paths on the street by chance, I won't miss him face-to-face. Yes, he's just as I imagined. Of course, his partially crippled little finger is the most reliable evidence. By my calculations, we have been separated for almost forty-five years, starting from early 1977.

When I saw his photo at Costco, I was shocked. Later, while I was on my way to show the house to my clients, I was so preoccupied that I couldn't focus. The client was bombarding me with questions, but I couldn't absorb a single word and I had to send them away. I just want to talk to someone now, about my brother, about what has happened to me for most of my life, and another brother who shared your Chinese heritage. Alas, it's fate when I think of it. My life has been profoundly influenced by you Chinese people. I couldn't have survived without Chinese. I fell in love with Chinese people, and now I make a living counting on Chinese. I was not a superstitious person, but having suffered so much and encountered so many strange people, I became more and more superstitious. And now, again, it's you guys who helped me find my long-lost brother. Truly, I am overwhelmed with excitement! Thank you so much! Please excuse me if my words come out disorganized and incoherent. Right now, I just need to talk to you. Having bottled up so much for so many years, I have too many words inside me, wanting to come out. Moreover, I heard from your wife that you are a writer, constantly working on books. I have been eager to talk to you about some of the people and things I have encountered in my life, mainly about my brother, who you now refer to as Miller, and about my boyfriend. I would like to ask you to write a book about them, especially my brother, to help him clear his name from the unjust accusations. Of course, I would first ask you to help me meet—oh, right, Miller—as soon as possible. The sooner, the better, the faster, the better, and if I can see him tonight, I wouldn't have to wait until tomorrow!"

"But we don't have Miller's phone number, and to meet him we'd have to wait until the weekend," I said.

"It's alright, it's alright. I was just saying—anyway, alas, I'm just worried that the longer the night, the more nightmares there might be. I'm afraid that he would disappear again and be gone."

"That won't happen. Miller said he's always there every Saturday and Sunday, no matter what," I said reassuringly.

"That's good, that's good. That eases my mind. Saturday is just the day after tomorrow, isn't it? I can wait, I'm able to wait. I have been searching for him for nearly half a century, and I can wait a few more days."

"Well, it's a bit sultry inside," said my wife, upon seeing us standing at the entrance. "I think you should sit on the balcony. I'll go make some coffee for you."

I led Tutu through the porch and dining room, opened the east-facing sliding glass door, and we stepped out onto the balcony. The sun had not yet set. The undulating mountain ridges in the distance and the nearby houses, densely spaced and staggered, were painted with a golden afterglow of the setting sun. At the turn of autumn and winter, it was a warm hue that some people responded to with all kinds of reverie and myth.

Tutu, acting as a seller's agent, sold us this house, and she was quite familiar with the views, so she didn't give it much thought at first. But as she rested her hand on the balcony railing and swept her gaze over the courtyard below, taking in the lush green grass, the bamboo grove, the fountain, the wooden Chinese classical pavilion, and the winding bridge, she couldn't help but exclaim, "Wow, you guys have done a beautiful job — it's truly stunning!"

As we spoke, my wife came out with two cups of coffee and placed them on the small coffee table. We then sat down facing each other in a pair of swiveling wicker rocking chairs while my wife brought another cup of coffee and dragged another wooden chair to join us, so that we sat in an isosceles triangle formation.

Tutu lowered her head to take a sip of the coffee, then cradled the cup in her hands. She glanced at me, looking hesitant and unsure, as if she didn't know where to start.

"There's no rush; take it easy," I said in a comforting tone. "Just treat it as a chit-chat. It's OK if you don't want to talk about it."

"No, I rushed over here to confide — to pour everything out. 'Confide'? Am I using the right word?" I nodded, and she continued with relief, "I, in fact, always wanted to find someone to pour my heart out to, but I could never find the right person. Some things can't be understood unless experienced. In this world, it is not only hard to find someone who understands and loves you but it's also hard to find someone to confide in. It really depends on fate. I have been going to Xilai Temple a lot lately, where most of the monks are female nuns. They all seem to have their stories and have suffered emotional trauma. What they often say to me is that 'phenomena arise from causes and conditions and cease when such cause and conditions are not present.' My brother used to say this to me too, but at that time I couldn't understand it at all. Only now do I realize that in life, there is good karma, bad karma, and even sinful karma. After so many years — how do I put it? I still can't figure out whether these two people who once had the closest relationships with me were good, bad, or sinful karma? But one thing is for sure — they have always been the greatest pain in my heart ...

"Now I'm almost old enough to be a grandmother, yet the ones I dream about the most at night are still those two. One had long been gone from the earth, but this one — you now call Miller, I ... alas, I thought I would only see him again in the next life, but unexpectedly ... However, I want to give you a heads-up in advance; please don't share with anyone else what I am about to tell you about Miller. I don't know exactly what his current situation is; for example, does he have legal status? Does he have a family? You said he had been to five or six countries and spent time in Europe, but do you know why? You certainly don't know, because he wouldn't tell you. Only I know. He has been on the run and without a home because his name has been on the Cambodian government's global wanted list. However, he is very different from many of the Chinese who have fled or smuggled themselves here. He didn't leave his hometown purely for political reasons or to chase fortune. He fled for reasons that are difficult to explain in a few words ... Alas, he is now in his seventies and can no longer withstand life's bumps. But someone should know the truth of the matter. I don't want such a good person with a high state of mind to bear a tarnished reputation, not only misunderstood by his countrymen but also tarnishing the religion he believed in. All these years, I have been feeling guilty. I often hear the Chinese say that 'a beauty brings disaster.' I might just be such a person, that kind of disaster. If it weren't for me, they might have ..."

She suddenly paused, her chest heaving rapidly. Her hands trembled as she picked up the coffee cup from the table, seemingly trying to take a sip to calm the raging tide of emotions. However, just as the cup reached her lips, she put it down again. Two thin lines of tears streamed from her eyes, and she covered her face and began to weep. "You know, I want to see him right now. For decades, I've longed for him day and night, and finally, there's news of him. It can't be a dream, can it? He's not just my brother, he is also my savior. But I — I ruined him. Tell me, do I still have the face to see him?" she said, before breaking down into uncontrollable tears.

My wife, whose eyes were already red, quickly went back into the house and returned with a box of tissues. She pulled out a few and handed them to Tutu, saying, "Oh, Tutu, don't, please don't. If it hurts too much to talk about it, then don't."

Tutu first nodded and then shook her head, still convulsing. Once she finally managed to stop sobbing, she wiped away her tears and lifted her head again. She took a deep breath and slowly began to uncover the gauze on the long-unhealed wound in her heart, revealing to us, little by little, black scars and bright red flesh...

CHAPTER 8

Tutu told us her brother was born Jochen in a village on the outskirts of Phnom Penh. His father was a rural teacher who taught English, and their family was quite well-off.

Like Thailand and Myanmar, Cambodia is a Buddhist country with an exceptional number of temples and monks. One day, when Jochen was three or four years old, he accidentally fell into a pond at the end of the village while playing hide-and-seek with other boys. An old traveling mendicant monk saw it and rescued him in time. The old monk was quite eccentric and later insisted on taking Jochen as his disciple. Jochen's parents refused at first, but the old monk persistently visited, coaxing and pleading, and claimed that the child could only escape a deadly fate by following him. Despite their doubts, his parents consented, thinking that if it weren't for the monk's rescue, their son might have already lost his life.

The old monk did not reside in a temple. He typically wore a gray robe and a pair of cloth or straw shoes with leg bindings, living a life governed by fate and staying wherever was convenient. Whether under large trees, on piles of grass, in bridge archways, or on rocky riverbanks, he traveled and rested wherever he found it suitable. In that region, he was renowned for his expertise in the dharma of Wu Lou; "Wu Lou" is the Chinese term for non-leakage and signifies a state free from the leaks of mental defilements or flaws. This practice was said to be extremely challenging and nearly lost in Cambodia. Therefore, those who knew him referred to him as the Wu Lou Monk or Wu Lou Master. Besides, he was also skilled in physiognomy, medicine, and herbalism. During his walking meditations, he often helped people diagnose their illnesses or he read their faces. His treatments were usually effective, and his predictions often came true, so much so that many villagers who were unfamiliar with him thought he was a wandering physician or a fortune teller, thus holding him in even higher esteem.

There was a saying that had been circulating in the Buddhist world for a long time, which was that it was difficult for a disciple to find a master and even more difficult for a master to find a disciple. After passing the age of fifty, the Master Wu Lou also began to treat finding a successor as a matter of utmost importance in his life. His hanging heart finally settled after he found Jochen, whom people later referred to as Little Master Wu Lou or Little Wu Lou Monk.

Thereafter, in the early 1970s, when Lon Nol overthrew King Sihanouk in a coup d'état and the Khmer Rouge established the Cambodian National United Front with Prince Sihanouk and Prince Binh Ngu in Beijing, the old monk, seeing the turbulent times and the chaos in the country, decided not to travel anymore but to settle down and concentrate on teaching his disciple. The old monk, whose ancestors came from Chaozhou, China, not only spoke some Chaozhou dialect but also could write Chinese calligraphy, so he was very close to some monks of Chinese descent. Among them was Elder He Tong, originally a Taoist. He had revered Laozi's *Tao Te Ching* as "the fore-most sutra in the world." Later, he read the *Platform Sutra* of Huineng, the Sixth Patriarch of Zen Buddhism, and had an instant realization, converting to Buddhism. He was deeply impressed by the practice of alms gathering in Theravada Buddhism and traveled to India, Thailand, and Burma before finally settling in Cambodia. Coincidently, Elder He Tong passed away after the old monk took Jochen as his disciple, leaving a small courtyard temple in the jungle vacant. So, he and little Jochen settled there. In addition to planting crops and tending the vegetable garden daily, he taught Little Wu Lou Monk to read and write in Chinese and Khmer, as well as to meditate and cultivate the Buddha's dharma of non-leakage or dharma that is free of leaks or flaws. Sometimes, he also explained Buddhist scriptures to Little Monk, especially the *Lotus Sutra*, *Diamond Sutra*, *Shurangama Sutra*, and so forth, emphasizing that while practicing was important, reciting the scriptures was indispensable; only by fully understanding the essence of the scripture could he truly understand the essence of the dharma of non-leakage, which could also be said to be the highest state of Buddhist practice, and usually required many lifetimes to achieve.

"So have I been cultivating for many lifetimes?" Little Wu Lou once asked.

The old monk nodded and then told him, "You began your practice during the time of Buddha Dipankara. However, there have always been causes and conditions that interrupted and interfered with your progress, which is why you have yet to achieve anything. However, you should attain accomplishment in this life."

"But, Master, how do I know I have achieved a body free of leaks?" asked the little monk, who was not yet ten years old.

"Well, you might not fully understand even if I tell you this now. Once you have achieved it, you will be unhindered in both worldly and transcendental dharmas, without any leaks. Of course, when it comes to a man, there is another very important way to measure whether he has achieved a state of non-leakage: not even a drop of semen flows out, not even in a dream."

Not understanding, the Little Monk asked, "What is semen, Master?"

"You are still too young now; you will naturally know when you grow up."

"But where would the drop leak from?" asked Little Wu Lou, characteristically leaving no stone unturned as he continued to probe for a loophole while pinching and squeezing his body up and down.

The master laughed and said, "The conditions are not yet mature. When they are, you will naturally understand."

Then, Little Wu Lou let go of this thought.

It was also a twist of fate; when he was eleven years old, he went out with his master and ran into a little girl in ragged clothes, sallow-faced and starved to skin and bones. The little girl seemed to be only about four or five years old. They learned that she had been digging for mushrooms in the woods when she saw two robbers breaking into her house. Frightened, she didn't dare to go back and hid behind a bush until she saw the robbers fleeing her house, carrying two large bags. She rushed home only to find that her parents had been stabbed to death. Terrified, she cried for a long time watching her parents lying motionless in a pool of blood, and eventually fell asleep. When she woke up, fearing the robbers might return, she dared not stay at home and ran away.

They also learned that there was no one nearby that the little girl could turn to for help, so Little Wu Lou asked the master to take her in. The old monk was hesitant at first, concerned that the female aura's interference would spoil Little Wu Lou's practice. But then he thought again, reflecting on the compassionate nature of monks. How could he stand by and not save a life? Besides, he reasoned, this was also a part of Little Wu Lou's karmic path, not to be interfered with, so he agreed.

Many years passed by in a flash, and Little Wu Lou got along with the little girl just like brother and sister. While he was meditating and chanting with his master, she was in the vegetable garden chasing butterflies and playing with grass; while he was helping the master cook by tending the fires, she would clumsily assist by adding wood to it. After meals, she would stand on a low stool to help him scrub the pots and pans and wash the dishes together. Life was poor but joyful, especially for Little Wu Lou, whose face was always overflowing with uncontrollable smiles.

But probably because the tragic image of her parents lying in a pool of blood was too overwhelming, the little girl never smiled or could not smile. She would quietly stare at an ant, a bird, or even a weed or a wildflower for a long time. Once, while watching birds bouncing on the grass, she suddenly asked Little Wu Lou, "Brother, do birds die?" Without waiting for his response, she looked up at the sky and murmured, "I wish I were a bird; then I could fly to the sky to find my mom and dad."

Hearing this, Little Wu Lou felt his nose tingle. On the verge of tears, he raised his hand and began to stroke her head to comfort her. "Don't worry," he said in a soothing voice. "You still have your brother; this brother will protect you forever."

"But I also want a home. Brother, will you marry me someday?" she said, looking up earnestly at him.

"This…." Little Wu Lou blushed, not knowing how to respond properly. After thinking for a while, he resolutely said, "That can't be, I want to follow Master and cultivate the dharma of non-leakage."

"I knew it," she said, pouting. "I am not the one you like the most."

"Then who else?" he asked, somewhat puzzled.

"Wu Lou. You are always talking about Wu Lou; you must love yourself the most."

"This…" he said, lost for words.

"But, Brother, can you tell me what Wu Lou or non-leakage really is?"

"Um. Wu Lou isn't a thing, it's, well, that's—ahem, how can I tell you, it's like a valve to enlightenment."

"A valve? Like a water faucet? We saw those when we went into town last time."

"No, not that kind of valve. It's a metaphorical valve, one that controls the passage to dharma, the path we monks follow to learn Buddhism."

This confused Tutu. "Why do you need a metaphorical valve to learn Buddhism? Are real valves broken?"

"No, not like that," he said, struggling to provide her with a patient explanation. "Brother studies Buddhism to become a Buddha. One can also become a Buddha by cultivating a leak-free body, a state of 'anasrava' or a defilement-free state. Master often says that Buddhism is the most harmonious and thorough. Let's see," he said. Taking note of a small, purple, round-bellied teapot on a nearby tea table, he picked it up and pointed at it. "Look at Master's teapot," he said. "What is it for?"

"To drink tea. Who doesn't know that?"

"Let me ask you, what is the teapot used for?"

"To hold water and tea."

"Right. But let me ask you, if the teapot has cracks, can it still hold water?"

"It cannot; it will leak."

"That's right. The Master means our body is like this teapot—no cracks, no leaks. That's a good teapot, capable of holding the teachings of Buddhism."

"But not us girls," said Tutu, pouting and rolling her eyes.

"Why?"

"I once heard a granny offering an incense say that boys are like teapots because they have a spout, while girls don't, so girls can only be vases and are meant to marry boys when they grow up."

"Ha, where are you going with this? I'm done talking to you," Wu Lou said, turning to walk away.

But Tutu grabbed his sleeve and continued to pester him. "But doesn't the water still have to be poured out of the teapot?"

"Yes."

"Then isn't that also leaking?"

"It's ... it's pouring, not leaking ..."

"It's leaking, it's leaking; you're trying to fool me. You just don't want to marry me, so you make up these words to fool me! I'm not talking to you anymore," she said, before turning and running out the door.

He later found her under the guava tree in the backyard. Seeing her so disappointed and aggrieved, her face wet with tears, he ran to catch a beautiful yellow butterfly that happened by and rushed over to give it to her.

"I don't want it," she said, taking the butterfly and letting it fly away. "It has a mommy and daddy too." As she watched it flutter away, she brought her arms up to cover her face and cried, "I miss my mom and dad ..."

He immediately picked her up, kissed her on the face, and said, "OK. Tutu does not cry. Tutu good girl. Brother promise you, OK?"

"Really?" She rubbed her eyes and looked at him dubiously. Their faces were so close that their eyes were almost touching.

"Yes." He nodded emphatically.

Smiling through her tears, she hugged his head tightly.

The old monk happened to come by the backyard right then, and hearing their conversation, he shook his head and said, "Alas, the power of Buddha is always overshadowed by the power of karma."

Later, shortly before he died, he called the seventeen-year-old Little Wu Lou to his bedside and said to him, "You should let her go."

"Master, but why? Why?"

The old monk looked at him for a long time before saying, "Your bedsheets, I've seen them; you already had a leak."

He was alarmed and rushed to his bed to check it out. Sure enough, the center of the sheet had a palm-sized brown stain. He then recalled that in his dream the previous night, he had been anxiously riding a horse in the jungle in search of his sister. The horse galloped up and down, upsetting him so much that he suddenly felt something flowing out of his body. After waking up, he reached down to his lower body, felt a sticky puddle, and smelled something funny. He initially thought he had wet the bed, but it turned out to be…

"What should I do? What can be done, Master?"

"I also don't know what to do," the master replied. "To be honest with you, I—in fact, have had leaks, but they all occurred in dreams. Alas, after so many years, I have come to some understanding that being non-leakage is not truly being without leaks; it is just called non-leakage. One should not be overly attached to it. You can't be too attached to the idea of life, nor death. There is no duality between life and death." After that, the master began to sit in seclusion, without lying down, eating only once a day.

One day, Little Wu Lou brought a bowl of water for the master, only to discover that Master had quietly passed away while sitting there.

From then on, Little Wu Lou and his sister lived in the small temple, depending on each other.

CHAPTER 9

Time passed swiftly, year by year, and before they knew it, nearly a decade had elapsed since they started living on their own and depending solely on each other. One day, while pulling weeds in the vegetable garden, he noticed that his sister's forehead was covered with beads of sweat, like a budding, dewy wild chrysanthemum, blooming like a flower. And over time, she started to act in ways that were somewhat odd.

When he was chanting or meditating, she no longer messed with him by doing things like poking his ear with a chicken feather or coughing incessantly to draw his attention. Instead, she sat staring intently without moving a muscle. When he happened to turn around and meet her gaze, a flush of red would immediately spread across her face, and she would lower her head shyly and fiddle with the buttons of her sweater.

By then, the war had ended, gunfire was seldom heard in the jungle, the Khmer Rouge had marched into Phnom Penh, the Lon Nol government had collapsed, and Cambodia was now Democratic Kampuchea.

Still, no matter how the world changed, the temple remained tranquil as always.

The number of people coming to worship the Buddha dwindled, and the offerings decreased sharply with each passing day, slightly affecting their livelihood. Nevertheless, the fruits and vegetables in their garden thrived under their meticulous care, yielding a bountiful harvest sufficient to sustain their living.

Occasionally, they felt as though the temple was forgotten by the world. Yet, being forgotten also had its benefits; it allowed them to live more peacefully, more comfortably, and without worries...

On a beautiful autumn night, the full moon rose gradually from behind the whirling trees and hung high in the sky. White clouds, like a veil, kept wrapping around the moon's bright face. The birds seemed to have returned to their nests. It was quiet, but one could hear the endless chirping of the autumn insects. At the time, he was already in his mid-twenties, and she had passed her fifteenth birthday.

After dinner, seeing how beautiful the moonlight was, they sat together on a cyan stone bench in the courtyard and craned their necks to view the moon.

But she was not looking at the moon but at him.

"What are you looking at me for?" he said, gently poking the center of her forehead with his index finger. "It's not like you don't know me!"

With an angry pout, she turned away, refusing to look at him. Then she lowered her head again, looking preoccupied.

"Do you have something on your mind? What is it?" he asked.

She gave him a look and said nothing.

"Please tell me. I'm your brother, your only family in this world.

If you don't tell me, who else can you tell?" He pressed the question with some urgency.

She remained silent.

Later, under his persistent urging, she plucked up the courage to look up at him affectionately, then lowered her head again and said softly, like a mosquito whisper, but clearly, "Brother, I want to know—when will you...marry me..."

He couldn't believe his ears. "What? Did I ever say I would marry you?"

"You did. You said it when you caught a butterfly for me in the vegetable garden. You can't deny it!"

"But—even if I did say that, I was just wheedling you out of crying. Don't you know that I am your brother! How could—and..."

"It's not like you're my real brother," she said sharply.

"But you said that I was dearer to you than a blood brother!"

"That's a different thing."

"No way. That can't possibly happen!"

"Shame on you. You lied!" She balled up her fists and pounded on him.

"Ah, that's not true; you were just a child then, and I just didn't want to upset you. Marry you? How could that be possible? I am a monk, and to marry you, I'd have to return to the secular, but if I did, I would never be able to cultivate a leak-free body.

"Is a leak-free body really so important?"

"Of course. As the master said—"

"You've got leaks too. I overheard it at the door that day when the master was speaking to you. He said there was already something on your bed...I saw it too...Also, I once helped wash your shorts and saw a stubborn stain that wouldn't wash off..." she said, blushing.

His face turned even redder than hers in an instant, because, although the leak occurred in a dream, unseen and unknown to anyone, he knew it was because of her. And now, his sister was looking at him with pure eyes full of trust and expectation, as if she had peeked into the secret of his dreams. All of a sudden, he was flustered and did not know what to say. Once he composed himself, he firmly shook his head and said, "No, I can't. The master said I have already cultivated countless lifetimes and am close to success with just a little more effort. I cannot waste all my previous efforts. Even if there is indeed a leak, I must seal it promptly; I will not smash a pot because of a single crack."

With that, he stood up from the stone bench, walked into the hall, stood at the base of the Buddha statue, and bowed deeply to Maitreya Buddha with his palms pressed together. He then chanted the Great Compassion Mantra and the Medicine Buddha Mantra, over and over again.

Later, he stayed up almost all night.

The next day, after completing his morning chants, he wanted to have a serious talk with his sister to completely dispel her unrealistic thought. But seeing her eyes swollen from crying, he couldn't bring himself to do it. Finally, it was his sister who spoke first. "You don't need to comfort me anymore. I understand. Since childhood, I've always dreamed of having a home, a home that truly belongs to both you and me, but I forget you are determined to be a monk... Don't worry, I won't pressure you anymore. All I ask is that you let me stay by your side forever, never leaving or forsaking, and be your dharma protector..."

He was touched by her words and wanted to hold her in his arms, kiss her, and wipe away her tears, just as he had done when she was little. But seeing her now, grown into such a beautiful young woman, her eyes radiant, her chest bulging as if concealing a pair of wooden fish, he couldn't help reminding himself of the master's frequent admonitions to him: "Women are like tigers; the more beautiful a woman is, the more dangerous she is."

He then tried hard to suppress the impulse.

After lunch, having thought long and hard, with great resolve, he finally spoke to her nervously. "Sister," he said, "this is the situation. Well, um, mid-next month will be the tenth anniversary of the master's passing. Last night, I dreamed of him saying to me, 'My disciple, cultivation is like rowing a boat—if you do not advance, you retreat. You must not stop halfway!' So since then I've been thinking about doing something to express my deep gratitude for the master and, of course, to strengthen my monastic heart."

"What are you going to do?" she asked, not quite understanding.

"I will offer a burning finger to Buddha," he said.

"What? Burning a finger—to offer to Buddha?" Having never heard of such a thing, she stared at him wide-eyed.

"The master once told me about this, and the Buddha also spoke of it in the *Shurangama Sutra*: 'If, after my passing, there be a bhiksu who is determined to practice samadhi, and in front of the image of the Tathagata, lights a lamp on his body, or burns a finger joint, or lights a stick of incense on his body, I say this person has paid his boundless past debts in a single moment, will bow out of the world and be forever free from all leaks. Though not yet fully enlightened, he is on the path to supreme enlightenment. This person has already devoted himself to the Dharma. If he does not perform this act and instead sacrifices his body for minor causes, even if he achieves a state of non-leakage, he will still return to the world and repay his longstanding past debts.' Think about it, what does it mean to be forever free from all leaks? Isn't it the state of Nirvana?" he said, speaking faster and faster, in his eyes two star-like spots sparkling constantly.

"You mean you want to burn your own fingers as an offering to the Buddha?" She heard it clearly this time, her eyes widening even more.

"Yes."

"But how? Fingers are not twigs or firewood. How can they be lit?" She was skeptical.

"Master had told me about this. When he was in a large temple in Phnom Penh to place orders, he saw people performing this ritual. They would tie the finger to be burned tightly with thread or gauze to cut off the blood circulation. After three or four days, they would unwrap it to find the skin and flesh turned black. When they feel no pain even when poked with a knife, they then rewrap the finger, pour incense oil, and light a fire on it."

"It is easier to say. That must still be excruciating! What's more, the finger would certainly be ruined after the burn. How are you supposed to do things in the future?" Although she had not seen him do it, she was horrified at the thought of it. She would scream from the pain of an ant bite, let alone the pain of an open flame. She was stunned.

"Don't worry. I'll use the little finger of my left hand; at most it will end up slightly shortened, and that won't affect the cultivation and daily life." He tried to sound casual, downplaying it as if it were as easy as taking a few sips of hot porridge.

"So, you've made up your mind?"

"Yes."

"Is it a well-thought-out decision that will not be changed or swayed?"

"A commander's rank can be stripped away, but the resolve of even an ordinary person cannot be taken from them," he responded.

"But isn't it self-harming? To cripple your body, even if it's just a small finger, isn't it still a defilement, a leak?"

Hearing her words, he was stunned for a moment but still said, unwaveringly, "If a minor physical impairment can be traded for the undefiled and non-leakage state of the dharma mind, then it is worth it."

She saw in his eyes the steely determined look, the fervent desire to devote himself, and his ardent yearning to cultivate a leak-free body. As much as she admired his fortitude and was deeply touched by his commitment, she was also heartbroken. Because she knew very well that it was not about burning a finger as an offering to Buddha; it was his declaration, by resorting to a cruel ritual, to completely sever ties with all worldly matters, including marriage, family, and those emotions, buried one day, bubbling the next, that hindered his quest for the enlightenment. In short, having chosen to be a monk, a renouncer, he could no longer remain entangled with this world of passions and desires. At best, all she could do as a younger sister was to be an assistant or a nurse to help him prepare the threads, gauze, wet towels, incense oil, salted water, incense ash, and so on.

He chose the eighth day of the fourth lunar month, the Buddha's birthday, to burn his finger as an offering to Buddha.

He rose at dawn to bathe. He had originally planned to do so in the Shadow Pond, less than a mile away, where they often went together. However, due to constant rain, the water there was a bit muddy and not pristine enough at that time. He then decided to draw water from an ancient well, surrounded by a stone fence, in the middle of the courtyard. He lifted a small wooden bucket full of water over his head and poured it down over and over again.

After ensuring that he was thoroughly cleansed, he carefully dried all parts of his body with a new towel, changed into a clean cassock, and lit scented candles and an altar lamp. He then knelt straight in front of the Maitreya Buddha statue in the hall, chanting the Great Compassion Mantra, the Shurangama Mantra, and the Medicine Buddha Heart Mantra, over and over again until the clouds cleared and the sun rose and shone and the hall was bright. Then, he had her help him rewrap the gauze around the little finger of his left hand and tighten it with cotton thread at the first knuckle. Using a small porcelain spoon, he carefully scooped out half a spoonful of scented oil from the bowl used to light the altar lamp, and carefully dripped it onto his already completely disfigured little finger.

It was she who struck the matches for him, but after lighting the first two matches, she grew increasingly nervous, her hands trembling so much that the flame went out before it reached his finger.

"Don't be nervous. I don't even take it seriously. Think about it," he said reassuringly. "You should be happy for me now that I will be 'forever free from all leaks!'"

She then closed her eyes and hard-heartedly poked the third burning match at the tip of his upright little finger. The fire, upon touching the scented oil, ignited with a sizzling sound, quickly forming a flame the size of an olive, resembling the old monk's bright, wise eye, often half-open and half-closed.

When the fire first popped, perhaps because it had not yet touched the skin through layers of gauze, Wu Lou was not aching and still wearing a smile. But soon, the smile faded, and his forehead began to spill large beads of sweat. Then, the excruciating pain spread from the burning finger to the adjacent fingers and the back of the hand. Seeing this, she quickly took a pre-prepared wet towel to wrap around his little finger.

After about five or six minutes, the air was filled with the choking smell of burnt flesh.

She then hurriedly said to him, "Brother, that should be enough, right? I think that should be enough."

But he shook his head firmly. "No, as I said, at least fifteen minutes."

She could only continue to follow his instructions, pouring scented oil on the shrinking finger. Gradually, the mixture of the scented oil and the flesh emitted subtle sizzling and crackling sounds.

The pain Wu Lou felt must have been immense, but she felt that her suffering was greater than his, not only because his pain distressed her deeply but also because his action drove her to despair. Although it was his finger that burned, what was extinguished was the last flicker of hope in her heart for having a home with him. While he took a big leap towards the supreme state of non-leakage, he also built a wall between them, one that would be exceedingly difficult to tear down both mentally and physically.

When the monk finally accomplished the feat of burning his finger for the Buddha amidst unbearable pain and sweat, Tutu tended his wounds with trembling hands, her eyes tearing and her heart dripping blood. When she finally put his charred finger into a bowl of salted water to reduce inflammation, seeing his bitten lips and hearing the rattling sound between his teeth, she could no longer keep from bursting into tears.

CHAPTER 10

The incident caused a rift in their relationship. Although they lived in the same courtyard, one in the east room, and the other in the west room, it was as if they were separated by the Mekong River or Tonle Sap River, often going days without speaking to each other. Her face and eyes became as cold as ice and snow.

Meanwhile, the world outside the small temple was undergoing earthshaking changes.

What the Khmer Rouge did after coming to power was so extreme that it left not only their enemies but also their like-minded supporters in disbelief and astonishment.

The portrait of their leader, Pol Pot, was often featured in the newspaper — dressed in a Mao-style tunic suit, with short hair, a side-parted hairstyle, eyebrows that were short and black, a high forehead, large ears, full cheeks, a slightly upturned chin, and a mouth slightly open to reveal a row of straight, snow-white teeth, always maintaining a quiet smile.

Yet it was this gentle-looking man who turned Cambodia restless and upside down.

Private ownership was abolished, trading of goods prohibited; currency circulation was strictly forbidden, and even bartering, the most primitive form of trade, was not allowed. They also orchestrated a massive relocation of nearly two million people from Phnom Penh, leading to hundreds of thousands of deaths.

The new regime classified everyone into "old people" and "new people." The "old people" were those who were already in the liberated areas before the capture of Phnom Penh, primarily peasants. The "new people" consisted of military and political personnel, intellectuals, monks, skilled workers, businessmen, and urban residents from the former regime. The "new people" had to undergo rehabilitation to be reborn and were required to re-register, giving an account of their past histories. Anyone who had served the Lon Nol regime, was discontent with the new government, was wealthy, or refused to voluntarily leave Phnom Penh was summarily executed without a trial. They also launched a campaign to purge class ranks. Property owners, business owners, intellectuals, teachers, doctors, and other professionals who were not part of the proletariat were targeted for purging. Individuals who wore glasses and those who spoke foreign languages were also marked, with the latter considered a capital offense. At the same time, the government banned all religious beliefs, closed or destroyed all churches and temples, forced Buddhists to return to secular life, and compelled Muslims to eat pork. Party dissenters, as well as ordinary citizens, were often regarded as spies for Vietnam or the Soviet Union, or as American agents, and were arrested and executed.

Some of those who escaped from the more remote jungles said things like, "It's hard to know how many bamboo houses we've built over these years," "The most I've seen in my life were bears, snakes, and yellow deer," "We ate anything we could swallow, such as red ants, rats, snakes, tubers, and so on. We also used cages to catch birds, but before eating them, we had to take the seeds out of their throats and save them for planting."

The new regime regarded knowledge as a sin. They established no formal schools, banned books and printed materials, and only revolutionary songs and dances were allowed; traditional songs, dances, and theaters were outlawed, and the spread of Western culture was strictly prohibited. Men and women were separated and lived in large communal dwellings by the fields. Married couples were only allowed to meet once a week.

It was as if people had been organized to cultivate the leak-free body collectively.

Only the troops who watched over these townspeople enjoyed a bit of freedom. They used their patrols as an opportunity to wander around and even go hunting for various types of game from the jungle such as wild boar, hares, and pheasants.

One day at dusk, a young officer of such a troop was hunting near a small temple and unexpectedly encountered a beautiful girl by the Shadow Pond, who caught his eyes more than the wildlife.

The so-called Shadow Pond was actually named by Little Wu Lou's master. One day, they went to a household to perform a Buddhist ritual for the deceased. On their way back, they took a shortcut along a winding mountain stream. As they walked, they saw that the stream was blocked by several dark boulders on three sides at a sharp bend, forming a pond over five feet deep, about the size of a patio, with crystal clear water that reflected not only the sky and the clouds but also the shadows of trees and people. The master said, "The shadows of the clouds, the people, and the trees are all like bubbles in a

dream; thus, let's call it 'Shadow Pond' henceforth." On the opposite side of the three boulders lay a rocky slope, inclined at approxi-
mately forty-five degrees. From its peak, one could vaguely make out
the small temple, nested within the lush green jungle.

The young officer climbed to the top of the rocky slope from the
other side and looked around. He spotted a young girl bathing in the
clear water at the foot of the slope. Taken aback, he turned quickly
away and backed down the rocky slope. But he soon stopped and
rubbed his eyes, thinking that what he had just seen was nothing
more than an illusion.

He was a young man in his early twenties from Guangxi, China,
but he had been serving in the Cambodian military for over seven
years. The scene he had stumbled upon reminded him of a folktale
that he had read in his middle school Chinese literature textbook: A
fairy secretly descends to the mortal world, bathing in a lake, only
to be stumbled upon by a young man who hides her clothes, and
later they become husband and wife. Reflecting on this, he turned
around, climbed back up to the top of the slope, and lay flat on the
hard rocks, holding his breath as he peered down from above.

By then, the girl had emerged from the water and was standing
on the rocky shore of the pond, her back to him, using a towel to dry
her wet hair and water-drenched, newly developed torso. She then
bent down to pick up a blue floral top and a pair of gray-white trousers from the ground and put them on. She seemed to hesitate for a
while, then sat down on the rocky beach, pulling the long hair that
fell over her chest, biting her lips, appearing somewhat unhappy. After
some time, as if having thoroughly thought through something and
made a decision, she flung her hair back, picked up a pebble from
beside her, and hurled it with all her might into the pond. Watching

the ripples spread out in circles on the water's surface, she gradually smoothed her tightly furrowed brow.

He was momentarily stunned, thinking that it was a dream.

The sun began to set in the west, and the twilight gradually closed in. The girl finally stood up, patted her body gently a few times, stepped through a rock crevice, and disappeared.

It was only after a while that he caught a trace of her blue floral cloth top through the distant trees and watched it flutter into a courtyard with a tall, crooked-necked elm tree in front of the door.

He had passed by the courtyard before and knew it was also a small temple.

"Could she be a nun? But how could a nun have such long hair?" he wondered.

In order to find out, he often made use of his patrols and hunting excursions to roam around the area of Shadow Pond. However, since that day, she seemed to never go to Shadow Pond, except for once when he spotted her accompanied by a young man who looked like a monk. As she bathed in the pond, he sat quietly at the top of the rocky slope, his back to the Shadow Pond, reading a book while keeping watch for her.

At his wits' end, the young officer came to their residence under the guise of checking household registration and monitoring itinerant people. This is when they became officially acquainted. But when he saw her close-up, he saw that the girl was just sixteen or seventeen years old—around the same age he was when he finished middle school—and still childlike in appearance.

Monk Wu Lou and his sister noticed that the young officer had very fair skin, not typical of Cambodians. They learned that he was originally from Guanxi, China. His given name was Wu Huaiyu, with "Yu" meaning jade. However, during the world-famous Great Proletarian Cultural Revolution, when it was fashionable to rename roads, streets, stores, and people, he altered his name to be in line with the spirit of the times. While keeping the phonetic sound the same, he changed the character "Yu" from jade to universe, making it appear more revolutionary, combative.

After they got to know each other better, Wu Huaiyu told them bluntly that his arrival in Cambodia was entirely due to a twist of fate. But he also confidently told them, "I have never regretted it. I don't hide my opinions either; I never believed in such a thing as Buddhism — it's a superstition. But fate, well, I think there might be such a thing," he said, shooting her a meaningful look. But she didn't understand that he was alluding to his encounter with her at the Shadow Pond.

CHAPTER 11

Wu Huaiyu later voluntarily disclosed to Wu Lou and Tutu that he had run away from home secretly when he was about her current age. He had since become a battle-hardened company commander in the Overseas Chinese Battalion under Khieu Samphan.

What surprised Wu Lou was Wu Huaiyu's apparent hatred for his family, especially his father. He shared that he had left home without telling his family.

"Do you miss home?" Wu Lou asked.

"Yes, of course, mostly my mom and my sister. But once the war started, you couldn't care about anything else."

"Then why do you hate your father? Don't your Chinese people emphasize filial piety towards parents? When I was young, my master even taught me the Chinese *Three Character Classic*, which says, 'When one's parents are alive, one shouldn't travel far.' "

"Ah, that's old history, relics of feudalism and revisionism. Kinship is determined by class. To us revolutionaries, the entire world is our home."

Wu Lou was bewildered, especially when he heard novel words from Wu Huaiyu every now and then, such as "revolution," "class," "feudalism," and "revisionism," words he had never heard before.

Eventually, though, he figured out why Wu Huaiyu harbored resentment towards his father and journeyed thousands of miles to Cambodia.

His father was a tailor in the town where they lived and owned a small tailor shop with a single storefront. Although stubborn and even a bit bull-headed, he was a good craftsman, hardworking and thrifty, never easily discarding a scrap of thread or a piece of leftover fabric. He saved up for a family business over time. Against the opposition of his entire family, he purchased over ten acres of land in the nearby countryside in the tumultuous days approaching liberation, not anticipating that it would soon be confiscated by the new red regime under their campaign to "fight the local tyrants and redistribute the land."

After losing his land, he could only resign himself to his bad luck and try to put it behind him. However, he didn't anticipate that during the subsequent land reforms and class-restructuring movements, he would be labeled as an enemy of the new regime, grouped among landlords, rich peasants, and small business owners. He had never cared much about the world's happenings, but he had not been spared by them. From the Three-anti and Five-anti Campaign to the Cultural Revolution, one movement after another. He endured public criticism and humiliation outside, and when he returned home, unable to vent his frustration elsewhere, he often took it out on his wife and children, breaking into rages, throwing tantrums, and slamming pots and pans, much like a prison warden.

As a child of a member of the "four enemy classes," Wu Huaiyu was seen as inherently inferior, and even if he did well, he was at best considered an "educable youth." When he returned home, he still had to face the double oppression from his father, a member of the "enemy class." Life seemed unbearably dark to him. Therefore, from the age of ten, he began planning to run away from home one day, to completely break away from his family and start a new life in a place where no one knew about his past.

Perhaps to be accountable for his newly changed name, after finishing junior high, he made a life-changing decision. Inspired by the revolutionary song "Go wherever you are needed, settle wherever hardship lies," and by the revolutionary zeal of "exploring the world with your homeland in heart" in the newspapers and magazines, he decided to follow some of his classmates, hide in a train, and sneak across the border into Vietnam to join the fight against the United States in support of Vietnam.

The group consisted of four people, all childhood classmates and friends. The other three came from good backgrounds, while he was the only one from an exploitative class. At first, they were hesitant to accept him, but they knew he was acquainted with a woman who had fled from Vietnam. This woman, married to his disabled neighbor, was shunned by the townspeople except for Wu, the only person who respected and showed sympathy for her. She expressed her gratitude by offering him special treats when her husband was not around; she would stop him and slip an egg or a baked sweet potato or something into his pocket when he passed by her house on his way to school. Through these interactions, he actually picked up some everyday Vietnamese, a skill that was extremely valuable to the group. So, they decided to bring him along. He would serve as a sort of interpreter; at least it would be easier to ask for directions.

It was early autumn and still very hot. They took a train from Chongzuo to Nanning, then transferred from Nanning to Friendship Pass and waded across the border river so they would reach the other side after dusk and avoid the sentry's surveillance. Once ashore, they followed a group of Vietnamese who crossed the border for business, hoping to blend in and board a train or long-distance bus to Hanoi. But they saw that the border guards on the Vietnamese side were strict in their checks, and it was difficult for them to get on board without Vietnamese ID cards. After weighing their options, they decided to emulate the spirit of the Red Army's Long March, walking on two legs.

"It's only a 180-kilometer-long journey; if we walk fast, we can make it in four days," Wu Huaiyu said confidently.

Unfortunately, his thinking was a bit too optimistic.

Their feet began to blister after only one day of walking, causing drilling pain. Fearing that they would be interrogated and repatriated before reaching Hanoi, they did not march along the road openly; instead, they walked off the road, often climbing up and down the hills or hobbling on narrow paths, resting during the day and walking at night. Very soon, they exhausted their supply of dry food, so they were forced to sleep in bridge underpasses or haystacks during the day and venture out at night to steal the tender corn or thumb-sized sweet potatoes from the fields. Once, they were caught by a nightguard who nearly beat them up. Thanks to Wu's quick wit, they pretended to be homeless and mute, chirping and shrieking, looking pathetic. When the night guard saw that they were just a group of homeless and disabled youths, he became sympathetic towards them and let them off the hook.

After that, they simply disguised themselves as beggars — not that they needed much disguise, as their clothes had long been in rags, their hair disheveled like a bird's nest, and they were thin and tanned, looking every bit like starving ghosts. In this way, they dined in the wind, slept in the open air, begged all the way, and in an early morning nine days later, finally reached Hanoi, the capital of North Vietnam.

Walking on the asphalt boulevard, they saw the ubiquitous red Vietnamese national flags with a large, yellow five-pointed star in the middle. It felt as if they were looking at their homeland's five-star red flag, evoking a profound sense of closeness. Their exhaustion immediately vanished.

Later, as they passed a gate that resembled a government agency, they stopped and saw a statue of an affable old man with a white beard in the courtyard. "Look, Ho Chi Minh!" they exclaimed, feeling even more at home. Wu Huaiyu hurriedly asked a passerby in Vietnamese, "What is this place?" The man told them, "It's the district government." Overjoyed that finding the place had been so easy, they eagerly swarmed into the courtyard.

They found it truly heartening to see an elderly man in the reception room who understood Chinese. After listening to what they had to say, he picked up a black hand-cranked telephone receiver on a desk near a window and made a call to some department. Shortly after, a thin, short, competent-looking man in grass-green military fatigues, without any cap badge or collar insignia, came down the wide concrete staircase leading downstairs, his face expressionless.

"Where are you from?" he asked, in stilted Vietnamese that seemed to buzz and rattle through his nose.

"Guangxi, China," Wu Huaiyu replied in Vietnamese. As soon as the words were out of his mouth, a classmate behind him added enthusiastically in Chinese, "Your rear base!"

The Vietnamese officer showed no reaction; perhaps he didn't grasp the meaning of "rear base" or he had become accustomed to the many Chinese who, like them, had come to fight the "American Imperialists" on the front line.

"Where are you headed?" he asked.

"To South Vietnam, to fight the American Imperialists!" Wu Huaiyu replied. Before he could say more, another student eagerly cut in to add, "And the puppet army, and all the reactionaries!"

"Do you have a letter of introduction?" the officer asked abruptly in Chinese, apparently unmoved and extending his dark, thin fingers towards them.

"A letter of introduction? What letter of introduction?" They looked at each other with baffled expressions. "A letter of introduction to fight against the US in support of Vietnam?" exclaimed Wu Huaiyu, perhaps a bit too loudly.

"Of course. As per our policy, we need to verify your identities."

"Is there such a thing? But we didn't know. We don't have one. We came voluntarily," said Wu Huaiyu, feeling compelled to answer as the others fell silent. "We want to join the Chinese People's Volunteer Army."

"Where did you hear there is a Chinese People's Volunteer Army in our country?" asked the Vietnamese officer, scrutinizing them gravely. His once indifferent gaze now took on an added layer of vigilance, as if he suspected they might be spies sent from the South.

Feeling panicked, helpless, and deeply regretful for not having done their homework thoroughly, they all wondered how not one of them had thought of getting a letter of introduction. They had heard adults say that a letter of introduction was necessary for business trips, travels, and hotel stays within the country. Vietnam, a socialist country like theirs, would of course require a letter of introduction to prove one's identity! But who would write a letter of introduction for those who ran away from school and families?

Fortunately, after staring at them for several uncomfortable minutes, the Vietnamese cadre, probably concluding that they did not look like bad guys, softened his tone somewhat. "Wait here for a moment," he said, and headed to the reception room to make a call.

While he was on the phone, these unofficial "Chinese People's Volunteer Army" soldiers waiting outside, not knowing where fate would take them, had mixed feelings.

They thought to themselves: Didn't Uncle Ho Chi Minh say, "The friendship between Vietnam and China is profound, akin to comrades plus brothers?" He held such deep affection for China, visiting China more frequently than one would visit relatives, sometimes staying for years. How warmly did we welcome him? We not only rolled out the red carpet but also had female students present him with flowers. Yet here we are, coming voluntarily to help them fight the Americans, and they...

Besides, we had been through such a challenging journey, trekking through the mountains, nearly giving up multiple times. But we persevered, driven by our deep proletarian feelings for the Vietnamese people and our intense hatred towards American imperialism, gritting our teeth all the way. Who would have thought that when we finally met our "comrades plus brothers," we were not offered a sip of hot water, nor a single word of comfort, but instead were met with suspicion... What should we do? What could we do? Do we really have to produce a letter of introduction? How and where would we even obtain one?

Thankfully, just when they felt hopeless, the Vietnamese cadre came out of the reception room looking much more relaxed. In a cordial tone, he told them, "A car will pick you up later."

Thrilled, they thanked him profusely in their newly learned Vietnamese, "Thank you, thank you, thank you!"

Soon, a familiar Chinese-made Jiefang truck appeared at the gate and drove slowly into the courtyard. After parking the truck, an elderly driver in his fifties, one eye slightly misaligned, got out. The Vietnamese cadre approached him, spoke to him briefly, then turned back to them and said, "This Shifu will take you there today."

"Where to? The front line?" someone asked.

"You'll know when you get there," the cadre replied with a slight smile. With their worries turned to joy, they were so exhilarated that they jumped up, spontaneously chanting slogans: "Long live, Chairman Ho Chi Minh!" "Long live Vietnam-China friendship!" "Long live Chairman Mao, forever and ever!" At the same time, they competed to shake hands with the Vietnamese cadre to say goodbye.

The older driver pulled open the front passenger side door, one eye on the seat and the other on the group, indicating that one of them could sit there.

They then looked at each other. Since Wu Huaiyu had been the one mainly responsible for communication throughout the trip and he was the only one who knew a bit of Vietnamese, they unanimously elected him to sit in the driver's cab.

Wu Huaiyu did not excuse himself; after watching the other three climb into the open bed of the truck, he grabbed the door handle, stepped onto the high footboard, leapt up, and then slid into the seat in the cab.

After the car started, the driver turned his head around—not looking at Wu Huaiyu but simply pointing at his mouth—and asked in Vietnamese, "Have you had breakfast?"

"Not yet" he replied, recalling that he had not had a full meal in days and his stomach had been rumbling nonstop.

After the car left Hanoi, the driver stopped in front of a roadside shop. He spoke to the proprietress, who came rushing out, gestured to the group in the open truck bed to get out, and had everyone sit around a round table on the roadside. Later, the driver paid for everyone to have two bowls of Vietnamese rice noodles and two Vietnamese spring rolls. He also asked her for a receipt.

After being fed and getting back on the road, feeling warm and fuzzy, Wu Huaiyu asked the driver in Vietnamese, "Shifu, are we going to Ho Chi Minh Trail?"

He asked this because he had heard from a veteran who fought in Vietnam that the only way for North Vietnamese troops to enter the South was through the Ho Chi Minh Trail, which passed through not only Laos but also Cambodian territory, where the Americans could not strike North Vietnamese troops in compliance with international laws. Therefore, a significant number of North Vietnamese combatants and logistical supplies were transported to the South via this trail.

The driver did not look at him or respond to his question, probably in strict observance of military secrecy. Instead, he said in a low, muffled voice, "You will find out when you arrive."

Wu Huaiyu did not dare to ask anything more. Exhausted from the lack of food and sleep, and further lulled by the movement of the car, he became very drowsy. Soon he fell asleep with his head resting against the window.

CHAPTER 12

An hour later, the Jiefang truck began to shake violently, as if it had caught malaria, so intensely that one's skeleton could have fallen apart.

The driver stopped the truck. First he looked under the hood, then he crawled underneath the vehicle, touching and knocking around, and carefully tightened some loose screws with a wrench. The people in the back also got out and stood around to watch. Seemingly interested in the construction of the Jiefang truck, they squatted down one after another, their hands on the ground, peering intently at the vehicle's underside. The driver turned around and waved them off with a greasy hand. "What are you looking at?" he asked, gazing at them coldly. "Go away, go away! Just you people, I don't see you guys fighting the Americans on the front line. You would have been wiped out before seeing them. Nothing but troublemakers!"

He fiddled under the car for a while before his legs, followed by the rest of his body, wriggled out from underneath like an earthworm.

"What? Hurry up and get in!" he barked at them once he stood up, waving his wrench at the dazed onlookers.

They exchanged glances as they realized that, despite the scowl on the driver's face and his eyes not looking in the same direction, he was speaking Chinese.

"You speak Chinese! You are Chinese?" one of them asked in amazement.

"No. I am Vietnamese, a Vietnamese who speaks your Chinese," the driver snapped, seemingly at the end of his patience. He then commanded, "Get in!"

For the rest of the journey there was silence.

Sitting in the cab, Wu Huaiyu kept turning to the old driver, wanting to say something, but was blocked by the man's cold face and the uncertainty of where he was gazing.

The only time they interacted was when the driver, presumably sensing Wu's thirst, took the initiative and unhooked a worn military water bottle hanging behind his seat and handed it to him.

After drinking some water, he fell back into a deep sleep and had a dream. In the dream, he was officially accepted as a soldier in the Chinese People's Volunteer Army. He was riding in an artillery vehicle headed to the front line, with his former middle school teacher surprisinlgy serving as the company commander.

When he woke up, he was dismayed to find that their car had returned to Friendship Pass, and the driver was negotiating with the Chinese border guards. Then, a bearded Chinese soldier wearing an armband shouted, "Get out quickly!"

Once they all complied, the soldier let out a laugh as he surveyed them, with their heads bowed and bodies stooped as if defeated on the front line. "You're really something," he said sarcastically. "A trip to Hanoi and chauffeured back. But tonight, you'll have to make do with sleeping on the large communal bed." Then he added, "Tomorrow morning, I will arrange a car to send you back to Chongzuo."

"Back to Chongzuo? How do you know we came from Chongzuo?" Wu Huaiyu asked.

The bearded man laughed again. "You have been missing for so many days. The higher-ups have informed us and sent us the photos. You—" he flipped through a few sheets of paper in his hand. "You are Wu Huaiyu, right?"

Wu Huaiyu nodded hastily, feeling utterly defeated inside.

Meanwhile, his classmates were in fairly good spirits, even a bit cheerful, especially after a hearty meal. With all the turmoil they had been through for so many days, their original ambition and spirit to become combat heroes had long since evaporated. Now, all they wanted was a peaceful rest in bed, free from any disturbances.

Therefore, as soon as their heads touched the pillows on the wooden plank communal bed, they fell into a deep sleep, as if magnetized, and they would not wake up even if someone were to carry them away.

But not Wu Huaiyu.

His classmates could chicken out and turn back, but he couldn't.

He did not want to be a weak-willed revolutionary, let alone return to face his "prison warden" father. The only way out of his life was to leave behind his lifeless, caged home, enveloped in layers of iron curtains, so that he could breathe and live. Once he was certain that his buddies were in slumber, he quietly sat up, got out of bed, and opened the door.

All was silent. The lookout guards were dozing as he tiptoed quietly into the dark night.

He ran with uneven steps for a long time. It was not until dawn that he heard the sound of cars. Knowing that the road was not far away, he ran toward the sound of the vehicles.

He decided not to walk all the way to Hanoi. It would take too long and be too arduous. It seemed more sensible to hitch a ride. The border was farther away, and there were no more checkpoints, so the risk would be much less.

What he least expected was for the first vehicle he stopped to be the Jiefang truck that transported them back to Friendship Pass.

When he and the old driver, whom he had just parted with the night before, suddenly recognized each other in the thick morning fog, his first instinct was to flee. But before he could turn and run, the old driver shouted, "Don't run! Don't worry—I won't send you back!"

Seeing him standing there, hesitant and half-believing, the old driver mumbled, "I found out last night when I handed you over that we are fellow villagers. My ancestors were also from Chongzuo; they fought in the Taiping Rebellion, Shi Dakai's troops. Unable to stay in in Guangxi after their defeat, they fled to Vietnam."

Wu Huaiyu got into the car, and the driver looked him over again with one eye, keeping the other eye on the road. "But why do you want to go to the front?"

Wu Huaiyu didn't want to say anything at first, but the old driver seemed different now, his tone sincere and gentle, his gaze kind. As they talked more, Wu found out that the man's ancestral home was only about five kilometers away from the small town where he himself now lived. Wu Huaiyu ended up sharing his thoughts with the driver in full detail.

The old driver heaved a deep, long sigh and said, "Kiddo, you're oversimplifying some things. These days, it's better to turn a blind eye." He closed one eye and looked at Wu with the other, adding, "But it's hard to say that the dead end is not a turning point. Life is a gamble; you are still young; maybe it's worth taking risks."

Thus, along the way, they chatted amiably, almost like a father and son.

"Who did you learn your Chinese from? You speak it even better than me," Wu Huaiyu asked.

"My family always spoke Chinese, and it was also taught in schools."

"They taught Chinese at school in Vietnam?"

"Yes, they used to. It's different now. Speaking Chinese might bring troubles."

"What kind of trouble?" Wu asked.

"Well, I shouldn't be telling you this. But it might be good for you to know more. Do you know the first thing Ho Chi Minh did after China supported Vietnam's independence?"

"What was it?"

"He immediately ordered the abolition of Chinese characters and promoted Vietnamese written in Latin alphabet. He also mandated in the constitution that only citizens who could read and write Vietnamese would have the right to be elected. You know what? Vietnamese books and newspapers were once in Chinese, and they had been using Chinese characters for thousands of years. Nobody expected Chinese characters to be banned once Ho Chi Minh came to power."

"How can this be? We grew up hearing that Uncle Ho Chi Minh had lived in China for over twenty years. He not only speaks fluent Chinese but also writes beautiful calligraphy. He was also good friends with both Chairman Mao and Premier Zhou and often said that China was the great rear base for the Vietnamese people. But what happened? How could it be possible?" Just then, the truck broke down again due to a leaking water tank, causing the engine to overheat. Fortunately, there was a large bottle of coolant in the back of the driver's seat, and after it was added, the engine started up again.

The car resumed its normal speed on the winding mountain road. The old driver, gripping a steering wheel that had been reduced to just

a greasy, shiny iron ring, turned to Wu Huanyu with an affectionate expression and continued speaking as if there had been no inter-
ruption. "You, kid, look a bit like the Vietnamese, except your skin
is too fair. But I must remind you that these things are best kept in
your mind and not spoken aloud. Between nations, morality is one
thing, but interests are the most fundamental. Alas, we, the disap-
pointing Chinese, are to blame; the weapons and ammunition we
aid other nations with are not as good as those of the Soviets, just
like this broken car we're driving, far inferior in quality. Also, whenever our anti-aircraft radar units started up, they would be detected
by the Americans, and a missile would come flying, wiping out an
area the size of a basketball court, and eventually we didn't dare turn
on the radar. But without the radar, how do you detect the enemy
aircraft sneaking up on you? The Soviets, on the other hand, assisted
them with rocket artillery and missiles. Because of this, some Vietnamese look down on the Chinese, or at least on our equipment,
thinking that we support them with outdated or soon-to-be-obso-
lete stuff... Besides, in history... well, long story again. We indeed
often oppressed them; Hanoi had been Chinese territory at least five
times in history.

They talked until noon, and then they stopped for lunch at a restaurant in a small town. As Wu Huaiyu got out of the car, he felt a
tingling sensation in his legs, and he walked back and forth in front
of the restaurant. He then caught sight of an elementary school with
a not-so-tall flagpole in front of it and a Vietnamese flag flying in the
wind. As he approached it to get a better look, it occurred to him that
although both countries have a five-starred red flag, the red color in
each was slightly different — the Vietnamese flag was crimson while
the Chinese flag was scarlet.

As they ate lunch, he told the old driver about his observation. The driver laughed and patted him on the shoulder, saying, "Good boy. With your keen eye, if the bullets can't hit you and shrapnel can't reach you, you're sure to be a great soldier in the future!" Thinking for a moment, he then added, "In that case, I'd better take you straight to the military station over the Ho Chi Minh trail. I know their head well; he often asks for my help with things. He'll find a way to send you to the southern troops."

Once they had arrived at the military station and connected with the person in charge, as they were about to part ways, Wu Huaiyu hugged the old driver with heartfelt emotion. "Thank you! Thank you, Shifu," he said. "For making this possible! I will definitely work hard in the army and strive to win more battles and achieve more merits to repay you."

"No need to repay me. As long as you are still alive and kicking the next time I see you, I couldn't be happier," the old driver said, gently patting him on the head.

A few days later, although Wu Huaiyu was now alone, unlike when he first left China, he had nevertheless fulfilled his aspirations and ideals. He set out with a unit that routinely transported arms, personnel, and other strategic supplies to the South through the Ho Chi Minh Trail.

They first walked through the mountainous terrain along the Vietnam-Laos border, crossed the Mu Gia pass along the Truong Son Range on the Vietnam-Laos-Cambodia border, entered Xieng Khouang, and then crossed the Kong River and Savannakhet area to reach the Cambodian border. They planned to travel through eastern Cambodia to enter the Western Highlands region in southern Vietnam.

But just at that moment, their movements were detected by American reconnaissance planes. At that time, the Americans no longer cared about international law, often crossing the border to bomb inside Cambodian territory. So, as soon as they spotted the Vietnamese transport convoy, they immediately summoned several armed helicopters, which swooped down with a roar. In less than ten minutes, gunfire and cannon fire rang out, deafening, followed by incendiary bombs that fell from the sky, one after another, turning the lush green jungle canopy into a sea of fire.

Wu Huaiyu used to love watching movies, especially war films. However, when the sounds of guns and cannons suddenly erupted beside him, he was so scared that he wet his pants. He saw some soldiers whose heads had been blown off by the machine guns from the helicopters before they could even raise their guns, their blood splattered everywhere. Some were hit by incendiary bombs, their bodies disfigured and turned instantly into black charcoal by the burst of flame. Smelling the pungent odor of burnt flesh and watching severed limbs flying through the air, he felt his horror intensify. He started to run frantically through the dense forest, across rivers, over hillocks until he had run a great distance, and when he could no longer hear the gunfire or see the flames, he finally collapsed in shock under a large banyan tree.

Just like that, he found himself separated from the troops transporting personnel and supplies. He wandered in the jungle for several days as if trapped in an endless maze, surviving only on rainwater and wild fruits. By a twist of fate, he stumbled upon a Khmer Rouge guerrilla group and joined them after learning that the group was also led by the Communist Party.

CHAPTER 13

After attentively listening to Wu Huaiyu recount his journey in pursuit of the revolutionary ideal, Wu Lou, sitting with his feet folded on a worship mat in front of the Buddha statue, felt both moved and sympathetic. He half-jokingly said, "In that case, we are the same: both renunciates."

"Who is the same as you? Let me tell you, we are revolutionaries who call the world our home; we give up our own small personal homes for everyone else in the world. Unlike you guys, who only think about cultivating yourselves to become Buddhas and not about rescuing the suffering masses. You are actually very selfish."

Wu Lou was taken aback. "How could you say that? We renunciates also forsake our personal small homes for the greater good of all the people under heaven. You might not yet understand the dharma—it is the crystallization of Buddha Shakyamuni's enlightenment. Buddhists spread the dharma to save beings trapped in the ignorance and obsession of the five aggregates and six consciousnesses. However, it primarily seeks to save the minds and souls of sentient beings, not just their basic physical needs."

Wu Lou was about to keep going, but Wu Huaiyu abruptly cut him off with a sweeping gesture. "Enough, enough, please don't preach any more of your dharma. In my opinion, you are not spreading the dharma, but releasing toxins, trafficking drugs, and poisoning the masses."

"Toxins? Drugs? Poisoning?" The monk had never heard such an offensive argument before, and he found it bewildering.

"Haven't heard of it, huh? The revolutionary mentor Marx once said, 'Religion is the opium of the people.' What is opium? Don't you know? Isn't it a drug? What you all are spreading and dealing is just spiritual opium."

Unimpressed, Wu Lou retorted with a smile, "Then don't you think your ideal of world revolution is a kind of spiritual opium?"

The remark left Wu Huaiyu dumbstruck for quite some time, almost to the point of anger. But he held back since Wu Lou was, after all, Tutu's brother.

But Wu Lou continued, "Also, in this world, no matter who is right or wrong, it is always wrong to kill with weapons."

Now Wu Huaiyu was enraged. He jumped up from where he sat in a low bamboo chair by the door and retorted angrily, "What do you mean by that? Are you saying that we Khmer Rouge are bad people? Let me tell you, if someone else heard this, they could immediately label you as a counterrevolutionary. If not for the fact that your sister is an orphan, a member of our proletarian class, and that you once saved her, I could have demolished your damn temple right away." He then violently yanked open the slightly ajar door, slammed it shut with a loud bang, and stormed out.

His words were not alarmist.

Despite being in the jungle, where information was scarce, Wu

Lou still learned from worshipers and travelers that after the Khmer Rouge took power, at least a quarter of Cambodia's eight million people had been eradicated as enemies. He made a trip home to check on his father, an English teacher at a school, only to discover that his entire family had disappeared without a trace.

As a devout Buddhist living in the jungle, who considered the killing of a mosquito or the stepping on an ant as a sin, how could he comprehend humans killing and massacring each other over differences in political views and backgrounds? Moreover, Buddhists were viewed as parasites and were actively suppressed and forced to disband from many big temples both in and outside the cities, with countless temples already destroyed. It was a miracle that this small temple, looking more like a residence, where Wu Lou and Tutu stayed, survived.

So from then on, he firmly opposed Tutu's continued involvement with Wu Huaiyu.

However, she didn't see it that way.

She did not know much about what Wu Huaiyu believed and advocated for; she felt that Wu Huaiyu and Wu Lou were remarkably similar: once they believed in something, they would do everything and anything to pursue it. One strived to cultivate a state of non-leakage, while the other sought the complete liberation of all humanity. Both left their families as if driven by mysterious forces. Wu Huaiyu, though also like a devotee, was not as extreme as Wu Lou in matters between men and women. She could tell Wu Huaiyu was genuinely fond of her and treated her with kindness, just as Wu Lou did. When they were together, Wu Huaiyu would often affectionately stroke her head, squeeze her hand, and call her "little rabbit," pronounced "Tu" in Chinese. In the jungle, he would pick beautiful wildflowers, delicious wild fruits, and catch lovely butterflies to bring to her.

In contrast, Wu Lou became increasingly averse to any physical contact with her, and guarded against her like one would a tiger, fearing that he might inadvertently touch her hands, arms, thighs, or other parts of her body. Whether talking, eating, or working, Wu Lou made sure to keep a few feet away from her, as if in fear that she might devour him.

Gradually, the scales of her emotions began to tip towards Wu Huaiyu. Sometimes when Wu Huaiyu was occupied with training and hadn't visited for a long time, she would run out of the mountain gate alone, standing under the crooked elm tree on the roadside slope, gazing into the distance, eagerly awaiting his arrival.

Tutu also grew increasingly fond of the smell of his sweat; she relished looking at the fuzz on his face and arms and liked touching the maroon leather belt tied around his waist, an award for his meritorious service. She liked listening to his many amusing stories about his time in China, tales of fighting teachers with his classmates, giving them yin-yang haircuts and drawing big black faces on them. Although she continued to love her Wu Lou brother as always and believed that he would achieve great things on his path of cultivation, her body seemed to be on a very special pill as her fascination with Wu Huaiyu increased. She yearned to grow like the guavas on the guava trees, ripening quickly for Wu Huaiyu to pick.

Wu Huaiyu visited her often, not just because she was genuinely adorable, but also because he felt their unexpected encounter was arranged by fate itself. He was sympathetic towards her orphan status, feeling that they were in the same boat. This often sparked an urge in him to take her under his protection. Years had passed since he ran away from home. In the dead of night, amid conflict and friction with those around him, particularly the native Cambodians, or when he sensed that some of his superiors were suspicious of him, fearing that he was a Chinese eye on them, he would feel like a homeless orphan in the Cambodian jungle. He would often think of home and miss his mother and siblings, his schoolmates and close friends — especially those "comrades" with whom he had once secretly crossed the border, traversed mountains, and wanted to fight the Americans in South Vietnam. He would wonder how they all were now.

Moreover, he knew that their Overseas Chinese Battalion was not ironclad.

The cadres and soldiers from worker and peasant backgrounds often held different views and objectives than those anti-Lon Nol officials and guards once on the side of Prince Sihanouk. Being only temporary fellow travelers, they constantly engaged in infighting, leaving him in a difficult situation, alternatively embraced and then forsaken by both sides like an orphan. Therefore, he treasured his feelings and friendship with Tutu even more.

Nevertheless, whenever he faced Wu Lou in the small temple, although they were of similar age, he increasingly felt they were polar opposites. His anxiety and fear grew more intense. He feared that if Tutu stayed by the monk's side for too long, Wu Lou's influence would only deepen, and perhaps one day she might part ways with him to become a nun.

He and Tutu had known each other for more than half a year; many in the military camp had come to know about his Cambodian "sister" in the jungle, and they constantly teased and made fun of him.

"Company Commander Wu, we heard that your girl is pretty. When are you going to introduce her to us?"

Some of them, who would stop moving at the sight of a women or enjoyed dirty jokes, asked lewdly, "What? Have you opened the bud? Is it tight?"

Wu Huaiyu blushed but couldn't turn against them, especially those with whom he had gone through life-and-death experiences together, fought side-by-side, and supported each other along the way. So he would just respond, "Stop that nonsense; she is just sixteen years old, still a child."

As soon as he said that, someone would start to jeer, "You see? Our company commander has a unique taste; he likes tender grass, so tender that water could drop out of the grass. Wow, only sixteen years old. What a treat!"

At that time, Battalion Commander Song, who was once King Sihanouk's personal guard, happened to walk by. Hearing their conversation, he grew curious and stopped to ask, "Company Commander Wu, why don't you bring her over for us to have a look sometime? We are soldiers, and if you really like her, don't beat around the bush with this so-called sister thing…make her your fiancée instead. You can get married when she turns eighteen. How about letting me be your matchmaker or officiate at your wedding? However," he said, pausing for a moment and feigning a serious glare at Wu Huaiyu, "the three disciplines and eight precautions must still be observed. Before marriage, keep that thing below in check, and don't make any mistakes."

The crowd guffawed again in unanimous praise for Battalion Commander Song. "Good reminder, timely reminder!" cried some. Several commanders of the same rank were also deliberately provocative, calling out, "So how can we know if Company Commander Wu has made a mistake? Should we mark it there?" As they spoke, the group closed in on him, gesturing as if to pull down his pants.

"You bunch of lowlifes," spat out Wu Huaiyu bitterly, before turning and running off.

Then one day he met up with Tutu, and he was surprised to hear her ask, "Can I visit your military camp?"

He was taken aback and hesitated.

"Take me there, please. Don't you always say that your place is also a big school of Mao Zedong's thoughts? If it's a school, shouldn't it allow visitors? Besides, I'm not a bad person," she said, pouting.

"Well, today is not good. How about Sunday? I need to talk to the battalion commander first."

She leapt with joy and grabbed his hand, saying, "Let's make a pinky promise! You can't break your promise now."

CHAPTER 14

It was a gorgeous sunny day after the rain, and the jungle was filled with the pleasant aroma of leaves, fresh grass, and soil.

Wu Huaiyu had a previous commitment and couldn't come to pick her up, so he sent his messenger, an eighteen-year-old overseas Chinese, to take Tutu to his barracks, hoping to satisfy Tutu's curiosity and also comply with the battalion commander's order to avoid baseless speculation and rumors about his relationship with her. Their relationship couldn't have been more innocent, a typical class comaraderie born from his sympathy for her orphan status that elevated into a class friendship. At the same time, he thought it would be beneficial for Tutu to visit the barracks, learn about the revolutionary tradition, and understand that, apart from parasites like his brother, who deceived themselves and others through superstition and smooth talking, there were also those who toiled and courageously killed the enemy for the liberation of Cambodia's suffering masses.

But Wu Lou didn't think so.

Last night, when Tutu told him that Wu Huaiyu would take her to the barracks for a visit today, he was quite displeased. His brows furrowed tightly as he said, "You are a girl; why do you want to visit the military camp? Those people kill with guns and knives; they have a foul energy around them, and it's not good for you."

"I know that. But, Brother, please let me go. I'm curious to see if the Khmer Rouge people are really like what they say out there, with green faces and fangs and blood-red eyes."

"Not so much that. But it's possible they might detain you there and make you join them."

"I'm not afraid of that. I have Company Commander Wu's protection. He said I was an orphan, their class sister, and they wouldn't force me to join the army. He also mentioned that everyone joined the revolution of their own free will. I want to know more about them, to see what kind of people they really are. In case they find us displeasing one day, we can be prepared."

"You must return before it gets dark. It's chaotic outside, and we can't risk any incidents." Wu Lou, unable to stop her and recognizing that her words were sensible for someone her age, relented.

Tutu excitedly followed the silent, dark, and skinny messenger, walking briskly. She felt particularly blissful and happy at the thought that she now had two brothers who cared for and protected her despite having lost her parents. She couldn't help but softly hum a song Wu Huaiyu had taught her: "Other girls have flowers to wear, but my brother has no money to buy. He took a long red headband and tied it up for me, ah hey ah hey hey, tied it up for me..."

Hearing the song, the messenger looked back, slightly surprised. "Are you also an overseas Chinese?" he asked.

"No."

"Then how can you sing Chinese songs?"

"My brother—Company Commander Wu taught me."

"Hmm. But you sang it wrong. It is not 'my brother,' it's 'my father.'"

"But that's how Company Commander Wu taught me."

"Is that so? Well, I don't understand then. We always sing 'my father' or 'your father,'" the messenger said seriously as he rubbed his hand over his head.

"Do you sing a lot in the military camp?"

"Yeah."

"What kind of songs do you sing?"

"Revolutionary songs."

"I heard from your company commander that you also sing songs of Chairman Mao's quotations; is that right?"

"Yes."

"Chairman Mao is not our Cambodian; why do you sing his songs?"

"How can you say that? Only reactionaries and counterrevolutionaries would say such things." The boy suddenly stopped in his tracks and turned to stare at her. Seeing that she was confused and frightened, he softened his tone again and explained, "Chairman Mao is not only the great leader of the Chinese people but also of the world's people. His quotations should be learned not only by the Chinese people but also by us Cambodians, and we must apply what we learn. Our 'Number One Brother,' our greatest leader Pol Pot—that's what we call him—is a good student of Chairman Mao. He frequently visited China, and Chairman Mao often received him; he even shook hands with Chairman Mao. There are photos of it in the newspaper."

"Can you teach me to sing the Chairman Mao's quotation songs? That way we won't feel tired while walking."

The boy thought for a moment, looked back at her, and said, "But I don't sing very well."

"It doesn't matter. Just sing any way you like, and I'll hum along."

"OK, then, I'll sing a song called 'It's Right to Rebel.'" He cleared his throat and first explained the gist of the lyrics to Tutu in Cambodian before singing in a coarse voice: "The principles of Marxism are manifold, but in essence, they boil down to one phrase, 'It is right to rebel.' Based on this principle, we rebel, we struggle, and we build socialism."

"Is that all?"

"That's all. I mean, that's all for this song, but there are many more quotation songs."

"What are some other songs that you often sing?"

The boy raised a hand to his forehead, thinking. "Most often we sing these two as well," he said. He then began to sing, "The core force leading our cause is the Chinese Communist Party, and the theoretical basis guiding our thinking is Marxism-Leninism." When he was done, without waiting for her suggestion, he continued with another: "Be determined! Fear no sacrifice! Surmount all difficulties! Strive for victory!!!" After finishing, he loudly chanted the slogans: "Be determined! Fear no sacrifice! Surmount all difficulties! Strive for victory!!!" His loud voice, coupled with the sudden, vigorous stomp of his feet, startled many birds in the forest, causing them to chirp incessantly and flutter away in all directions.

They sang all the way through, passing through a banyan forest where single trees formed entire groves, wading across the winding rocky creek, trekking through the dense bamboo forest that blocked the sky, and finally arriving at the military camp around noon.

When they were a few hundred meters away from the camp, Tutu could already see Wu Huaiyu standing under a large banyan tree at the entrance, looking anxiously in their direction. He strode toward them as soon as he spotted them.

"Brother—"

They had agreed that Wu Huaiyu would call her Tutu, her name, or Tutu, as in Rabbit, and she would always call him Brother, and Tutu abided by the agreement.

"You must be exhausted from the trip," Wu Huaiyu said, as he led her into the camp while giving a military salute to the armed guards standing at attention at the gate. He gestured towards Tutu and said, "This is my guest." One guard immediately returned the salute, nodded, and said, "Yes, Commander!" Wu Huaiyu then turned to the messenger accompanying them and said, "Alright, Xiaohong, task completed. You can go back to the barracks now."

Then, turning his attention back toward Tutu, he looked her up and down and noted that her rosy cheeks were still dotted with fine beads of sweat. "You look different," he said. "You used to be cold, reticent, aloof."

"Is that bad?" She rolled her eyes at him.

"No, it's good, very good, more than I could have hoped for. I'll show you around the camp first, and then it'll be time for lunch in about an hour."

But Tutu didn't seem to be listening; her eyes were fixed on the messenger's retreating figure. Confused, she asked, "Why is his name Xiaohong? Sounds like a girl's name."

"It's 'Hong' as in flood, not 'Hong' as in the color red."

"Oh. I thought all Khmer Rouge people had the color red in their names, like little red, big red, old red, deep red, light red, orange red ..." she said, covering her mouth in an attempt to suppress her laughter.

"Don't be ridiculous. Now tell me, are you tired? Are you hungry?" Wu Huaiyu said, giving her a light pat on the head.

"Reporting company commander brother, not tired, not hungry,"

Tutu said, giving him a mischievous grin and raising her hand in salute, just as he had done.

"Really, not tired? It's several miles up the mountain."

"Not tired, I never lie. And, of course, thanks to the boy who asked me to sing along the way … "

"Is that so? But stop calling people boys in the future; they are all Khmer Rouge soldiers."

"Yes!" she said. Then, mimicking the guards' stance at attention, she put both feet together, but she stumbled and lurched forward a few steps — at which point she could not help laughing herself silly.

"What's with you today?" said Wu Huaiyu. "Looking so happy."

"What? Is it bad to be happy?" she responded, laughing again, the sound of it like a string of silver bells.

"Don't laugh so loudly," Wu Huaiyu shot back, lowering his voice. "I am the company commander, and many people in the Overseas Chinese Battalion know me; it would be embarrassing."

"I'm your younger *sister*. What's there to worry about?" she said, playfully using the term "sister" in the affectionate way common in Eastern cultureal traditions where lovers often refer to each other as "Brother" and "Sister."

"I know that. But many of them don't think the same way."

"They don't? Then what do they think then? Surely they won't think I'm your older sister, right?" Tutu said, again covering her mouth to laugh.

"You really are something," Wu Huaiyu said, shaking his head. "OK, no more messing around. Let me show you around first — look over there. Those rows of houses with bamboo roofs are our barracks, and over there, that's the drill ground where they are doing formation training. Beyond the drill ground is the mortar range.

The land to the right of the mortar range is what we cultivated this year. The seedlings are already over a foot tall, but they are fertilizing them — quite smelly." He unconsciously pinched his nose and said, "Let's not go over there."

But Tutu asked, "What kind of crops are those? How come I've never seen them before?"

"This…" Wu Huaiyu found himself at a loss for words.

"You don't recognize them either? But, no, you should know, right?"

Wu Huaiyu then looked around and whispered to her, "I'll tell you, but you mustn't repeat it to anyone."

"Mm-hmm," Tutu nodded.

"They're poppies."

"Poppies?"

"They're opium. When the flowers bloom, they are incredibly beautiful, a bright, vivid red. But the red is not quite the same as our usual red; almost too red, more like purple. Strangely, there's some sort of demonic aura in that purplish hue. Well, I can't describe it clearly. When they bloom, I'll bring you here to see them"

"But isn't opium a drug? What do you grow it for? Don't tell me you also—" Suddenly Tutu brought a hand to her mouth, her eyes widened, and she swallowed back the rest of her words.

"No way. We trade it for money to buy weapons and equipment. This is called self-reliance and being self-sufficient. Besides, only the rich and our enemies use opium, so we use it to break their morale and then use the money to buy weapons to eliminate them. Killing two birds with one stone."

She listened, seeming to understanding but looking more and more confused. "Why do you need to eliminate them?"

Just then, a group of soldiers passed by in formation. Tutu turned to look; their steps were orderly, but their clothing was not uniform. Some wore grass-green clothes, others black clothes; some had military caps, while some had towels wrapped in their heads. But all of them had rows of bulging canvas bags tied around their waist. Tutu asked, "What are those bags tied around their waists?"

"Bullet pouches."

"Why are some long and others short?"

"The long ones are for submachine guns. The short ones are for rifles. Why? Are you interested in these things?"

"Look how young they are, almost my age. Some might even be younger than me. I asked Xiaohong—he's only a year older than me," Tutu said, turning towards the group with confusion and bewilderment.

"The youngest in our Overseas Chinese Battalion is even younger than you, just fourteen, in the communications unit. What, have you thought it through and want to join the army too? I can talk to the battalion commander about it—there shouldn't be a problem."

"Oh, no, no, no," Tutu said, shaking her head fiercely. "Ever since I was little, following my brother, I wouldn't even step on an ant. But you have to kill—oh, no, I mean, eliminate enemies. I just can't do it, and my brother wouldn't allow it either."

He was about to take the opportunity to explain and guide her when he spotted the battalion messenger running towards them, waving his hand. "Company Commander Wu, please come to the battalion headquarters immediately. Battalion Commander Song is looking for you."

He quickly turned to Tutu and said, "Just walk around and look around for a little while. I'll be back in no time."

The words were barely out of his mouth when a Beijing jeep,

provided by Chinese support, drove through the military camp gate and screeched to a halt beside him. The car window rolled down and someone stuck his head out and shouted at him, "Company Commander Wu!"

It was the operations staff officer from the regiment headquarters. Before Wu Huaiyu could greet him, the staff officer pushed the car door open, got out, and pushed Wu into the car, saying urgently, "Hurry, come with me."

"No, I can't, the battalion commander is looking for me."

"Never mind him; it's probably about the same thing."

"What thing? You have to let me know!"

"I don't know either. The regimental commander ordered me to rush you to the regiment headquarters immediately. Sounds like a high-ranking officer has arrived from above and specifically asked to see you."

As they spoke, the driver had already turned the car around and slammed on the accelerator before Wu Huaiyu could wave goodbye to Tutu again. The car zoomed away at lightning speed, kicking up clouds of dust from the ground as if stirred by a horse's hoof.

CHAPTER 15

Wu Huaiyu left just like that, without any explanation and without even saying goodbye to her again, leaving Tutu feeling lost and disappointed. The strange glances of the soldiers on the drill ground, including some nakedly lecherous looks, made her feel even more uncomfortable. Fortunately, she soon saw the messenger Xiaohong heading in her direction and felt a bit more at ease.

But Xiaohong was not alone. He was accompanied by a much older man who looked like an officer. As they approached her, Xiaohong introduced him to her, saying, "This is our Battalion Commander Song."

Wu Huaiyu had once mentioned that Battalion Commander Song had been a personal bodyguard in Prince Sihanouk's Royal Guard. Recalling that, she couldn't help but steal a glance at him. There were earthworm-like scars on his forehead and chin, giving him a fierce appearance, which made her even more nervous. She feared that she must have violated some rule here that alarmed the battalion commander. In a voice as faint as a mosquito, she said, "Hello, Battalion Commander," then lowered her head as her hands fidgeted with the edges of her clothes.

"Not bad, not bad at all," said the battalion commander. She was surprised he did not scold her. He even smiled and extended his right hand towards her.

Misunderstanding his meaning, she thought he was asking her for something, so she looked at the messenger.

"Our commander wants to shake hands with you," Xiaohong said.

Only then did she hesitantly extend her left hand; because her body wasn't directly facing the commander, this hand was closer to him.

"Use your right hand," Xiaohong said with a laugh.

She quickly retracted her left hand and extended her right one, which was immediately surrounded by a rough, large, and thick palm, holding her tiny hand tightly in its hot and damp grip.

"Good, good, very good," Battalion Commander Song said, stretching out his left hand to gently pat the back of her hand several times before finally releasing it. He turned to Xiaohong. "Accompany Commander Wu's sister around," he said. "And then head to the battalion headquarters for lunch."

With that, Battalion Commander Song headed off towards the mortar range.

"What would you like to go and see?" Xiaohong then asked Tutu.

"I don't know. I'll follow your lead."

"Well…" Xiaohong thought for a moment, his hand on his forehead, and then said, "Let's go to the woods over there to watch the children's military training."

He led her out of the drill ground, through a bamboo fence, and into a wooded area where the sky was obscured by teak and rubber trees. Green vines from the roots of the rubber trees entwined up to the tops, then hung down in the air, brushing against people's faces and ruffling their hair, much like the mischievous forest spirits of the sort that liked to play tricks on people in the woods.

Twenty or thirty children in groups of five or six, all dressed in black shirts and pants, were receiving formal military training: learning how to fight hand-to-hand, use firearms, make traps, and lay mines. These children, no older than twelve or thirteen and some as young as eight or nine, looked up as they approached, their malnourished faces beaming with joy and happiness. Some children were training in tree climbing, leaping nimbly like monkeys from tree to tree. Some had reached the top and were sitting on the thick branches, leisurely swinging their legs, proudly overlooking the passersby below and every now and then pulling off leaves from the branches around them and throwing them down like flyers, declaring their high-up presence.

Tutu looked up, smiled at the children, and waved to them to show admiration. She then sat down on a wide tree root exposed on the ground, flicked the hair from her face, and pulled up the corner of her coat to wipe the sweat on her forehead and neck. Having walked the entire morning, she was not only tired but her heels also hurt. Not knowing when Brother Wu would return, she was feeling a little sullen and frowned without realizing it.

Noting her sour expression, Xiaohong quickly went to her and asked if she wanted to go back. Just then, they heard the loud sound of military bugles and saw children in the trees hugging the trunk and sliding down quickly. He knew that the companies were about to have lunch, so he quickly said to Tutu, "Good, time to eat, let's head back."

As they walked into the camp, they saw that the companies had already gathered in front of their respective units and were singing songs while heading towards rows of canteens with thatched roofs but no walls.

"What are they singing? Is it also a song of Chairman Mao's quotations?" Tutu asked.

"No, it's not. It's 'The Party's kindness is greater than the sky and earth; affection from Brother Number One is deeper than from our parents; nothing is better than socialism; the depth of our class friendship is greater than any river and sea; Mao Zedong's thought is the treasure of the revolution, and whoever opposes him is our enemy.'"

"Affection from Brother Number One is deeper than from our parents? Who is Brother Number One?"

"Our leader, the General Secretary. I told you about him on the way here. How could you forget? He's a great person, very approachable. He always put himself first in hardship and last in enjoyment. When Phnom Penh was liberated, he was advised to move to the city but refused, insisting on living in the jungle and mingling with the soldiers."

"Is that so?" asked Tutu, surprised. "Brother Number One means 'big brother?'"

"Yes. Many also refer to him as Big Brother. I heard that his family was very wealthy and he was once a novice monk. But he resolutely led us to take up arms for the liberation of our Cambodian people."

"Ah, you're only a year older than me, yet you know so much—that's really impressive," Tutu told him sincerely.

"Oh, what I know is nothing really. Our Company Commander is the truly impressive one; he knows everything. He often teaches us that Brother Number One, Pol Pot, mastered Chairman Mao's guerrilla warfare theory the best. He would often fight annihilative battles by concentrating superior forces to strike a single point when the enemy was beleaguered. He also uses, what's it called, yes, the spirit of ants gnawing on bones, nibbling the enemy bit by bit. During the dry seasons when the government forces had the advantage of heavy weaponry, we would defend, playing hide-and-seek in the jungle to exhaust them. During the rainy seasons, when they lost their advantages, we would attack everywhere, besiege cities, and expand the guerrilla zone. Just like that, Brother Number One finally led us to capture the capital city Phnom Penh and gain the world."

"Is that so! What else did Company Commander Wu tell you? Can you share it with me?"

The messenger thought for a moment before he said, "He told us many things, and I can't recall everything. But have you ever heard of the story of the Tang Monk's journey to the West to seek scriptures?"

Tutu shook her head.

"It's not a big deal if you don't know," the messenger continued. "It's about a monk during the Tang dynasty in China, about a thousand years ago, who took three disciples on a journey to the West to seek scriptures. Our Brother Number One, General Secretary Pol Pot, also made the most important choice of his life: to go to China to obtain the 'true scriptures.' Of course, what he sought was not the Buddhist scriptures of feudal superstition but the scriptures of Marxism-Leninism. He led his followers northward through the jungle, secretly entered Laos, and then infiltrated Hanoi, controlled by North Vietnam via the Ho Chi Minh Trail. However, he failed to gain the attention of North Vietnam and was instead treated as a dangerous person. He later learned that the Vietnamese had always considered the Communist parties of Cambodia and Laos as part of their Indo-Chinese alliance, denying us independence. So, he crossed the border once again, from Vietnam to China, and made his way all the way to Beijing. Later, he went to China multiple times. During the Chinese Cultural Revolution, he returned to the Cambodian jungle with the treasured *Selected Works of Mao Zedong*. When Chairman Mao received Brother Number One, he told him, 'Don't copy China exactly.' He also mentioned something about 'sickness in copying.' I also don't understand what that means. Better wait for Company Commander Wu to explain to you later."

Lunch was served in the battalion office, a thatched hut built with Moso bamboo framing. Inside, there were a few wooden square tables, surrounded by about a dozen bamboo chairs.

Tutu was seated between Battalion Commander Song and the politial instructor. The instructor, who was thin and taciturn, kept his head down and ate after offering her a casual greeting. Although Battalion Commander Song had introduced her to the other cadres, she couldn't remember them, only that among them were deputy battalion commanders, staff officers, and other officials. The meal consisted of white rice, a bowl of vegetable soup, and a fried egg. A little oil and bits of meat scraps floated in the soup. She carefully picked out the meat scraps with the intention of discarding them, but upon noticing Battalion Commander Song's gaze upon her, she felt embarrassed and returned them to the bowl.

Taking note, Battalion Commander Song quickly said, "Are you vegetarian? Then give them to me, don't throw them away. What a waste." With that, he reached his chopsticks into her bowl, picked out the small bits of fat, and transferred them deftly into his own mouth. He chewed and swallowed them with gusto, while his gaze remained fixed on her. He then turned to the people around him and praised them, saying, "Wu Huaiyu really has good taste." Seeing everyone nodding in agreement, he turned to Tutu and said, "Of course, this Tutu girl—I got your name right, didn't I?" Tutu nodded, and he continued, "Make an excellent choice too! Let me tell you, Company Commander Wu is one of the few big-name commanders in our Overseas Chinese Battalion, having been awarded third-class merit four or five times. The two of you together are just like what they say—what is it?" He suddenly scratched his head, thought for a moment, and then said, "Right, it's a hero coupled with beauty!"

At the sound of these words, everyone put down their bowls and chopsticks and flashed their eyes at her in unison, causing her to blush.

"Has Company Commander Wu encouraged you to join us?" asked Battalion Commander Song with a smile.

"Yes, he has. But I'm an orphan; my brother brought me up ... I want to ..."

"Are you referring to, what's his name, the Wu Lou monk? Let me tell you this: because your house looks more like a residence than a temple and doesn't attract attention, we haven't bothered with it until now. Of course, that's also because Company Commander Wu knew that you are an orphan and he was afraid that you would have nowhere to go, so he didn't want to force you out. However, according to our party's policy, Buddhism is a superstition that paralyzes and deceives the toiling masses, and Buddhists are also parasites. You won't be able to stay in that small temple for long. I think you should join our troops so that Company Commander Wu can have you close at hand and look after you in the future."

Just then, the box-style telephone sitting in front of the political instructor rang. He grabbed the receiver, spoke a few words, and frowned slightly. He then stretched the receiver over Tutu's rice bowl towards Battalion Commander Song, saying, "The political commissar is looking for you!"

Everyone immediately put down their chopsticks and turned towards Battalion Commander Song, who kept repeating, "Yes, yes, yes" on the phone. Then, to the diners' collective surprise, he stood up and snapped to attention.

He swept a glance over those seated at the table and said to the political instructor in an unmistakably condescending tone, "The political commissar's phone instruction: cancel all training activities this afternoon. The entire battalion is to assemble to hear Company Commander Wu's relay of the latest directives and the essence of the conversation with the superior chief."

"The superior chief?" "Which level of chief?" "Why did the political commissar personally make the call and ask Company Commander Wu to relay the message?" Everyone present, including Commander Song, felt momentarily as if in a thick fog.

Later, they all turned to look upon the baby-faced girl seated between the Battalion Commander and the political instructor, wondering if her arrival had anything to do with it.

Of course, when the jeep that had taken Company Commander Wu to the regimental headquarters returned to the camp, all these questions soon vanished like smoke.

People saw not only Company Commander Wu but also Shen, the regiment's political commissar, and two other officers from the political department, disembarking from the vehicle. When Battalion Commander Song saw Political Commissar Shen, he was about to salute, but Shen waved him off and said, "In the next few days, Company Commander Wu will not only be touring our regiment's battalions to deliver speeches but he will also visit neighboring units for the same purpose. You should find someone to temporarily cover his usual duties."

"Yes!" Battalion Commander Song exclaimed.

"Is the troop assembled?" Political Commissar Shen asked.

"All ready."

"Then let's get started," Political Commissar Shen said, taking note of Wu Huaiyu briskly walking over to a girl and speaking with her. He asked, "Whose kid is that? Why is she here?"

"Well, this—" Battalion Commander Song said, taking a quick step forward. He then whispered to the political commissar, "This is a girl Company Commander Wu has taken under his wing, likely his fiancée. I asked Company Commander Wu to bring her here so we could give him some advice. I've already checked; the girl has a clean political background and she is an orphan. She also views our Khmer Rouge favorably."

"Oh, that's very good. It shows that Company Commander Wu is beginning to think of Cambodia as his own home."

"So—" Battalion Commander Song moved his mouth slightly in the direction of Tutu, "should we also let this girl listen to his speeches to deepen her feelings and admiration for Company Commander Wu?"

Political Commissar Shen thought for a moment and then nodded.

CHAPTER 16

The sun had begun to set in the west but still gave off unbearable heat.

Amidst a mixture of chaotic whistles, commands, and footsteps, the three companies of the Overseas Chinese Battalion — the machine gun company, the mortar company, and the engineering company — along with the battalion headquarters, totaling nearly four hundred cadres and soldiers, quickly formed up, divided into four small squares, and sat on the damp yellow-black soil that had yet to dry.

Many soldiers had unbuttoned their shirt collars, hoping to sweat less and breathe more in the steamy atmosphere. They kept looking towards the western sky, hoping that the hideous-looking shade of the banyan tree would rise quickly enough to cover the repulsive sunlight that had lingered for too long.

"Why isn't the battalion commander delivering the speech?"

"Look, Political Commissar Shen has also come to lend support!"

* * *

The cadres and soldiers were all standing around talking, but when they saw Political Commissar Shen walk up to the makeshift podium—made from two small tables pushed together—and pick up the microphone, ready to speak, they suddenly fell silent.

"Comrades, today I am assigned by our superior leadership to accompany Company Commander Wu Huaiyu of your Overseas Chinese Battalion in conveying the latest directives from our superior leader. As you all know, the latest directives of the higher leaders should be delivered before the end of the day, a good revolutionary tradition that we have learned from China, the center of the world revolution. Of course, this time, I also had the honor of being present and listening when the supreme chief received Comrade Wu Huaiyu. I felt particularly happy and fortunate. Well, I won't say much more. Now, let's welcome Comrade Wu Huaiyu to the stage." Saying this, Political Commissar Shen raised his hands and led the applause.

Amidst a burst of warm and sustained applause, Wu Huaiyu stood up from the ground in front of the podium, facing the battalion's cadres and soldiers, and gave a military salute before walking up to the podium.

That day, he wore a well-fitting grass-green uniform with the crimson military leather belt he had been awarded as a special commendation for his third-class merit, which drew his waist in tightly and accentuated his broad shoulders and upright posture. His eyes also looked extraordinarily bright, as if lit from within by an unextinguishable fire.

Tutu sat next to Battalion Commander Song in the front row, her eyes on Wu Huaiyu. She was so close to him that she could see the beads of sweat seeping from his forehead and his Adam's apple moving up and down. And he, before starting his speech, also seemed to glance inadvertently at her, who was sitting right in front of him. Then, as if he had drawn endless strength from her, he cleared his throat with more confidence, straightened his chest, and began to speak.

"Chiefs and comrades, fellow soldiers, today I feel particularly honored to stand on this small podium to deliver the latest directives of our superior chief to our Overseas Chinese Battalion. Yet, at the same time, I feel nervous, concerned about whether I can accurately relay the spiritual essence of the superior chief's directives. Fortunately, Political Commissar Shen is right here, so I would like to ask him to promptly point out any mistakes," he said, glancing at Political Commissar Shen, who had already taken a seat in a bamboo chair nearby, and nodding to him.

Political Commissar Shen then waved at him, indicating not to be nervous and to go ahead and start.

Thus, he pressed his hands on the table, trying to calm himself and even out his breathing, and then continued to speak.

"Today at noon, the regiment chief sent a car to pick me up. On the way, I kept wondering: What was so important that he had to send a car for a grass-roots officer like me? After I arrived at the regimental headquarters, the political commissar led me to a house ensconced in the dense shade of trees behind the headquarters. A tall, kindly man, fluent in Chinese, stood up from his chair, greeted me, and reached out to shake my hand. It was then that I was incredibly surprised to discover that the person who specifically asked to see me was the General Secretary of the Communist Party of Cambodia, whom we affectionately call 'Brother Number One' or 'Big Brother,' Comrade Pol Pot."

"Ah, Pol Pot? Brother Number One? Big Brother?!" Hearing this, the cadres and soldiers in the audience were momentarily stunned and then erupted into a chorus of "Long live Brother Number One!

Long live Big Brother!" followed by roaring, long-lasting cheers and applause.

After the wave of cheering had subsided, Wu Huaiyu managed to contain his excitement and continued speaking.

General Secretary Pol Pot then kindly invited him to sit on a chair nearby, leaned forward, and asked amicabley, "You are Comrade Wu Huaiyu from Guangxi, China, aren't you?"

Wu Huaiyu nodded.

"Comrade Khieu Samphan told me long ago that there was a Chinese comrade in his Overseas Chinese Battalion who fought bravely and was very smart. I remembered this and thought about it today when I came to visit your area, so I had them bring you here. Let's talk. You probably already know, I have been to China often, visited Guangxi many times, and met Chairman Mao several times. He was very concerned about our revolutionary cause in Cambodia and cared about us. When I first met him, I said, 'I come to China to learn from the Chinese experience. The revolutionary practice in Cambodia over these years has made me realize that your statement "Political power grows out of the barrel of a gun" is an unshakable truth. After many discussions, our leadership has decided to model and learn from the experience of the Chinese revolution and socialist construction.' Shortly after we gained power, on April 17th of this year, 1975, Chairman Mao met with us again in Zhongnanhai and warmly shook our hands."

When Wu Huaiyu heard this, he couldn't help but interrupt. "Brother Number One, you shook hands with Chairman Mao?"

"Of course," Pol Pot replied with a slight smile.

He then asked, "May I shake your hand again?"

Pol Pot immediately agreed. Wu Huaiyu jumped up from his seat and eagerly clasped Brother Number One's warm, thick hands.

Indeed, he felt extremely fortunate at that moment, because through Brother Number One's hands, he felt as though he was holding the hand of Chairman Mao, the Red Sun in the hearts of the people around the world, and even sensed the warmth from Chairman Mao's own hands!

Later, Brother Number One continued, "I was so excited that I told Chairman Mao that we are very happy to see him, the great leader. Chairman Mao then said he wouldn't talk about our combat, warfare, politics, military, economy, diplomacy, or united front because we did well. During the hour-long meeting, Chairman Mao elaborated on the issue of line struggle. He said, 'We approve of you. Many of your experiences are better than ours. China is not in a position to criticize you. In fifty years, we made ten line-struggle mistakes, some nationwide, some local. You are fundamentally correct. As for flaws, I am not sure. There will always be some, and you will correct them yourselves.' Mao added, 'You are now transitioning from a democratic revolution to a socialist path, with two possibilities: socialism and capitalism. We are now what Lenin described as a bourgeois state without capitalists, a state that exists to protect bourgeois legal rights. Wages are not equal, and inequality is practiced under the guise of equality. In the next fifty years, or even a hundred years, there will still be two lines of struggle, and in ten thousand years, there will still be two lines of struggle. Even under communism, there will be two lines of struggle. Otherwise, we are not Marxists.' I agreed with Chairman Mao and said, 'Chairman Mao, discussiong the issue of line struggle with us is a very important and strategic matter. We will definitely heed your words in the future. I have studied many of your writings since my youth, especially those concerning people's war. Your writings have guided our entire Party.

We must also pay special attention to class struggle and line struggle in the future.' Chairman Mao smiled slightly at this and added, 'I remember in 1966, at the beginning of the Cultural Revolution, you came here wanting to learn from China. At that time, I introduced you to two dharma teachers spreading Marxism-Leninism; one was Chen Boda, and the other Zhang Chunqiao. Unfortunately, Chen Boda later joined the wrong side with Lin Biao. However, Comrade Zhang Chunqiao should still be a very competent teacher. His theoretical level is unparalleled in our Politburo.

At this point, Brother Number One suddenly asked him, "Do you know Zhang Chunqiao?" Wu Huaiyu responded, "Of course. At the beginning of the Cultural Revolution, he led the 'January Storm' in Shanghai, seizing power from the old Shanghai Municipal Committee and establishing the first truly proletarian red regime — the Shanghai Municipal Revolutionary Committee."

"But are you aware that Comrade Zhang Chunqiao recently wrote a notable article?" Brother Number One asked again.

"What article?"

"'*On the Total Dictatorship over the Bourgeoisie*,' General Secretary Pol Pot said. After a pause, he continued, "I've read that article many times, and it's excellently written. It comprehensively discusses how to continue the revolution under the dictatorship of the proletariat, how to further restrict bourgeois rights, and how to prevent capitalist resurgence after establishing the socialist system. It's insightful and hits the mark precisely. Of course, China's revolution and development have also taken some detours. For instance, the communal dining halls in the People's Communes were initally effective and even commended by Chairman Mao. However, they eventually failed due to some natural disasters and resistance within the Party. Also, I personally feel that it is inappropriate for leaders to move into the royal palace after the victory of the revolution. It can lead to a disconnect from the masses and become a breeding ground for the bourgeoisie. Therefore, after we, Khmer Rouge, took over Phnom Penh, I decided to set an example by continuing to live in the jungle alongside cadres, fighters, and working people. Only by doing this can we ensure that our party's leadership will never be corrupted by the bourgeois right. In summary, we are confident that we will accomplish what the Chinese comrades have done. We will also strive to achieve what the Chinese comrades have not, and we aim to do it the best, most thoroughly, and most purely. We will drive the bourgeoisie, businessmen, intellectuals, and citizens in the cities to the countryside, thereby vacating the cities. We will reconstruct the socio-economic system of the cities based on the principle of 'from each according to his ability, to each according to his needs,' and we will declare to the world that Cambodia is the realm of workers, peasants, and other laborers. We should also gradually abolish money, commodities, trading, and the family. Why keep the box when all the apples inside have rotted? Merely transforming labor practices is not sufficient. Cambodia's poverty stems not only from industrial and urban pollution but, most fundamentally, from the erosion of old ideologies. Therefore, we must diligently learn from the experiences of the Great Proletarian Cultural Revolution in China, embarking on a thorough cultural transformation of our society. This includes closing all schools, burning all books, confiscating all radios, and eliminating any soil for the survival of various old traditional cultures. Moreover, we must eradicate all old things, including the concept of family. Regarding young people in love, they too must be matched by the Angkar (organization), implementing a planned allocation system. Even after marriage, couples must live apart and be allowed to meet only once every half month. Children will be taken from their families and placed under the unified management of Angkar, and parents are only allowed to see them once a month..."

At this point in Wu Huaiyu's speech, the audience erupted in another long and enthusiastic round of applause, led by Political Commissar Shen. After the applause subsided, he took a sip of water from the cup brought over by the messenger, moistened his mouth, cleared his throat, and then continued with his speech.

Later, Brother Number One recalled his experience of joining the revolution. He came from a wealthy peasant family that owned twenty hectares of land and the largest number of houses in the village. When he was two years old, his cousin married the king, making his family royal relatives. To receive a better education, he went to Phnom Penh at the age of six with his brother to live with a cousin. He spent a year and a half at the Lotus Temple, where he became a monk at nine and left the monastic life at twelve. He did not begin formal schooling until he was fifteen. Influenced by his mother, a gentle Buddhist, he grew up a timid child, distressed by the sight of bystanders killing a chicken. He excelled in his studies, earning a scholarship to study in France where he met like-minded friends, such as Khieu Samphan, Ieng Sary, and others. All of these individuals later became his key aides and right-hand men. Wu Huaiyu also recalled a story he read on a mimeographed tabloid at the beginning of the Cultural Revolution: It was during the Sino-Soviet polemic, when Premier Zhou Enlai attended a summit of the Communist parties in Moscow. At the reception, Khrushchev, having consumed a lot of liquor, approached Premier Zhou Enlai with a tipsy air and provocatively said, "Although we are both leaders of the Communist Party, my parents and grandparents were workers, whereas you come from a capitalist family." He then looked at Premier Zhou smugly and raised his glass to toast. This led all the leaders of the Communist parties to turn their attention to Premier Zhou, curious as to how he would respond to this provocation. Premier Zhou smiled slightly and said deliberately to Khrushchev, "Mr. General Secretary, you are right, and these are indeed facts, but unfortunately, you have forgotten the second half of the sentence."

"The second half?" Khrushchev was momentarily stunned. Premier Zhou then solemnly said, "But you and I have both betrayed our own families!"

At this point, Wu Huaiyu raised his voice and exclaimed, "Like Premier Zhou Enlai, our beloved Brother Number One betrayed his own family and devoted everything to the grand cause of liberating Cambodia and all of humanity!"

Thunderous applause once again erupted from the audience.

But despite the applause, Wu Huaiyu found himself distracted by the realization that he, too, had betrayed his own exploitative-class family to join the fervent Cambodian revolutionary cause. But who knew that, two years earlier, when the relevant department had asked him to fill out the party membership application form, he had hesitated at the "family background" section. He knew that if he wrote "small business owner," his chance for party membership would go down the drain. Yet he couldn't lie to the organization. So, in the end, he steeled his heart and filled in those words, which felt like signing his own death warrant. Fortunately, although his background delayed his party memebership for a long time, he eventually won the trust of most party members and comrades through his relentless "Fear neither hardship nor death" efforts.

Thinking of this, he glanced at Tutu in the audience again.

She was listening intently to every word he said, every syllable, completely captivated by the sound of his voice, the expression on his face, and the various gestures he made to emphasize his tone. She realized that if before she had simply adored him as another brother, now, right at that moment, as he stood with his hands on the lectern, looking straight into the distance, passionately delivering his speech, his voice sometimes low, sometimes high, sometimes gentle, sometimes resounding, she had hopelessly fallen in love with him as an attractive, handsome, and heroic man. Every glance he shot her was like Cupid's arrow, striking and piercing her heart, hitting the softest, most vulnerable part of her emotions, transforming her from a girl into a young woman.

No longer feeling the desire to listen to what he was saying, she instead hoped for the presentation to end quickly so she could be with him. Then he would belong only to her, and she to him, without any ulterior motives or schemes. She no longer wanted to do this just to provoke her brother; now she genuinely wanted to become Wu Huaiyu's shadow, to follow him wherever he went and to always keep her possibly homeless brother close by their side.

With these thoughts, it felt to her as if time was passing excruciatingly slowly.

After the report finally concluded, the Battalion Commander announced the dismissal and all the cadres and soldiers swarmed toward Wu Huaiyu like a tide, eagerly rushing to shake his hand. They believed that by holding his hand, they were also holding the hand of their beloved Big Brother, as well as the hands of Chairman Mao, the Red Sun in the hearts of people around the world, even though the actual sun at that moment was intensely hot, burning, blazing, and roasting them.

They bombarded Wu Huaiyu with questions, asking what Brother Number One meant by "abolishing the family" and whether it implied communal wives in the future. He could only shake his head and tell them that Brother Number One had not provided specific details. They continued discussing the topic.

"It seems that in the future, choosing a woman will be based on political performance. Whoever fights bravely and earns more merits will have the priority in choosing a woman, and can even pick the beautiful ones."

"But what if a man is an ugly man that women don't like, and they are unwilling to be with him?"

"You don't need to worry about that. Angkar will take care of it for you."

"Ah, but then, won't that lead to polygamy or polyandry? And surely there will be people who starve and people who are stuffed."

After much anticipation, dinner was finally ready, and people gradually dispersed, seemingly reluctant to leave.

Tutu finally had the opportunity to be alone with Wu Huaiyu.

Their true moment of relaxation together came after dinner, as Wu Huaiyu escorted her home.

By that time, the moon had risen, and the mysterious passions and desires she had hidden deep in her heart began to surface.

For the first time, Tutu took his hand as they walked. As they neared the small temple, she allowed him to kiss her on the cheek. That single kiss was electrifying, leaving her dazed for a long time. That night, lying in bed, she felt her cheeks burning with such heat she lay awake almost the entire night.

CHAPTER 17

After returning from the overseas Chinese camp, Tutu felt as if she had become a different person. One one hand, she was deeply captivated by Wu Huaiyu's tiger-like vibrant military temperament. At the same time, she started to have reservations about Wu Lou's lack of concern for national affairs and his sole focus on practicing the flawless Dharma.

Whenever Wu Lou reproached her for her frequent interactions with Wu Huaiyu, she would either argue with him or say, "If I ignore him, he really might bring people to demolish our temple and force us to live in communal housing. Don't doubt it; he has already mentioned that he participated in the destruction of many temples when he was in China."

"That's still no excuse. I would rather have the temple destroyed than see you mix with a murderer and risk damnation."

"What do you expect me to do? Spend my life practicing like you, and eventually become a nun? Who will take care of me when you're gone one day? Don't mistake my intentions; I'm also doing this for you. You have heard it too; many big temples have been destroyed, and one day it could be ours. Knowing someone in power can't be entirely bad."

"No, it's not OK. I don't feel safe with you being around those people. You are young and innocent, and in this dharma-ending era, there are many evildoers out there."

"I won't listen, I just won't!" Tutu suddenly covered her ears and screamed as she never had before, "It's all your fault for not agreeing to marry me! If you change your mind, I'll cut ties with him immediately and follow you to the ends of the earth."

He was momentarily speechless, torn and in pain, but in the end he shook his head firmly and cruelly. He could not let go of the great ideal that he and his master shared: to achieve an unparalleled flawless body, a body without leaks.

She burst into tears, her nose running and her eyes watering, as she shouted at him, "Wu Lou, Wu Lou, you only have yourself in your heart, never me. But I don't believe there's such a thing as a leak-free body in this world, unless they are made of clay, carved from stone, or an emperor's eunuch."

From then on, she seemed to feel more justified to embrace Wu Huaiyu, seizing every opportunity to learn Chinese from him, planning to one day become his wife and return with him to China, the sacred land of the world revolution.

Wu Huaiyu took every chance to educate her about the revolution, telling her that two-thirds of the world's population were still living in misery, awaiting their liberation. He also often earnestly advised her, "Although Wu Lou is your brother and you owe him gratitude, he owns a house and land, and receives offerings from believers, making him a member of the exploiting class. You, on the other hand, are an orphan and belong to the proletariat. Kinship is secondary to class. If you aspire to continue the revolutionary cause of the proletariat, you should foster a deep-seated hatred for the exploiting class. You must distance yourself from him, and not be deceived by his hypocritical savior facade."

She felt as though she was living in a crevice, being contested over by two men who were like older brothers to her, and even more so by the immense spiritual backgrounds behind them. It was as if they both needed her support to succeed in the causes they were fighting for. Yet she felt lost, neither interested in cultivating a leak-free body nor willing to be a revolutionary constantly filled with hatred. She simply wanted to live the normal life of an ordinary girl, to marry a man she loved, and to have a cozy home of her own. She often wondered, Why do women always long for a home, while men seem to always think about leaving home or being away from home?

Wu Lou gradually realized that times had changed. He could no longer use his Dharma teachings to resist or counter Wu Huaiyu's gun, nor could he use them to calm the inner turmoil of a girl's budding passions. He had no choice but to turn a blind eye to the developing relationship between his sister and Wu Huaiyu.

Unexpectedly, Wu Huaiyu found him increasingly objectionable. He despised the merciful yet slightly mocking look in Wu Lou's eyes every time they met, as well as his benevolent smile towards everything and everyone, which he found hypocritical. Wu Huaiyu repeatedly argued with Wu Lou that beings could not be equal; only class, class struggle, and class hatred were the true realities of human society and the driving forces behind historical development.

Over time, the relationship between them grew more and more tense.

One day it occurred to Wu Huaiyu that since he had been received by Pol Pot, many people felt that he would go far. Rumors constantly circulated that he would be transferred to a neighboring unit to serve as a regimental political commissar. Additionally, it was said that Pol Pot himself highly valued him and was in discussion with Khieu Samphan about appointing him as his secretary or assistant, mainly responsible for handling affairs related to China, with the rank of a full division commander.

Because of this, those who envied him began to question his family background again, alleging that he had come from Vietnam with a dubious past, possibly as a spy planted by the Vietnamese. At that time, the relations between the Vietcong and the Khmer Rouge were tense due to their respective backers, the Soviet Union and China, as well as territorial disputes, leading to frequent skirmishes along the border. Consequently, higher authorities had to discreetly investigate him further. Although Wu Huaiyu knew that as long as he stood upright, his shadow would not be crooked, he was still disheartened by these rumors. Recently, some people had been using Tutu's brother Wu Lou against him, pointing out that Wu Lou clearly belonged to the reactionary side, yet he remained untouched and lived a laid-back, pampered life in the small temple, supposedly under Wu Huaiyu's protective red umbrella. This was a damaging public narrative that Wu Hauiyu had never seriously considered. If investigated thoroughly, he would have to suffer in silence, like a mute person tasting coptis, unable to speak of its bitterness. After much deliberation, Wu Huaiyu concluded that he needed to act decisively about Wu Lou, even if it meant damaging his relationship with Tutu. If necessary, he could lay evertyhing out to Tutu, explain the stakes and tell her there were only two paths: one was for him to take her away from Wu Lou, like Chinese Dachun took the white-haired girl or Hong Changqing took Wu Qionghua to join the revolution, sever ties with Wu Lou, and embark on the revolutionary path together as comrades, fully committing to the great cause of the Cambodian revolution. The other path was to be destroyed along with Wu Lou and his small temple.

But he also knew that to achieve this, he must first completely free her from Wu Lou's influence. Strategically, he decided to begin by toppling and shattering the statue of Maitreya Buddha in the small temple. Since Maitreya Buddha was Wu Lou's idol, and Wu Lou was Tutu's idol, he believed in attacking the most crucial point, akin to defeating a python by targeting its heart. By demolishing the idol, he thought the ideological framework of feudalism, capitalism, and revisionism that Wu Lou had instilled in her mind would crumble. This would simplify his task of re-educating her. Thinking of this, he felt excited and somewhat smugly said to Tutu, "Remember, one day I will be Cambodia's Dachun, and you will be Cambodia's White-Haired Girl. Our love story will be written into Cambodia's future proletarian literature and be recounted by future generations."

However, to his great despair, he later found that her thoughts and feelings remained deeply entwined with Wu Lou. She still considered him her lifesaver, but now she was also emotionally attached to him. She would most likely choose to wander the world with Wu Lou if he were to disrobe. This was something that Wu Huaiyu absolutely could not tolerate. Thus, he decided to accelerate the execution of his plan.

One morning, taking advantage of Wu Lou's trip to the city to buy daily necessities like oil, salt, soy sauce, and vinegar, he came to the small temple carrying a bundle of thick hemp rope he had found on a construction site.

When Tutu discovered his intention, she hastily intervened, plead-ing, "No, you mustn't do this; this could cost my brother his life."

"The reactionary class uses these clay and wooden sculptures as tools to numb the people's fighting spirit and extract their hard-earned money for incense offerings. You must sharpen your eyes and not be deceived by him. I'm not exaggerating to tell you that almost all the temples in the city have been demolished; it is only a matter of time before this one is too. You must understand—the world is now ours, the state is ours. If we don't do it, who will? Although in order to jointly deal with the American-backed Lon Nol regime, the doll-looking Prince Sihanouk and Penn Nouth, who shakes his head like a rattle drum, still hold leadership roles in the National United Front, they are merely vases, just for show. The real power is in our hands. You must be clear about this. I am doing this for your own good and for the good of our future."

"Then—can we wait for my brother to come back and discuss it with him first?" she asked, taking a step back after hearing his words.

"No. A revolutionary must have a decisive and swift fighting style, 'Strike when it's time to strike, act when it's time to act.' We will never achieve anything if we keep dillydallying."

She couldn't convince him, nor could she stop him, so she just stood aside and let him be.

However, just as Wu Huaiyu finished tying the thick hemp rope around the neck of the Maitreya Buddha, Wu Lou unexpectedly returned. He had forgotten to bring the shopping vouchers recently issued by the new regime and had hurried back to retrieve them, only to walk in on this scene. He was instantly stunned.

"What are you doing? Why on earth are you doing this?" he demanded loudly from Wu Huaiyu.

"To smash the symbols of feudalism, capitalism, and revisionism, and to bring down the executioners who fool and exploit the working people!" Wu Huaiyu replied righteously and fearlessly.

"This small temple and everything in it were left to me by my master; you can't do it without my consent."

"What? What did you say? You say this temple is yours?" Wu Huaiyu laughed. "Are you dreaming? Don't you know that times have changed? There's no private property in the country and society anymore; everything belongs to the peasants' associations; everything belongs to the new red government. Do you understand?"

"I don't care. As long as I'm here, I won't let you succeed," he said, and with a swift stride, he climbed onto the half-human-high base of the Buddha statue. Standing resolutely in front of the Maitreya Buddha, he spread his arms and declared unflinchingly, "If you pull, pull me along. I will live or die with the Buddha today."

This action and his unwavering stance shocked Wu Huaiyu, who could only stare at him hatefully, panting heavily, unable to speak for quite some time. But Wu Huaiyu eventually blustered, "You, you, you don't get in my way of enforcing the law!"

"What law? Whose law?"

"The law of the new regime. It's all over the newspapers! What? You want to oppose it? Do you want to be an active counterrevolutionary?"

Tutu quickly ran over and clung to Wu Lou's legs, pleading, "Brother, let go of it. It's like this everywhere now. He's just following orders from above. The arm cannot take on the leg. Don't be stubborn. Let him do it."

"Yes, I'm here under orders. Do you really want to oppose the new red regime?" Wu Huaiyu tactically stepped back, while raising his right hand to touch the pistol case at his waist, as if to embolden himself, yet it seemed more like a threat.

Tutu became even more nervous, her eyes brimming with tears as she pleaded with Wu Lou, "Brother, please listen to your sister and come down. Even if I've been wrong in a thousand ways, please listen to your sister this time, OK?"

Wu Lou lowered his head to look at her, rasied a hand to gently stroke her head, a rare gesture for him, and then turned back to gaze up at the Maitreya Buddha statue, which had been his companion day and night for over a decade, always bringing him joy and confidence. Tears streamed down his face.

"Alright. I'll listen to you this time," he slowly said to her, and stepped down from the base of the statue. He then cast a meaningful glance at Wu Huaiyu and added, "But this brother from China, whether you like to hear it or not, let me advise you: the Buddha is not something that can be pulled down by human force. Those who try to pull him down often end up dropping stones on their own feet."

Wu Huaiyu remained unmoved. "Well, we shall see!" he sneered. With that, he wound the rope around his arm, gathered his strength, took a few steps back, and pulled on it sharply.

However, the Buddha statue stood rock steady.

Feeling somewhat embarrassed, Wu Huaiyu turned around again, bent down, and pulled using his shoulder strength, yet this only made the Buddha statue nod slightly.

He looked up again at the Buddha, then at Wu Lou standing aside, and noticed they both seemed to be giving him the same mocking smile, ridiculing him. Bursting with anger, he took two strides toward the Buddha statue. He then wrapped the rope around his waist, coiled it over his arms, faced the statue, and planted his feet firmly, leaning his body down as much as possible while counting silently to three before exerting all his strength.

Finally, the Maitreya Buddha statue was brought down.

However, at the very moment the Buddha statue landed like thunder, Wu Huaiyu slipped and fell backward. At the same time, the statue seemed to lunge straight at him as if to embrace him.

Tutu, watching close by, let out a loud cry of shock and jumped backward several steps, bumping into Wu Lou, who quickly held her in his arms.

Once the dust stirred up by the Buddha statue had settled, Wu Lou pulled the frightened Tutu and rushed over to examine the fallen statue.

Wu Huaiyu's head had been struck squarely by the head of the Maitreya Buddha—cracked open—leaving only a puddle of blood and a deep indentation in the mud on the ground.

Wu Lou was stunned. He had always believed the Buddha statue was made of clay, but upon seeing a large chunk fall from the Buddha's head and shoulders, revealing the statue's pristine white core, he realized that it was actually carved from a precious block of white jade. He then took a closer look at Wu Huaiyu, who was embraced by the Buddha statue. Although he had not been smashed to pieces, his face was contorted, completely devoid of life.

Wu Lou regretted uttering the phrase about "dropping stones on their own feet" earlier. Although a part of him had hoped that the Buddha would show some divine powers to warn Wu Huaiyu, who often professed to be a materialist and did not believe in gods or Buddha, he had never wished for his life to end in such a brutally bloody way. Moreover, he still admired Wu Huaiyu's courage and audacity in leaving home to join the world revolution right after junior high school. He also knew that although Wu Huaiyu was a bit extreme and paranoid, his mistakes were likely the result of an endless cycle of causes and conditions, and the interplay of karmic forces.

As he pondered this, Wu Lou suddenly felt a weight in his arms. Looking down, he realized that Tutu had fainted into his embrace.

CHAPTER 18

He bent down, gently picked her up, turned around, crossed the high threshold of the hall, and walked over the brick path worn uneven by the passage of time. He softly nudged open the slightly ajar, askew wooden door of the west wing with his body and placed her on a makeshift bed assembled from two long benches and a door plank. Then he poured a small porcelain cup of hot water from the thermos beside the bed and scooped up half a spoonful with an iron spoon, intending to feed her some water. He knew she had only fainted from shock and her blood phobia, and that drinking some water would help her come around quicker. But the water was a bit hot, and her lips were tightly closed, making it difficult for him to proceed. He hesitated, suddenly remembering the time shortly after he had taken her in when she had fallen ill with high fever, then became delirious, and, unable to eat properly, incessantly called out for her mother and father. So, as his mother had done for him in his childhood, he cooled the hot water and the rice porridge in his mouth and chewed the pickled vegetables before feeding her mouth-to-mouth, bit by bit.

However, back then she was just a child, and neither he nor his master thought much of it.

But now, she had grown into a young lady. Her slightly upturned, bright red lips were full, like a bud about to bloom, making him hesitate and falter, no longer daring to feed her mouth-to-mouth as innocently as before. Seeing from her cracked lips that her body was in dire need of water, he remembered a story his master once told: A young monk was troubled after seeing his master carry a young woman across a river on his back, thinking the master had harbored lustful thoughts and broken his vows. Upon returning to the temple, he couldn't help but reproachfully ask his master why he did such a thing. The master smiled and replied, "I put her down as soon as we crossed the river. Why do you still carry her in your mind?" The young monk suddenly became enlightened, and the words "Let go, let go, let go …" echoed inside his head.

Adopting a mindset free from attachment, he fed her water mouth-to-mouth against her slightly upturned, rosy lips. He no longer felt they were the lips of a beautiful young girl but rather the buds of a lotus flower in a pond on the verge of drying up in the summer heat.

As if nourished and watered by his tenderness, the bud abrutly opened up, followed by her starry, sparkling eyes. In a trance, she wrapped her arms around his neck and pressed her lips tightly against his. But soon she was fully awake and abruptly released her embrace, rolled out of bed, and ran barefoot towards the main hall.

"Is this a dream?" She covered her face with her hands, leaving only her eyes peeking through her fingers.

Of course, it was not a dream.

A dream was not a dream; therefore, it was called a dream.

The Buddha said, "All phenomena are like dreams and bubbles, or dew and lightning, and should be viewed as such." But that is, after all, a statement in a different context.

Now, Wu Huaiyu's body lay at the center of the main hall, already stiff, his head shattered like a watermelon, brownish blood blended with the dust on the ground and, a few steps away, a fallen grass-green rubber shoe … All were displayed before her in stark reality, far from what Wu Lou used to call the "moon in the water" or "flowers in the mirror."

This was an ending she never could have imagined would befall him, a distinguished Khmer Rouge officer, the future head of the household, to whom she had entrusted her body and heart. That he was not lost on the battlefield in a hail of gunfire but killed in a freak accident by a falling Buddha statue.

Everything went black before her eyes; she let out a cry of "Ah," and fainted again into Wu Lou's arms.

A few moments later, she woke up, immediately wanting to see the first person who had given her complete love in this earthly life, now returned to nature. Yet, before she could take a step, she stumbled and nearly fell. Acting quickly, Wu Lou helped her back to the west wing room, away from the horrific and bloody scene. Sitting together on the small bed, after she had finally stopped crying, he took her hands and said, "Sister, don't be too heartbroken. It's all my fault, not being able to stop him. Don't worry, I'll go and report to their superiors exactly what happened. A look at the scene will prove that it was an accident of his own making."

Her mind was a void, and she seemed to be frozen. After hearing his words, her lips started to twitch uncontrollably. "No, Brother," she shouted. "You must not go!"

"But why?"

"No one will believe you. Surely they'll think you're engaging in class retaliation. Huaiyu told me they are revolutionary soildiers who will never show mercy to class enemies. They will put all kinds of charges on class enemies, making them disgraced men who will never recover. Going there would be walking into a trap. Besides, people in the military camp are all in it together—they will definitely hold biases against you."

"But the scene is right there, the rope on his body, the angle at which the Buddha statue fell; anyone with eyes can see it clearly."

"But what if they say you killed him first and then staged the scene?"

"How could that be possible? How could I possibly have moved such a heavy Buddha statue to crush him? How is that possible?"

"Brother, stop talking about it. He has told me many stories of them fighting the property owners and redistributing the land. They have vowed to overthrow and shatter the old world and will not be constrained by any morals or laws. He admitted that they were often brutally violent and insane when they fought the enemy on the battlefield. There is one thing that I've never told you. Wu Huaiyu once told me that he highly suspected that the two robbers who broke into my house and killed my dad and mom were from the Khmer Rouge. Because he had heard from the older soldiers that during the hardest times, when they hadn't eaten for days, they had resorted to murder and looting in the jungle."

"Then what should we do?" For the first time in his life, he felt so helpless that he had no choice but to rely on a sister six or seven years younger for advice.

"Escape. Flee immediately to the Thai border, then find a way to the United States, where they accept refugees like you. Only by escaping, and the farther the better, can you have a chance to live, to continue."

"What about you? Aren't you going to flee with me?"

"I won't flee. If we both try to escape, we'll be caught quickly, and then even jumping into the Mekong River won't clear our names. Their battalion commander and political commissar are quite nice to me. They won't do anything to me if I stay, and I can still speak and testify for you."

"No, if I escape, you come with me. I will never leave you behind," he insisted.

"I've told you, I won't flee. I have my reasons and justifications."

"What reasons and justifications? Tell me!"

"I don't want to say now, but I will in the future."

"You have to tell me now, or I will never leave you behind."

At her wits' end, she looked at him quietly for a moment. Finally, she said, "You promise to leave immediately after I tell you?"

"Alright," he said, nodding, then added, "If it makes sense to me."

"I'm pregnant with his child. I'm his woman. He has no relatives here, and I must stay to take care of his funeral."

He lowered his head for a while, deep in thought, before looking up at her with red eyes. "Then how about I find a place to hide first? I haven't heard from my family yet, and I don't know what happened to them."

"No, that's even worse. Not to mention that they might already have encountered trouble. Even if everything's fine, you are doing them harm by visiting them at this point."

"Alright. I'll listen to you," he said. Thinking about it, he finally nodded.

CHAPTER 19

As Tutu spoke, her eyes were already brimming with tears, but she did not reach for a tissue to wipe them; instead, she let the tears seep out little by little and hang in the corners of her eyes. She quietly turned her head aside, gazing into the distance as if searching for her hometown and retrieving the youth and dreams she had left behind in its jungle.

The sun had already set, and the last glimpse of the sunset on the opposite mountaintop had long dissipated into the misty sky. The tall pine tree in the neighbor's yard to the right stood out starkly against the backdrop in the shadow of twilight. Rows of large, dark birds were sitting on a snake-like, zigzagging trunk growing sideways at the top of the tree. Ususally, they would chirp incessantly, as if holding a meeting or a parade, with some birds giving speeches, others cheering or protesting. But today they were silent, as if they too were listening attentively to a woman from the eastern Buddhist land recounting such a thrilling and somewhat elusive story.

"Then—what happened afterward?" Staring blankly at Tutu's silhouette, my wife was completely immersed in Tutu's narration of the characters and plot, especially since she knew the two protagonists, one of whom was right in front of her, within her reach, as if she had just stepped out of the movie screen.

Tutu turned her face back, moved the corners of her pursed lips, trying to show a little smile, and continued her story. "After that, I helped him pack his belongings simply—just a few sets of clothes for changing, some cookies and peach-flavored biscuits we usually find too precious to eat, and some incense money and worshippers' offerings we saved from frugality. I put the money in his inner pocket and wrapped the other items in a bedsheet that I tied in a knot so he could carry it on his shoulder.

Anticipating that he might be pursued on the way, I also found a map and helped him plot the best route to take to the Thai border. We decided he should not head directly west through Kampong Speu and Koh Kong provinces, but north to Kampong Chhnang province, then cross to Pursat, which was a longer detour, but the path went exclusively through jungles. He was used to living in the jungle. He knew what wild fruits and mushrooms were edible and what water was drinkable; he would not die of hunger. I also thought that, as a Buddhist traveling through Pursat, he would receive the blessing and protection of the Bodhisattva, which would help to keep him out of danger. All at once I became unusually calm and collected; I could not believe that this was me. It was as if I had grown up in the blink of an eye.

It was only when I pushed my brother, who was reluctant to take a step, out of the mountain gate and watched his figure disappearing, turning back every few steps, that I could no longer take it anymore. I ran after him, held him, tearfully pressed my lips to his, the lips that had fed me water and rice many times, and kissed him frantically while sobbing uncontrollably.

'Brother, remember, you must remember, even if you flee to the ends of the earth, the person I love the most will always be you, my dearest brother.'

He said nothing, just hugged me tightly, then abruptly turned around and strode into the depths of the jungle, eventually disappearing behind a large tree. I stared blankly at the shadow of the tree, at the flickering daylight shimmering within the shadows, for a long time before numbly returning to the temple and closing the mountain gate. I gazed at the suddenly deserted courtyard, then ran to the main hall to look at the person with whom I had the most intimate skin-to-skin contact, still lying on the ground. Thinking of all the kindness he had shown me, I knelt beside him and burst into loud sobs.

He treated me well and respected me. Although he often had strong physical urges, he never forced me to do the male-female thing with him. He always said that we should save the best for marriage.

Later on, I was the one who couldn't bear it any longer. Seeing him in apparent agony, I felt the urge to take the initiative to undress.

I remember one afternoon, when Wu Lou was assigned to go to work at the construction site, he made a special visit to see me. As soon as he entered my small room, I threw myself at him and hugged him tightly. When I was kissing him crazily, I could feel his response below. Feeling completely weak, I collapsed onto the bed and began to fumble with the buttons of my clothes. He grabbed my hand to stop me, saying, "No, not yet, what if—didn't we agree? It will be even more beautiful then…"

After a while, probably worried that I would feel embarrassed, he took my hand again and pressed it to his face, saying affectionately, 'It's not that I don't want to, but I need to be ready and also be responsible for you. You know? The human body is always dirty, only the soul is clean. The body always drags one down, and only the spirit can lift one up. ' He continued, 'I suddenly remembered something. When I was in the fourth grade, our class held a self-criticism review session to fight selfishness and repudiate revisionism. No matter how hard I racked my brain, I couldn't think of a single instance that would reflect that I was truly "revolutionary in my soul." Then I remembered a movie I had watched recently called *Ode to Yimeng*, in which a young woman named Aunt Red comes across a wounded PLA soldier who has fainted on a hillside. His lips are so dry and cracked from thirst that he is nearly at death's door. Unable to find any water, hesitantly at first, she ultimately lifts her clothes, squeezes her breast milk into his military canteen, and feeds him bit by bit. I raised my hand to ask if I could speak.

"Alright," the teacher said. "Wu Huaiyu, go ahead."

I lowered my head, stuttering, 'Teacher, um, I watched the movie *Ode to Yimeng*, and I had a troubling thought.'

'What's troubling about it? Elaborate,' the teacher asked.

My head dropped even lower, and I didn't dare to look at anyone as I stuttered out, 'Um, this, I think I want to be a PLA soldier when I grow up.'

'That's good, a good thing; no need for self-criticism,' the teacher responded.

I became more anxious, and finally, with determination and closed eyes, I said in a hoarse voice, "Teacher, it's not like that. I, I, I …"

I repeated "I" several more times before I finally confessed, "I think being a PLA soldier would be great, because if you're wounded, you might get to drink Aunt Red's milk."

The teacher was stunned at first, but then he couldn't help but burst out laughing. Then my classmates joined in the laughter.

The teacher gestured to me and said, "Alright, sit down now."

But I refused, saying, "I haven't finished yet."

"Not finished?" the teacher said. "Well, then, go ahead."

Gathering all my courage, I continued, "I don't just want to drink it from the canteen; I want to drink it directly, like how I used to drink my mother's milk when I was little. This thought, really, was wrong."

The entire room erupted into uproarious laughter. But after my confession, I felt relieved and dared to look up at the teacher and my classmates. Just then, I realized that the teacher had, at some point, come to stand beside me. I saw his mouth moving slightly, his tongue gently licking his lips, his Adam's apple visibly bulging a little, as if he had swallowed something. I became a little suspicious. Did the teacher also have troubling thoughts like mine? Two of my buddies, children of cadres, later told me that Aunt Red fed the soldier directly in the real story, but the movie had to modify it.

They also mentioned that Aunt AhQing, who ran the Spring Tea House in Shajiabang, actually had a questionable lifestyle, and Uncle AhQing was driven away by anger.

They said, "You are so naive; your troubling thought is nothing; we all have them, but nobody says them out loud."

But how could they understand that if I didn't dig deeper and more thoroughly than they did? How could I demonstrate my determination to reform myself and become an "educable youth of the exploiting class"?

Of course, telling you this is probably pointless; you surely won't understand. But because I had exposed my 'troubling thought' very sincerely and thoroughly, the teacher gave me a very good evaluation and marked it as "Excellent."

'So, you know? Our current leader — Brother Number One — is

actively applying Marxism and Mao Zedong thought according to the specific realities of the revolutionary struggle in Cambodia, leading us in a 360-degree, deep into the marrow, social transformation of Cambodia. This includes a thorough transformation of the human spirit, undertaking efforts never attempted by our predecessors, to build the world's purest, most pristine, most unadulterated socialist state. However, truly, I hate how I'm always dragged down by my physical body, influenced by bourgeois ideology and lifestyle, my will often not firm enough.'

I was both surprised and somewhat disappointed that he would say such things. But I also noticed that while he said this, his gaze kept darting towards my chest. My shirt was almost too tight to button. Once, when I bent down to pick something up, two buttons popped off and I pulled the hem of my shirt down, but he suddenly leaned over and whispered, 'Can I — can I touch there?'

I instantly knew what he meant. But I firmly replied, 'No!'

'Just once,' he had the cheek to request, rare for him.

'You're not thinking about the world revolution and serving the people now?'

'I thought of Aunt Red again. Just quickly, please. Revolutionaries have emotions and desires too, you know.'

I pinched his cheek and said, "Such cheek!" But he understood that meant yes.

Then he raised one hand, and with a white, thin, slender finger, he lightly, very lightly, pressed against one of my nipples through the cloth, and then bent down to take a gentle suck on it...

Instantly, I was struck by a current of electricity, bewildering yet intoxicating, like nothing I had ever experienced before, causing my whole body to tremble violently.

After that, I grew quite fond of his girl-like, delicate and slender hands; his fingers were particularly pale, resembling jade or five white candles. When we met, I often took his hands to admire them closely, as if appreciating a priceless artifact of God's creation. Those hands were also exceptionally dexterous. According to him, he taught himself embroidery as a child. He always carried needles and thread with him, mending his clothes or trousers whenever they tore. I'd seen it; the stitches were fine and neat, something even most girls would struggle to achieve. If not for the revolution and war, I think he could very well have been a fashion designer or an artist. Of course, I particularly appreciated his hands because of the way they touched me — like a bug leisurely crawling on your body, or like hands chanting scriptures, not missing a single word.

He was like a girl in many ways; he had all the trappings of a girl: attention to detail and patience. He always carried three things that we girls like to carry: a square mirror the size of a poker card, a small wooden comb with several teeth missing, and a pair of stainless-steel tweezers.

Once, when I saw him comb his hair with his fingers, I asked, 'Why don't you use your comb?'

'How do you know I have a comb?'

'Not only do I know you have a comb, but I also know you have a small mirror and tweezers. But I don't understand what you need small tweezers for. Do soldiers have to trim their eyebrows too?'

He blushed and smiled at me. 'We have other places to fix, too.'

'What places?' I probed.

He wouldn't say, but I insisted.

He then said I had to agree to a condition.

'What condition?' I asked.

He said he wanted to kiss there. Seeing that I was skeptical, he added, 'through the clothes.'

I said, 'OK.'

Only then did he tell me it was for plucking the beard. 'In the jungle, we encounter the enemy at any moment; there's no time to shave. I just pull out the tweezers and pluck whenever I get a chance.'

I then looked more closely around his lips, and indeed, I couldn't see a single whisker. This made him look more like a girl. Yet this very man, who in many ways resembled a girl, whose mind was consumed with the grand ideals of world revolution, aspired to fight, to save the world. Little did he know that it was precisely because of the revolution that his family had become targeted by it.

He sometimes felt homesick, for he had not heard a word from his loved ones since he left, and he wondered how his mother was doing. But he would soon admonish himself for harboring such petty bourgeois sentimentality. In short, he lived amidst the contradictions that the world had set for him, and in his inner passions, which were beyond my comprehension…

He was neat and hygienic, a rare exception in their army. He told me that many of their Cambodian comrades had worms, and during breaks in the battles they would often gather to pick lice off each other, even popping them in their mouths with a crackling sound. But whenever this happened, he would take the opportunity to wash his clothes, which was why he rarely had the sweaty smell that was typical of his comrades.

I gazed at him, lost in thought, as if he were asleep on the ground. It took a while for me to stop crying. I was no longer too terrified to look at him, and I began to carefully make out his bloodstained figure. His once fair and handsome face was unrecognizable, smashed, with a crooked mouth and an askew nose darkened with blood and mud. Only the brain matter oozing from his forehead showed an unusual and somewhat fierce and terrifying whiteness. One of his hands emerged from the waist of the Buddha statue as if trying to grasp something. I wanted to wipe the blood off the bridge of his nose and lips but ended up grabbing his outstretched hand instead. I bent over and pressed it to my face. Then I noticed something that had fallen out of his pocket, half buried in the dust. I picked it up and realized it was his wooden comb with several teeth broken off. My heart ached again, but it suddenly struck me that I should immediately report such a serious incident to his unit, so I quickly changed clothes and trotted out the door."

CHAPTER 20

Tutu paused again, reaching for the cup that still had most of its coffee left.

"It must have gotten cold. Let me go make you another one," my wife said, rising to her feet and reaching for the cup in her hand.

But Tutu stopped her, saying, "No need. I don't usually drink coffee. I just want to hold it for a while."

"Then — what happened next?" my wife asked.

"It's a long story. That day, I finally reached their barrack, relying on memory and by asking people along the way. At the gate of the barracks, I unexpectedly came across Battalion Commander Song being hogtied and pushed onto an old, beaten-up truck. When he looked up and saw me, I was surprised to hear him ask, 'Have you seen Company Commander Wu?'

I shook my head. He then said, 'Please tell him for me, we can only meet again in the next life!'

I was stunned and wanted to ask him what he meant, but an instructor came towards me and pushed me away. Then I saw the truck carrying Battalion Commander Song lurch forward and then drive away from the barracks, disappearing into the dust.

'Tutu, what are you doing here? Where is Company Commander Wu?' I watched in shock as the flashes of gun spikes on the shoulders of those escorts faded in the misty distance. I suddenly heard someone beside me speak. I turned and saw Xiaohong, Wu Huaiyu's messenger. I quickly briefed him on everything that had happened. He refused to believe it. 'Impossible, absolutely impossible. You must be lying to me!' he said. 'Impossible, impossible. I don't believe that both the battalion commander and the company commander would leave us on the same day…'

'What happened to Battalion Commander Song?'

He looked around, and after seeing that the instructor and his gang seemed to have left to savor their victory, he started speaking incoherently. Still, what he said shocked me.

'They said that he—he—he was Sihanouk's lackey, a traitor infiltrated into the Khmer Rouge. He always—always spoke up for the people from the palace… also opposed—the further purge of class ranks, har—harbor his relatives and—and friends…'

'So, where are they taking him?' I asked urgently.

'To the military court for trial. I heard it's already been decided—execution by shooting…' Xiaohong said, then buried his face in his arms and began to sob.

Just as I was about to comfort him—knowing well that Battalion Commander Song and Wu Huaiyu had always been quite close—I saw Xiaohong had already stopped crying. He turned around to avoid the gaze of the sentries at the gate and nervously wiped his eyes. However, before he could dry them, more tears started to flow. No longer concerned about the surroundings, he frantically shook my shoulders and said urgently, 'You—you just said—what did you say? You're lying to me, joking with me, right? I was supposed to go with the Company Commander, but he—he didn't let…me.'

Then it was my turn to no longer hold back and start crying loudly.

Then Xiaohong led me to the battalion headquarters.

The atmosphere there was solemn and tense. Some appeared bereaved, while others wore looks of triumph.

After listening to Xiaohong's report and my account, the instructor looked relieved and even showed a hint of a smile that was hard to discern. He immediately called the regiment to report Wu Huaiyu's situation. The call was answered by Political Commissar Shen, who, upon hearing that I was there, immediately instructed that I be put on the phone.

In the call, he inquired about the situation and offered some words of comfort before saying, 'Wu Huaiyu was a good comrade; it's a shame that we delayed him. The higher-ups had decided to transfer him to the regiment as chief of staff, but we were still waiting for the results of the political examination from China's side. Alas, these pointless political examinations are really deadly. If we were to subject many of our leaders to such political scrutiny, there would be no revolutionary cause in Cambodia left.'

Then he asked me if I had any requests for the organization or if I wanted to join the Khmer Rouge.

To be honest, on the way here, I had a flash of thought: having suddenly lost two brothers who had cared for and protected me, I became an orphan again. I might as well listen to Wu Huaiyu and join their ranks.

But then it occurred to me that the two bandits who killed my parents might be the Khmer Rouge people. How could I join when there's a blood feud? And now I've just seen Battalion Commander Song, who was close to Wu Huaiyu, being escorted away to be executed. Clearly, they kill not just their enemies but also their own. And I, under the influence of Wu Lou, had long made ahimsa one of life's most important tenets, ingrained in my blood.

I completely dismissed the idea and tactfully said to Political Commissar Shen, 'I'm not in the mood to think about this yet; I just want to first take care of Company Commander Wu's affairs.'

Political Commissar Shen said, 'That's alright.'

He then asked me to hand the phone to the instructor. I could hear Commissar Shen repeatedly stressing to the instructor over the phone, 'You must immediately investigate and report to me the cause of Company Commander Wu's death!'

But this instructor later refused to accept my testimony at all, insisting on characterizing Wu Lou as a heinous murderer who brutally killed a revolutionary soldier, and issued a nationwide warrant for his arrest. He also claimed that Wu Lou was the leader of a cult that practiced the so-called dharma of non-leakage to gain money and sex and then fled with all the money, making me the biggest victim.

As a girl, I couldn't overpower them, so I had no choice but to follow their orders. Fortunately, they never managed to catch my brother, and for that I am immensely thankful to heaven! Later, the troops wanted to hold a memorial service for Wu Huaiyu, and I asked Political Commissar Shen for some of his ashes as a keepsake, which they agreed to. They later gave me a teacup with a lid like this," she said, gently tapping the teacup she held in her hand.

"What about later? How could you, a young girl, be allowed to live on?" I couldn't help but ask.

"They said I was young, a class sister who had been poisoned and deceived, and that they would welcome me to join their ranks as long as I was willing to draw a clear line and fight against the counterrevolutionary, murderer, and cult leader Wu Lou."

"Did you agree to it?" my wife asked anxiously.

"Of course not," she said, her gaze shifting to the distance. She then spoke quietly into the blank space, "I told them that I was carrying Wu Huaiyu's child, that I belonged to him. I told them that all I really wanted was one thing, and I hoped the leadership would grant me this. They asked me what it was, and I said I would like your help to find Wu Huaiyu's family in China. I want to return his ashes and the baby inside me back to his hometown, to his parents' side."

With those words, she turned her face back toward us, stood up, and asked my wife, "May I use your restroom?"

"Of course," my wife quickly said, getting up to lead her inside. But Tutu pressed down on her shoulder to stop her, saying, "I know your house very well; I was here every day when the house was for sale."

As Tutu disappeared from sight and we heard the bathroom door shut, my wife, her eyes reddened again, sighed deeply. "Alas, to be so young when all the miseries happened to her, losing both parents, and her boyfriend being crushed to death ... alas, such a hard life ..."

I didn't respond, or perhaps I didn't even notice what my wife was saying. My mind was completely immersed in deep thoughts about Tutu, Miller, and Wu Huaiyu's fate. It was like a vast, multidimensional oil painting, both specific and general, realistic yet abstract, spanning many eras and lands. In the painting, words that Wu Lou, depicted in the scene, said to Wu Huaiyu, were inscribed like a caption for the canvas: "In that case, we are the same, both renunciates."

He might have said it jokingly to Wu Huaiyu at the time, but I now find these words filled with mystery. It even seems as though they were also spoken to me.

What is home, really? Do the characters you recognize, the books you've read, the cultural heritage and the spiritual baptism you've received not come from your home? Otherwise, why would there be a notion of spiritual homeland? But then, where is my home? Is it merely the house and land beneath my feet? Is it my wife and children who had to stay shoulder-to-shoulder with me all day long due to the restrictions of the pandemic? Then why, when I dream, do I often find myself elsewhere, wandering in my homeland, encountering people with dark eyes and yellow skin, whether they be acquaintances from the past or ancient figures?

While I was lost in my thoughts, Tutu returned with light footsteps. Her face and spirit suddenly became clearer, like someone who had been suffering from a churning stomach having finally expelled poisonous food and bitter water.

Without waiting for us to ask, she continued.

"Actually, I forgot to mention, although the instructor believed I was not involved in the so-called murder of Wu Huaiyu—'murder' was how they labeled his death—I could tell from the way he eyed me up and down, finally fixing his gaze on my belly, that he was not quite convinced the child in my womb was definitely Wu Huaiyu's. Yes, I lived with Wu Lou daily and was in the prime of youth; how could someone like me, in such a situation, have maintained purity and upheld my virtue? He must also have been thinking that it was because I was carrying Wu Lou's child that Wu Huaiyu confronted him, leading to their fatal encounter. Nevertheless, he had no way to confirm that the child was not Wu Huaiyu's. Moreover, the political commissar not only believed every word I said but also, as anyone could see, sympathized with my plight and took good care of me in every possible way, leaving the instructor with no recourse.

Two months later, they helped me obtain a visa to China and sponsored my train trip to a small town in Chongzuo, Guangxi, situated on the banks of the Zuo River. There, I met Huaiyu's father, his younger brother, and three younger sisters, but unfortunately not his mother. After he left home, she cried so much that she went blind, and her health deteriorated day by day until she passed away before reaching fifty.

The classmates who smuggled themselves across the border to Vietnam with Wu Huaiyu, and were later deported, heard I was coming and quickly came to see me. Hearing how he died saddened them all greatly. Such a pity, such a pity! they said. Wu Huaiyu was the smartest and most strong-willed one among them; he was the last one they would have expected to die without any dignity. Dying on the battlefield would have at least earned him a hero's title and his family some compensation. The classmates then began to lament their own situations. Two of them worked in factories, one as an elementary school teacher, and they all felt that this was all their lives would ever amount to. Then they fell silent, sighing deeply.

Wu Huaiyu's ashes were later buried under a peach tree in their home yard. After attending the burial ceremony, the elementary school teacher told me with a bitter smile, 'Now when we get together, our classmates always talk about our old days and ridicule us as "Chongzuo's Gang of Four." Alas, had we had the capabilities of the Gang of Four, we would have been able to get a single room even in prison. To say the least, I blame the Gang of Four, who preached that learning is a waste of time and that turning in blank exam pages makes one a hero, leaving us today without any knowledge. But it's getting better now. The newspaper began to talk about "seeking truth from facts" and something about "reform and opening up." '

One day at noon, an elderly man came by—the fellow townsman Wu Huaiyu had met in Hanoi, the old driver with mismatched eyes. He had returned to China because the fight against the Khmer Rouge, supported by China, led to tensions between Vietnam and China and made life difficult for those of Chinese descent in the area, so he simply decided to come back to China. Having thought about Wu Huaiyu for many years, he especially came to inquire about him and had no idea he would run into me. He kept sighing, 'Alas, it must have been his fate. Why did he go to Cambodia to smash the Buddha statue? How can a Buddha be smashed at will?'

I lived with the Wu Huaiyu family, and it was OK at first. Before the baby was born, his entire family treated me like their own and patiently listened to me talk about Wu Huaiyu. But as time went on, gossip started to spread. First, there were suspicions about whether the child was really Wu Huaiyu's. Then, some people said that the child in my belly was the result of an affair with the monk, who later killed Wu Huaiyu out of jealousy, and that now the stupid Wu family had to help raise the enemy's child. For a time, I really didn't know how to defend myself. Fortunately, I gave birth soon after, and the child not only looked a lot like Wu Huaiyu but also had his fair skin, so the rumors died down. But later, his oldest younger sister, who was already married, came back home and, after a disagreement with me, started spreading that I was a jinx, claiming that her big brother wouldn't have died if it weren't for me. The people there were superstitious, and after a while, even I began to feel that I was indeed a jinx. His younger brother and sister-in-law were afraid that my son would compete with them for the inheritance, so they were not nice to me. In that family, I was like a pariah, expected to do everything without any status or say. So, when I lay in bed at night, nursing my child and staring at the dark ceiling beams, I would often deeply miss those simple, free days with my brother.

His father and his two other sisters were kind enough, but they also didn't dare to offend the others, so they said to me, 'You'd better go back. Leave the child here, and we will take care of him.' But how could I return to a Cambodia that had become unrecognizable, completely changed, so frightening, and with no glimpse of a future? Moreover, I heard that the Khmer Rouge and Vietnam had finally fallen out and were fighting at the border. And now, with my child, the only person with whom I shared blood ties, how could I heartlessly leave him to seek my own happiness? After much thought, I decided to leave home to work outside for a while, to first gain financial independence. Once I'd saved some money and become financially stable, I would take my child and then try to go to America to find my brother.

Fortunately, before this, both my brother and Wu Huaiyu had taught me some Chinese, and I had learned quite a bit of Guangxi dialect during my stay of more than a year with the Wu family, so I had no major problems conversationally. I borrowed some money from his second younger sister and went to Nanning alone to find work. At that time, China was already in the midst of reform and opening up, and the management of the floating population was not as strict as before. I initially worked in a restaurant, washing dishes and serving tables, and later I went to a construction site to wash clothes for people. After saving some money, I bought a resident ID card from the underworld and then enrolled in an ethnic night school to study Chinese.

While I was in Nanning, I visited the Jiuquwan Hot Spring Resort with friends, where they offered a service called 'hot spring fish therapy.' This involved placing special small fish in a pool of warm water, about 40 degrees Celsius, where they could survive. Those fish, about three centimeters long, would gather around to nibble on your skin without causing any pain or itchiness and actually felt quite pleasant. The advertisement claimed that this was a purely natural therapy. Without the use of medicine, it was effective against common skin diseases, scars, and athlete's foot, without any side effects. But when I soaked in the pool, all I could feel were Wu Huaiyu's fingers gliding over my body. You might laugh, but for this reason, my favorite place to go in Nanning was the Jiuquwan Hot Spring Resort, and my favorite pool was the fish therapy pool. I liked to lie in the pool with my eyes closed, feeling the small fish touching and occasionally nibbling on me. When no one else was around, I would quietly undo my bra and let it float on the water like two white lotus flowers, while underwater. I let the fish touch and nibble on me from time to time. At those times, I would recall the Shadow Pond near the small temple. Ah, Shadow Pond, Shadow Pond, it's too unforgettable. But let's not talk about it; well, it's better not to talk about it."

Then she paused for a moment, turned her head to look into the distance, her eyes shimmering like those of a teenage girl deeply in love, her cheeks and the area around her eyebrows also covered with a subtle flush. Then she continued, "But later, what I thought of more and more was still my brother, Jochen. For years, I hadn't heard anything from him, nor could I find any way to inquire about his whereabouts. He must have escaped from Cambodia, because I would have found out through people in the Khmer Rouge if he had been caught. But whether he had left Thailand for America? That was hard to say. I also regretted not arranging a way to contact him in America at that time, but I knew nothing about America then. I was also concerned about whether he had attained a leak-free body, the goal for which he sacrificed so much in life. If he had, then all the suffering I had endured and the ordeals he went through would have been worth it, and it could be taken lightly, almost with a laugh. But ... So, from that time on, I had another urgent desire: to go to America to find my brother. I believed he must have already made it to America. I'd had several dreams where I saw him there, driving his own beautiful black car.

As luck would have it, just as I was making these plans, I met Tom, a white teacher from America who had also spent time in Cambodia. He taught English and was very fond of me. One day, out of nowhere, he asked me if I would marry him and go back to America with him. Of course, I was delighted and immediately said yes.

I went back to Wu Huaiyu's family to talk things over. I told them that I was going to marry someone and move to America, and I wanted to take my son, little Wu Fei, with me. To my surprise, his father refused to let me take my son. And the fact was, because I was hardly ever at home, my son had grown distant from me, and he would cry for his grandfather when he was not around. With this realization, I felt I had no choice but to harden my heart and leave him behind in China as a temporary solution. I would return and bring him to America when he was old enough to go to school. I didn't expect this to drag on for seven or eight years. Nor did I expect the world to be so big, the United States to be so big. I had asked many friends to look for my brother and advertised in the newspaper, but there was still no news of him at all. I started to think he might still be in Thailand, or maybe ... Over time, I gave up.

Tom died of lung cancer seven years after our marriage, and I never remarried. After Wu Fei came, I focused on raising him. He is now in his early forties, but he still lives with me—a mother and son dependent on each other. Thank you both for helping me find my brother. Thank heaven, you truly are my blessings. Someday when the pandemic quiets down, I must find a good restaurant to properly thank you both with a meal."

"Sure! We're also very happy for you! After you reunite, please come visit us. I'd really like to hear Miller talk about Zen and Buddhism, and preach his dharma of non-leakage."

Before I could finish, my wife quickly cut in, saying, "Don't talk about them; they just give me a headache and I don't understand them. I'm just happy to see him sitting there grinning. That alone fills me with joy."

"Great, great, then how about we go see him the day after tomorrow, early in the morning?"

"That works. How about we meet at my house at 8 a.m.? You can park in our yard and we'll go in our car," I said.

After a moment of thought, Tutu said, "Could we make it a bit earlier—how about 7 a.m.?"

"Sure. It's a deal," I said, nodding.

She stood up as if to leave, but hesitated and somewhat sheepishly asked my wife, "But—then—can you send me my brother's picture now?"

"Oh, of course. Haven't you got it yet? I sent it when you were in the bathroom. Check to see if you got it. If not, I'll resend it again right away," my wife said.

Tutu then checked her phone, confirmed she had received it, and thanked my wife profusely.

CHAPTER 21

Unfortunately, it rained all that weekend. Nevertheless, Tutu still arrived early, at 6:45 a.m.

I could understand her eagerness to see Miller. But as I watched the sky, which had just dawned, suddenly grow dark again and the wind bring rain that poured down like a torrent, I apologetically said to Tutu, "This is unfortunate … I'm afraid …" I frowned, hoping she would understand the difficulty and call off the plan.

"Will the market close?" she asked anxiously, her face becoming as overcast as the sky.

I nodded, confirming that it was inevitable.

"But is there any possibility that some vendors didn't hear the weather forecast and will show up anyway? And the rain might even stop."

My wife, having checked the weather forecast on her phone when she heard Tutu's hopeful but unrealistic speculation, blurted out, "No, impossible. This rain is going to last three to four days, one hundred percent, and it's all going to be a heavy downpour."

Tutu shrugged. "I've never had much faith in the weather forecast for Los Angeles," she said with a laugh.

I now understood that her longing to see her brother was so deep that she'd go to him even if it were raining knives. I turned to my wife and said, "In that case, since you didn't sleep well last night, why don't you get some more rest. I'll go with Tutu. If the market is closed and we can't see Miller, we'll come right back."

My wife could not argue against it, so she nodded. But as we started the car and were about to pass through the white iron gate, I suddenly saw her in the rearview mirror, running down the black granite steps at the entrance and frantically waving at us. I slowed down and rolled down the window a crack.

"Take this," she said, passing us a closed umbrella through the raging rain. "It's treacherous out there—be careful on the road! Be sure to drive slowly!"

"I know!" I replied, taking the umbrella and quickly closing the window with a hint of impatience before pressing on the gas. The car trembled on its way down the slope before merging into the boundless curtain of rain.

The rain kept falling harder, as if picking a fight with someone, unwilling to stop even for a moment. The raindrops striking the car made a relentless pitter-patter, as if arguing with someone and refusing to give in. This reminded me of how my wife sometimes lost her temper over trivial matters, bombarding me as intensely as the raindrops splatting against the car windows. I couldn't help but sigh.

Although the sigh was very soft, and it was masked by the sound of the rain, Tutu still heard it and immediately turned her head to apologize. "I'm really sorry for troubling you in such a downpour," she said, "and for making your wife worry."

"It's OK. She's always fussing over things, treating me like a child," I said, smiling lightly.

"Alas—" This time it was she who sighed deeply. "You men," she said. "Living in bliss but not recognizing it."

"But there are things that leave men speechless. For instance, this morning my wife started picking on me for not caring about her in her dreams. She was about to be pounced on by a bear, screaming for help, but I apparently told her to wait until I finished my hand of cards."

"Who were you playing cards with?" Tutu asked offhandedly.

"How would I know? It was her dream. " I shrugged and let out a wry laugh.

Tutu laughed too and advised me, "Well, home is not a place for reasoning. Even though your wife got mad at you, wasn't it because she was worried you'd get caught in the rain? You see, for a woman, love often turns into worry, and she wishes her man would worry about her twice as much. But men, they tend to be careless ... Alas, it's an unsolvable problem."

I didn't say anything. Different roles, different perspectives, different thoughts. Everyone has their own definition of what a so-called happy life is. In my view, couples should be grateful if they can tolerate each other and seek common ground while respecting differences. Isn't it the same between nations and ethnic groups?

"What about you? Was your American husband good to you?" I asked Tutu a moment later, trying to sound casual.

"Yes. Of course, good. Except for having chronic nephritis and not being interested in that sort of thing, everything else was pretty good. He gave me a lot of freedom and let me handle the household finances. That's something many white men wouldn't do. I have a few close girlfriends, all Asian, who always complain about how stingy their white husbands are and how demanding they are in that

department, almost unbearable. However, looking back now, I do
have some regrets. I should have been nicer to him. I thought about
this even when he was alive, but I just couldn't do it. Since my brother
left and Wu Huaiyu died, I've given all my love to my son, Wu Fei,
named by his great-uncle, a university professor. I could not figure
out the meaning of his name, but it is just a name, like a code."

"How old is Wu Fei?"

"Forty-four, born in the year of the snake. We just celebrated his
birthday last night."

"Really? How many children does he have?"

"..."

Not hearing a response, I turned to look at her.

"No children. He is not even married."

"Why not? Does he have a girlfriend?"

"He's always had one. Been through several, just doesn't want to
get married. He's very stubborn, truly his father's son," Tutu said, letting out another deep sigh.

I didn't ask anything further. Every family has its own set of problems, and if she wanted to talk about it, she would say more. I widened my eyes to focus on the road ahead, trying to remember my
wife's exhortation, always maintaining a good distance and paying
special attention to the movements of the vehicles in front of me, on
alert for any sudden stops or lane changes. I have had my share of
experience and lessons in this regard—it was a rainy day, and the car
ended up spinning 180 degrees. Thus, this incident has become an
indelible stain on my driving career, preserved not only in my official record but also in my wife's enduring memory, often brought up
as ammunition to criticize me when needed.

Sure enough, it wasn't long before Tutu initiated the conversation again. "Sounds like you have three children, right? I've heard from your wife, two daughters and a son. How are they doing?"

"They're OK, I guess. The second one had more issues, but that's all in the past now," I said.

"Well, alas, not to hide it from you, but it seems that my son still hasn't grown up. He's still in his rebellious stage. Last night, we got into a huge fight while we were having birthday cake."

"What happened?"

"Well. Everything went well until I mentioned—"

Suddenly, a bolt of lightning, jumping and twisting like a giant silver snake in the middle of the road ahead, ripped the huge, thick curtain of rain between heaven and earth in half. A thunderbolt boomed as if on the roof of the car, making my scalp tingle and my hands shake, and the car started to wobble. At the same time, the blood-red brake lights of a Mercedes-Benz up ahead glared at me, followed by the sound of many cars crashing all at once. I instinctively started to brake but didn't dare to press too hard, fearing that I would start to skid and lose direction and that the cars behind me would crash into me.

Fortunately, I was able to stop less than half a foot from the next car's bumper, and the car behind me didn't kiss my trunk.

Tutu and I looked at each other in shock and took a long, collective breath, like two people emerging from an arduous deepwater dive.

"That was close! Let's not talk anymore; you focus on driving! Or, let's turn back at the next exit?" Tutu said.

"No way. We're already halfway there. Not giving up is the only way to get what we want. Let's stay the course."

We drove slowly away from the scene of the accident and returned to the road.

"Why did you and your son fight? Was it related to you seeing Miller?" I asked.

She was a little surprised. "How did you know?"

"Well, just a guess," I said.

She sighed again and then said, "As soon as I mentioned my brother — ah, I'm still not used to calling him by his current name, Miller, my son's eyes flared with anger. When I said I wanted to visit my brother, he became even angrier. Hurling the cake plate he was holding onto the ground and smashing it, he shouted at me, 'You just can't get over him! Haven't we suffered enough because of him?'

" 'Fei Fei,' I said, 'how can you say that? He's your uncle; he's your mother's savior, and one of the main reasons that I came to America was to find him; we can't be ungrateful!' "

'What uncle?' he shot back. 'We're not even blood-related. I knew it, there's no place for my dad in your heart, only that bald ass! Let me make myself clear; if you go looking for him again, if you meet him you will no longer be my mother, and I will no longer be your son!'

"When I heard him talk like that and call his uncle a bald ass, I was enraged. I told him, 'Fei Fei, you may disown your uncle, but your mother will not disown her brother, nor will she allow you to insult him like that. Do you understand — huh? Insulting him is the same as insulting me. I … I … I …' I was so angry that I couldn't catch my breath. Then I raised my voice and said, 'I'm telling you, if I hear one more disrespectful word from you about your uncle, words that would invite divine punishment, I'll kick you out of this house!' But he was not intimidated by my words; instead, he became even more furious, running out, slamming the door, and not returning for the rest of the night."

"I see. I hope he won't be in any trouble, will he?"

"It's fine. He does this often. He'll slink back after a couple of days, his head bowed in apology. He knows very well that in this world, I am the one who treats him the best and loves him the most. Only I provide him a free house and cook his meals. But this time, he really did piss me off!"

"You also need to take it easy. We can't live our children's lives for them; they have their own blessings," I said.

"I don't dare to dream about blessings, but I'll be grateful if disasters don't come knocking on my door!"

"What do you mean?"

"This child has never given me peace of mind. In China, he was alright; he had his grandfather at home and teachers at school to disipline him, so he was at most somewhat autistic, not sociable, not fond of talking to people, let alone revealing his thoughts. But after he was brought to the United States at the age of ten, he became a bit fearless and turned into a real troublemaker. He would cheat on exams by copying from classmates, steal Transformers toys from the toy stores, smoke, and get involved in gang fights. After turning twenty-one, he started playing with all kinds of guns, claiming he wanted to protect me from being bullied. It's embarrassing, but he couldn't get into a decent school, and only managed to scrape through with a diploma from a community college. In his sophomore year, if I hadn't stopped him, he would have dropped out to join the military to fight in the war on terror in Afghanistan. There was no way I would let him go. His father might not have died in battle, but his death was related to his military service. I couldn't let my only son repeat the same mistake. He would not be deterred, so I told him, 'If you insist on going, I'll die in front of you!' That was what held him back. Then again, they tested him and he turned out to be color-blind. Alas, why am I telling you this? If we see my brother today, don't bring any of this up. He has suffered so much over the years, and for him, I will work on changing my son's mind slowly over time, hoping to eventually bring my brother home to live with us in the future."

We continued making sporadic conversation as we drove, and before we knew it we had arrived at our destination. As we approached, a quick glance told me that there was no need to enter the parking lot. There was not a single car parked there, let alone any vendors. It had become a wasteland.

I shook my head at Tutu and began to turn the car around.

Just then, Tutu's cell phone rang loudly.

Perhaps Tutu had accidentally activated the speakerphone, but it was loud enough for me to hear their conversation. The call was from her son, who was worried about her and wanted to know where she was. He told her he was sorry for losing his temper and that despite his mistakes, he hoped she would understand his feelings. He also mentioned having joined a support group for Black people and that he was planning to attend a protest downtown in a few days. Before he signed off, he also said he needed to return home that afternoon to pick up his clothes.

"Alas, always something to worry about . . .' Tutu said, sighing again.

Spotting a highway sign marked with the familiar McDonald's logo, she said, "Let's get some breakfast. You must be starving too; I thought I heard your stomach rumbling."

"It's only a quarter past eight. Is it open yet?"

"This one's open twenty-four hours."

"Alright then," I said, slowing the car down and moving into the right-hand lane.

CHAPTER 22

After exiting the highway and driving for about half a mile, I could see the large yellow "M" sign right up ahead. As we got closer, I found the McDonald's, with its red tiles and white walls, hidden behind two tall oak trees. Turning left into the parking lot, on the right side of the driveway were holly trees of a man's height. At the corner, to the left of the oak trees, stood three boulders with an irregular pond embedded among them. I had visited this place a few years ago and was quite impressed with this pond, which was so pristine and verdant that it felt surreal. Today, however, it felt different. Muddy water had overflowed and merged with the puddles on the road, and when vehicles drove by, they would stir up two streaks of gray waves, making it seem as if you were driving a boat, not a car.

Tutu chose a table by the window and asked me what I wanted.

"Anything is fine. What about you?" I asked, then turned to go to the cash register.

"No, let me," she said, quickly pulling me back and insisting I sit at the table. "You've been running around for me, and in such heavy rain. It's been tough; I'm terribly sorry."

I just had to respectfully comply.

As I surveyed the restaurant, I noticed that several tables had red "No Sitting" signs and red letters reminding diners to keep a six-foot distance. As a result, there were only four or five sparsely occupied tables, a world away from the pre-pandemic bustle when the place was often overcrowded.

I turned to look out the window, and the first thing that caught my eye was the pond encircled by those boulders. The heavy rain continued to pour down in torrents, as if the heavens too were battling a storm, short on manpower, with even the Jade Emperor himself holding a massive hose, unleashing a fierce and unending deluge upon the mortal world. So much so that the pond was like a giant cauldron boiled by the underworld's Yama, fervently bubbling with dense, large bubbles. The roiling pond made me think of Miller again. What was he doing in such stormy weather? Was he still thinking about going to the flea market to sell plants? Did that old car of his often break down? Did he have a place to store the plants? Was he still practicing his dharma of non-leakage?

Lost in thought, I saw Tutu returning to the table with a rectangular white paper box. "I got you a German Thuringer sausage, bacon and eggs, and crispy hash browns," she said, taking out a rouge-colored drink cup from the box and handing it to me. "I didn't know what you like to drink. Do you mind getting your own drink at the dispenser?"

She must have been hungry too. When I returned to the table with my Coke, I found that she had peeled a red-shelled boiled egg and was putting it into her mouth.

I was not shy either. As soon as I sat down, I grabbed a sausage and started chewing.

We didn't speak, each of us quietly enjoying one of life's rare peaceful moments, savoring the enticing aroma and the delightful tastes of a Western breakfast.

As we ate, Tutu kept her gaze on the pond outside and almost seemed to forget about my presence.

I was about to say something casual when she suddenly asked, "Do you think the child's personality and temperament are related to the weather at the time the child is conceived?"

I had no clue, but I had to say something. "Probably, maybe. I haven't looked into it. But—"

"I suspect that children conceived in bad weather might have violent temperaments. Like today's weather, it certainly isn't suitable for conception," she added.

"Hmm, that's quite possible. The political climate can also affect a person's character. There's a Chinese novel called *The Storm*, where the characters are especially prone to conflict, to fighting and killing…"

"Is that so?" she said, and gave a knowing smile.

Meanwhile, the rain kept pouring and showed no sign of letting up.

"Do you have anything pressing to do today?" she asked uneasily.

"No. Coming here with you is the most important thing I have today. It's a pity that the weather is not cooperating. I was just thinking about the flowerpots on the roof of Miller's car, whether they were brought down in such heavy rain. They must be drenched by now."

"Yes," she said, looking concerned. "He loves flowers, trees, and bonsai, probably because of his time living in the jungle. He used to say to me, 'Never underestimate a blade of grass; they are the same as an ant or an earthworm, all alive, all sentient.'"

Eventually, the subject turned back to her familial troubles. "What worries me the most now is my son. I don't know how to manage his relationship with his uncle in the future. How can I bring my brother back home if he refuses to accept him? This child is really immature; he's like a nemesis, born specifically to oppose me. The reason for the question I asked earlier is that he was reincarnated in my belly in this kind of weather, right by the Shadow Pond, very much like that one," she said, pointing out the window. "Whenever I pass by here, I come in, sit down, eat something, and reflect on those days—unsure whether they were a blessing or a curse. Alas, sometimes I think that my son's temperament and personality would be different if he had been conceived on a day when spring was in full bloom."

"Perhaps. But who knows?" I said.

"Sometimes, when I think about it, bad weather might just be my bad karma, and nothing good happens to me when I run into it. You're a writer, you must have heard of many strange people and bizarre stories, but you certainly haven't heard one like mine." She paused, seemingly hesitant, but then continued to follow the train of her thoughts. "Everyone has their first time, but mine was special because, um—" She looked up at the misty sky outside, then continued, "Because it happened during a storm, with thunder and lightning…"

As she spoke, she shyly ran her fingers through the grayish-white hair that hung over her forehead, as if trying to calm herself, and then told me the following story.

It was a Sunday, and Wu Huaiyu came early to take her to the woods to gather wood ears and mushrooms. Influenced by Wu Lou, she had always opposed his hunting, arguing that killing was wrong and would invite retaliation from vengeful spirits and creditors. Initially, he argued with her, citing "survival of the fittest" and "natural selection," but he eventually heeded her advice and at least never killed in her presence again.

The bamboo basket filled up quickly, and they began heading home. As they walked, the bright sky darkened within minutes, and soon came the sound of muffled thunder from the horizon.

They trotted back, and just as they were nearing the Shadow Pond, it began to pour with large, bean-sized raindrops. Wu Huaiyu grabbed her hand and ran along the creek toward the Shadow Pond. There, between several boulders, was a crevice with a pointed top, large enough to shelter two or three people from the rain.

"How do you know this place?" she asked, unable to contain her curiosity.

He smiled mysteriously at her. "Of course I know; I've even seen a fairy taking a bath here."

"A fairy?"

"That's you!"

"What do you mean?" she asked, taken aback. First she blushed, then she swung her fists at his chest and called him a "rouge." He quickly begged for mercy. "I'm telling the truth. I thought you were a fairy descended to earth; I dared not look; I saw nothing. We Chinese often say there's a Jade Rabbit, which is pronounced 'Tu' in Chinese, on the moon. Your name is Tutu. Maybe you were really sent down to earth because you offended the Queen Mother in heaven." Though she found his words pleasing, she retorted, "I don't want to be a 'Tu' for you to hunt!"

"How dare I? Tutu will be my mascot from now on, and I will protect her wholeheartedly."

"Forget it; you'd better serve the people wholeheartedly," she said, mimicking his tone.

He laughed, took one of her hands, and gazed at her face fondly, saying "You're so pretty."

"Thank you. But aren't you a revolutionary? Stop ogling me!" she said, feeling both uncomfortable and a bit cold due to her wet clothing. "I'm going to wring out my clothes," she said. "Turn your face away and don't look!" she commanded, before adding, "If you peek, I will go to your troops and report you for harassing me!"

At this, he obediently turned around.

She wrung out her top and put it back on, but still she shivered. Realizing that the shirt he was wearing underneath was fairly dry, he took it off and insisted she wear it. It was large and long on her, with the hem falling below her knees. They sat down facing each other on the damp gravel, waiting for the rain to lighten before running home, but the downpour seemed to have no end, with continuous thunder and lightning that sometimes struck so close overhead that she could not help but throw herself into his arms and cling tightly to his waist.

In response, the momentarily stunned Wu Huaiyu could only gaze at her foolishly, but eventually, as she continued clinging to him, he gave in and held her tightly in return. Then they simply stripped off their wet clothes, leaving only their shorts on, and huddled together for warmth. Later, as they lay side by side on the ground, they pulled the almost-dry white shirt over them.

"You are so fair-skinned," she remarked, admiring his snow-white arms.

He seemed displeased by the comment and responded,"What's good about being fair-skinned? A tan is the true mark of health. Fairness is characteristic of the bourgeois ladies and gentry. Back in school, I hated those kinds of comments, which insinuated that I was not from a worker or peasant family and even my skin color bore the mark of the exploiting class. During summer farm work, while others wore hats to protect from the sun, I purposely did not, often going bare-chested with rolled-up trousers. Unfortunately I remained fairer than the others, even with all that sun exposure. I also hated it when people looked at me with suspicion and talked behind my back, saying that I was a seed left behind by a white missionary, or that there was at least white blood or genes in my family … Of course, this wasn't entirely made up or baseless, because in our area there had been churches and nurseries run by white missionaries in the past, and indeed, such things had happened …"

"I don't care; I just like how fair you are!" she said, turning around to hug him tightly.

She must have been crazy at that moment, disregarding everything, including all of the teachings and admonitions of her brother Wu Lou, especially the one about not losing her chastity lightly. Everything flew out of her mind to the clouds in the sky all at once.

"Hold me, hold me tight, yes, just like that, don't let go …" she said, her breath short in a whirl of emotion, and they clumsily removed each other's shorts.

He grew increasingly excited, holding her tighter and frantically kissing her face and neck. It was only when she bit his tongue that it finally found its home in her mouth.

"Are you, are you still cold?" he asked her afterward.

"No, I'm not cold at all. And you?"

"Me neither; you're like a hot-water bottle," he said.

"So, do you want me?" she asked, reaching down to grasp that burning hot, candle-like thing, feeling the slippery, warm candle wax emerging from its tip. It reminded her of the candles on the altar in their small temple, the kind her brother Wu Lou used for burning his finger as an offering to Buddha. Lighting it inside her body would surely illuminate her from within. In this light, she could finally have a loved one and a warm, worldly home...

"Yeah..." he responded, but not knowing how to want, he aimlessly prodded and poked around her body like a blind man with a cane. Eventually, with her help and guidance, he managed to enter smoothly...

Suddenly, he saw she was in great pain. "Does it hurt? You look like you're in pain," he said anxiously.

She nodded but then shook her head.

Not comprehending that she was experiencing both pain and pleasure, he was confused by this gesture.

Even in these moments of ecstasy, he was meticulously caring, even holding his arms up to ease the pressure of the hard rocks beneath her. But this soon proved counterproductive as she kept pulling him tightly against her body, so much that her nails began to dig into the flesh of his buttocks.

She returned home very late. Her brother must have noticed that something was off about her demeanor. She had expected him to scold her, but he didn't say anything; instead, he silently reheated some dinner and brought it to her, saying, "Eat, you must be hungry."

Suddenly, she felt so ashamed that she wanted to slap herself and kneel before him to confess.

"Alas," Tutu said with a sigh, "looking back at it now, this male-female entanglement was no different from drug addiction. Once you've had the first time, you'll want it a second, and a third, until you're in so deep that you can't get out. Huaiyu later apologized to me many times, but whenever we saw each other we just couldn't control ourselves. He once jokingly said to me, 'You're not a fairy—you're more like a forest demon, sent by the heavens to seduce me and capture my soul.'"

I knew it was a joke, but it made me so mad that I refused to speak to him for several weeks.

"I finally understand now: the biggest setback or turning point in my life, in fact, started at the Shadow Pond. I once heard someone on TV talk about *Dream of the Red Chamber*, saying, 'All the sins originated in Ning House.' My body was essentially Shadow Pond. It was by the Shadow Pond, amid the violent storm, lightning, and thunder, that I became a woman ..."

She then looked out towards the boulders under the oak tree, towards the flooded pond that resembled a stage prop for "Flooding the Jinshan Temple."

CHAPTER 23

Another week passed in a blur.

Saturday was a day with clear skies and crisp air; although the sun had not yet risen, the glow of dawn had already reddened the eastern sky. Somehow, spending such a day reminiscing about the past seemed to render all previous storms and thunder less real, even trivial.

My wife didn't join us last time because she doesn't rest well at night, but this time she volunteered to come along despite her yawning and rubbing her eyes. She usually goes to bed late and rarely gets up this early, yet she was eager to witness the historic reunion of Tutu and Miller.

With one hand on the steering wheel and the other scrolling through music channels on the radio, I finally found a cello and violin ensemble. The music sounded soothing, capturing poetry and distant lands in the present moment.

I felt relaxed and enchanted by the sound of the music, which filled up the car like water, but from a glance into the rearview mirror I could tell from Tutu's bloodshot eyes that she was badly in need of rest.

"Tutu, did you sleep well last night?" I asked.

"Oh, no," she replied without looking up, "I only dozed off for two or three hours. I would wake up again and again, and I kept dreaming. I dreamed that I saw my brother, but he refused to acknowledge me."

"When did you dream about it? I asked. "In the first half of the night or the second?"

"I fell asleep at almost 2:30 in the morning. It must have been the second half."

"Dreams in the second half of the night usually turn out to be the opposite," my wife chimed in.

"Let's hope so," Tutu said, looking down at her phone.

"Are you looking at your brother's photo?" I asked, trying to lighten up the mood in the car.

"Mm, yes." Tutu looked up this time and smiled at my back, then added, "I'm all too familiar with my brother's eyes. They slant upwards at the corners, much like what you Chinese call 'upturned eyes.' If he weren't a Buddhist, he would have charmed away the hearts of many girls. Of course, there's also his mutilated little finger. Without it, I wouldn't be so certain it's really him. But now I'm suddenly worried. Since he's wearing a mask, I cannot clearly see his cheeks, lips, and chin clearly. What if I mistook him for someone else? Then it would be getting my hopes up for nothing and leading you guys on a wild goose chase!"

"Ah, that—I think it's impossible. Not to say it's 100 percent certain, but there's still a 99 percent chance. Besides, he told me himself that he was born in Cambodia. What are the odds? You, in my opinion, are having the symptoms of 'The closer one gets to home, the more unsettled one feels.' "

As we talked, I had switched from Highway 60 to the southbound

Interstate 5. Soon, the familiar towering billboard for the Commerce Casino gradually came into view. I pointed out the window and told Tutu, "That's where I used to work and where I met Miller."

"Oh, oh, that's also part of your karma too. I've never been here before, and I don't know how to gamble, neither would I enjoy it," Tutu said, looking in the direction of the casino. Suddenly, she lifted her phone and started clicking away, taking several photos in succession. Then she held up her phone, panning it slowly as if recording a video.

Her action made me think of a touching video snippet that I had seen recently on WeChat and watched again last night.

It was taken on a day in May 2010, at the Museum of Modern Art in New York, where an exhibition called "The Artist Is Present" was being held. A wooden table and two wooden chairs were set up in the space, one of which was occupied by the Serbian performance artist Marina Abramović. She had been sitting in that chair for over 700 hours. For two and a half months, more than 1,500 museumgoers took turns sitting across from her and engaging in eye contact for as long as they wanted to or were able. Abramović sat there calmly and serenely, showing no emotion. This detachment and immersion turned her into a vessel through which those who sat across from her saw themselves; some cried, some laughed, some made confessions, some were restless ... They were looking at Abramović, but also at the unreserved reflection of themselves in her eyes.

Until a man appeared and broke up the stare-down. His name was Ulay, and he had been Abramović's lover for more than a decade, but they had been apart for twenty-two years. During their years together, they created various performance art pieces that garnered global attention. They were a remarkably beautiful couple in the history of modern art, but in real life they ultimately went their separate ways.

Seeing Ulay take a seat across her, Abramović appeared slightly surprised, nodding gently, her mouth twitching into a faint smile. Ulay then slightly raised his eyebrows and exhaled, gently shaking his head. He then shrugged his shoulders, straightened up his back, and began looking into her eyes intently. Gradually, Abramović's eyes filled with tears, as did Ulay's. Finally, a few clear tears overflowed from her eyes, and her lips parted slightly as if she wanted to say something but could not. Seeing this, Ulay shook his head again, his eyes widening as if to say, "You don't have to say anything, I understand." Unable to hold back any longer, Abramović's tears fell like rain. No longer restraining herself and seeming to forget about the performance altogether, she leaned her body forward, almost resting on the table as she reached out her hands towards Ulay, who smiled and extended his hands to her. Their hands met in the middle of the table nearer to her side, her somewhat pale fingers gripped by his darker fingers, which gently tapped and caressed them.

During the 700-plus hours of eye contact, Abramović had been a vessel for everyone else, but at the moment Ulay appeared, she returned to herself. Thus, the narrator of the video clip said, her voice filled with emotion, "Reunion is crueler than parting. As in Byron's poem: 'If I should meet thee after long years, How should I greet thee? With silence and tears.'"

This video evoked a lot of emotions for me. I thought of Tutu and Miller, who had been separated for almost half a century and now were about to reunite. I felt fortunate to personally witness and take part in such a profoundly moving and unique reunion. This was not merely a simple reunion between loved ones after years of separation. As I saw it, this was a reunion between races, religions, histories, and destinies. But suddenly I felt a bit perturbed: how should I congratulate them upon witnessing their reunion? Like Byron, with silence and tears? No, I thought, I must record this reunion with my heart and my pen.

So, I asked Tutu, "What are your plans and thoughts after you reunite with your brother?"

"Ah, I have given it some thought. Of course, I'll also consider my son's opinion. I have emptied the study I used as an office, intending to bring him home to live there. Though my son hasn't budged yet, I'm confident I can persuade him. Afterwards, I plan to retire—after all, you can never make enough money—to be his nurse and care-giver full time, to take good care of him. In short, I will never again let him struggle and toil for a living on his own. I will do everything I can to make his later years peaceful and happy. Of course, if he feels that he hasn't yet achieved the dharma of non-leakage he had aspired to, I will support him to continue."

"That's great. Having such a devoted sister like you by his side, it can truly be said that his suffering has finally led to sweet outcomes. But," I pressed, "do you think your brother will agree to this arrangement?"

Tutu seemed hesitant, her gaze wandering to the window, her expression faintly clouded.

"This—I'm not sure."

My mind, however, was elsewhere.

As we got closer to the Cypress Flea Market, the word "reunion" began to echo in my mind with increasing frequency. My hands were on the steering wheel and my foot on the gas pedal, but my mind was churning with this word.

As my thoughts traveled down the highway of "reunion," I wondered if I would ever reunite with the casino, its colleagues and guests, and even those stiffers at the card table? Will I reunite with the mentors and friends who have drifted away over the years? With comrades from my military days? With the painful past or absurd eras? Or will history with history, era with era, event and event, also find their reunions? It's as if everyone is on an elliptical track in an infinite loop where, regardless of one's pace or when one joined, everyone will keep on encountering and reuniting with every point on that track. So, I wonder again, will each of us living in contemporary China reunite with the ancient emperor Qin Shihuang, the Boxers in the late Qing dynasty, and the Red Guards during the Cultural Revolution? Will we reunite with Ruan Ji, who often got drunk, showed his disdain openly through the whites of his eyes, drove his carriage alone, letting the horse wander aimlessly until reaching a roadless place, where he would then weep bitterly before returning home? Will we reunite with Ji Kang, who forged iron under the willow tree in the mountains and, before his death by execution, calmly played the ancient zither piece "Guangling San," a melody that has since vanished from the world? Will we reunite with Confucius, who traveled between states to offer his teachings to the rulers and ended up as weary as a dog with no owners? Moreover, it's only sensible to think that fortunes ebb and flow, so will we not only reunite with moments of prosperity and auspiciousness, such as the rise of great nations, wedding night, and success in the imperial examinations, but also encounter various forms of misfortune, bad luck, and even various viruses of the natural and spiritual realms?

As I considered this, several writer friends softly floated into my mind. First was the veteran Chinese author Liu, who wrote *A Second Kind of Loyalty* and *People or Monsters*. While I was studying at UCLA, he came as a visiting scholar and gave a lecture addressing the

Chinese community alongside me and another writer, Zhong, known for his distinctive style and grace. Once, during a car trip, the conversation turned to literature. Liu argued that literary writing should convey moral values, bear responsibilities, and speak for the people, underscoring the importance of responsibility and a sense of mission. Zhong, on the other hand, countered that "the most important thing about a good novel is that it's interesting. Writing should be enjoyable, and readers should find it fun too." Their views on art were clearly contradictory, but that did not hinder their mutual admiration.

I was out with Zhong one time when we accidentally rear-ended another car, causing a large dent on the left front side of the hood. Zhong then said that he was good at metal work, as skilled as an eighth-level fitter, and he could help me hammer it so flat that no trace would be visible. Following his instructions, I drove up to the trailer he had rented. Together, we took off the hood, and, under his demonstration and guidance, I used a small spade to level a piece of the ground beside the car, then broke up clods of earth with a metal hammer. As I worked, he sat on a small square stool, looking every bit the master craftsman in his duck-tongue cap, holding a Stalin-style pipe and smoking leisurely. Every now and then he would draw on the pipe and let wisps of smoke bulge out from his nose, but he always remained attentive to my task. When he saw that I had finally pounded the dirt into powder, he said, "It's ready," as he knocked the pipe, which was no longer sparking, face down on the leg of the stool. He then dragged over the car hood, placed the dented part on the crushed, soft dirt, squatted down, picked up the small hammer I had just used, and began to work on the dented areas, ringing and clanging. As he pounded, he turned his head towards me and winked. "Look over there," he said. "The people from the garage across the

street are watching us. They must hate me for taking their business."
I looked in the direction he pointed and indeed saw two mechanics
in blue shirts and trousers looking at us with confusion and curiosity.

"Why don't you rent a house?" I asked him, feeling somewhat per-
plexed by Zhong's choice to rent such a cramped trailer.

"To save money," he replied. "This trailer only costs 150 bucks a
month. It's small, but it has all the essentials: a kitchen, toilet, lights,
telephone, you name it. Of course, another bonus is it's earthquake-
proof. Now, I'm telling you the truth," he said, squinting and smiling. "Not only am I not afraid of earthquakes, I actually welcome
them—the bigger the better—just like Gorky looking forward to
more violent storms."

"Why?" I asked, feeling confused. "Are you sick?"

He lowered his voice and said somewhat mysteriously, "You don't
understand. That is how I get business. Just a gentle shake from the
Lord of heaven, a little twist of his hips, and all those antiques collected by rich people—porcelains, ceramics, and woodworks—are
damaged, and their rich owners need to come to me for repair. So,
the Lord of heaven knows better, often using such means to rob the
rich to help the poor." He then gave me a wild look, chuckled, and
said, "Remember, if one day you suddenly can't find me, it must be
that Los Angeles hasn't had a destructive earthquake for too long, and
I'm out of work, so I have to go elsewhere to make a living."

More than two decades have passed. Where are they now? I know
only a little about what happened with Liu. He relocated to the East
Coast, but then news of him gradually dwindled. A few years ago,
I heard he was diagnosed with rectal cancer and wished to return
to his homeland, but his request was not approved by the authorities and he passed away far from home. Fortunately, his ashes were

eventually brought back to China for burial. Since the early 1990s, there hasn't been a major destructive earthquake in Los Angeles, so it's safe to assume Zhong is no longer in the United States, or at least not in California. Perhaps God, in order to preserve more people's livelihoods, finally had to take away his. Fortunately, Zhong writes good novels, is able to trade his words for money, and possesses various other skills, so he likely won't go hungry.

Then, I thought of another friend, Zeng, whom I had seen in Los Angeles a few years ago. Both his novel and mine had received full-issue coverage in Shanghai's *Wenhui Daily*, and both were later adapted into comic strips and won the top prize in art. We met years later, and I was deeply moved hearing him talk about his experience on the run. After that incident, which the officials declared as turmoil, he quickly found himself on the wanted list. Initially, through connections, he worked under a pseudonym as a carpenter in a military logistics unit in northwestern China. He mentioned that the 14-inch black-and-white TV in the carpentry workshop was on day and night. Often, while he worked with a hammer in one hand and a chisel in the other, his name and picture would suddenly appear on the TV screen, playing back on a loop. Even though he had disguised himself and grown a long beard, he still feared being recognized. He repeatedly, almost obsessively, reminded himself, "Remember, you are not Zeng; you are Lao Wang, Lao Wang, Lao Wang! Do not turn around or react if someone calls you ZY. The person named ZY is dead—dead." Later, feeling the situation worsening and viewing the television in the workshop as a significant psychological threat, he decided to flee southward. For this, he meticulously created a fake ID card, on which he carefully drew every word, every pattern, and the public security department's seal. However, he could not complete the lamination process by himself and would need to visit a small shop for the final step. Having scouted the site multiple times and plotted a potential escape route if he were to be recognized, he finally stepped through the door and handed the shopkeeper the paper and photo that would determine his fate. His heart was in his throat; if the owner cast even the slightest suspicious glance at him, he planned to immediately bolt out of the shop and run.

But where is Zeng now? Will we ever meet again in this lifetime? Will we ever reunite?

Lost in my memory, I looked up and saw Tutu's face in the rear-view mirror, filled with hope and reverie, bringing my mind back to reality. I wondered: Miller has a sister who isn't his blood sister but is more than one; haven't I had someone like that too? But now, under the vast sky, in which corner of the world, at what coordinates of this global village, is she?

She was a girl I met and got to know during my internship at the newspaper, and for a time we became emotionally dependent on each other. She was intelligent and managed her relationship with my wife well, often coming over on weekends to cook with us. My daughter also liked her; she said her auntie was pretty and had a pleasant voice. At that time, we lived in the Tilanqiao area of Shanghai, and sometimes when she returned home late at night, I would walk her to the bus station about 500 meters away and wait with her. Only after seeing her get on the bus and it drive away would I leave with peace of mind. And she would always press her face against the bus window, waving goodbye to me with reluctance.

After I went abroad, as soon as I was able, I fulfilled her wish to study abroad. For this, she once wrote to me, saying, "Brother, I now realize that you are the one who loves me the most, cares for me the most, and understands me the most."

I once had a small office crammed with two tiny desks, where we often rushed to finish the day's press releases together. Sometimes, I would ask her to help me transcribe my newly written stories. In the evening, when most colleagues had left, the office became surprisingly quiet. We could hear the intermittent chirping of crickets on the balcony and the rustling sound of our pens moving across the paper. If one of our pens suddenly stopped rustling, we would both turn around and share a smile.

However, for various reasons, we eventually lost each other in the sea of people.

There are some people and things you shouldn't get too close to; otherwise, you might lose them.

Will she and I ever reunite one day? Feeling helpless at the thought, I let out a bitter laugh and glanced at my wife sitting in the passenger seat. When we first returned to China, my "sister" had asked to meet her in a park nearby, saying she wanted to marry me. But at that time, I could still face my wife's reproach, thinking it was at most emotional infidelity. But ... what about later?

Fortunately, her eyes are closed now; she appears to be asleep. Had she seen me at this moment, looking lost and immersed in a melancholic mood, and had Tutu not been sitting in the backseat, she would most likely sneer, "Look how lost you are. You must be missing your sister again, huh?"

She shows almost no interest or feeling towards many other matters, especially politics, but when it comes to discerning who might be in my heart, she hits the nail on the head every time.

CHAPTER 24

Because my mind was constantly wandering, the steering wheel in my hands seemed for a while not to be a steering wheel at all, but rather a watercolor brush that sometimes obeyed my command and at other times moved on its own, scribbling spontaneously. This brush had not only heavily marked my life's journey with many characters and symbols that astonished me with their beauty, or lack thereof, but also with many colorful and chaotic annotations. But now it seems to have also been fitted with four wheels, speeding along the endless path of life so fast that I can't make out anything, crushing everything in its path—leaving my heart empty for a moment, with only the vague traces and imprints of the wheels remaining.

The world is inherently chaotic.

But those traces and imprints suddenly appeared so clearly before my eyes and in my mind, then transformed into the vivid red strains of the coronavirus, one by one, grain by grain, stick by stick, strain by strain, row by row, line by line, covering the road ahead, filling the sunny sky, and permeating the spiritual and subconscious realm to which we have already lost immunity, somewhat like forest demons, somewhat like angels, somewhat like hedgehogs, and somewhat like crowns.

"Wrong! The 5!" my wife suddenly shouted.

It turned out that I had gotten confused and driven onto the wrong ramp at the intersection of two highways.

Her voice jolted me awake as if from a dream. With only a brief glance at the rearview mirror, I yanked the steering wheel to the left, forcefully pulling the car back into the rightmost lane of Highway 5.

My wife and Tutu, aghast at the sudden swaying of the car, screamed simultaneously.

I steadied the car as well as my emotions and apologized for scaring them, trying to sound calm and composed.

"Did you doze off? Or did you lose your soul?" demanded my wife.

I had no words to respond. My wife, knowing I was feeling guilty and in the wrong, and with Tutu sitting in the backseat, refrained from scolding me any further. But it was strange to both my wife and me that Tutu showed no other reaction or response except that scream.

My wife turned around to look at Tutu in the back seat, and when I looked at her in the rearview mirror I saw that her face was wet with tears, her eyes staring blankly into space with confusion. She seemed completely unaware of our presence, nor of what had just happened in the car.

"Tutu! Are you OK?" my wife asked, waving her hand in front of Tutu's face.

As if waking from a dream, Tutu looked at my wife attentively as if she had just become aware of her own existence. Then she straightened up and said nervously, "Ah, sorry! Are we... are we there yet?"

"No, but you're crying," my wife said, pulling out a tissue from the box beside her and offering it to her.

"Ah? I — ah … ah — was remembering some things from my child-hood." Tutu took the tissue, pressed it to her eyes, and then squeezed it in her palm. Seeming to regain a bit of her composure, she forced a smile.

"What things? What made you so sad?" my wife asked.

"Alas, it's not exactly sadness — it's just, I can't quite explain it. Any-way, I'm about to see my brother, and although I was really happy at first, I suddenly started to feel a little scared, even afraid of meet-ing him. So many things, alas, just too many, like a dried-up spring suddenly bubbling up from the ground again."

"Then, you might as well let them bubble up and share them with us, to keep me from dozing off," I said. "I bet you're unaware that I almost took a wrong turn earlier."

"Wrong turn? No, I didn't notice."

"You did cry out though."

"Did I? I had no idea. It was like watching a movie in a dream … I was a little girl, about six or seven, maybe eight years old, catching butterflies in the vegetable garden behind the house. Suddenly, I noticed a big, ripe yellow guava fruit on a guava tree against the east wall. I was worried that the birds and bugs would eat it, or it would fall to the ground and be ruined, which would be such a waste. That was the only guava fruit left, so I tried to find a way to pick it and save it for my brother. We had two guava trees: the one by the west-ern wall produced crunchy and sweet fruits, which were my favor-ite; the one by the eastern wall produced fruits that were a bit sticky, the softer, the sweeter, which my brother loved the most. Without thinking too much, I climbed up the tree, trying to pick the guava fruit for my brother. But just as I made it to the top of the tree, hold-ing the trunk with one hand and reaching for the guava with the other, the branch broke, and I slipped and fell from the tree. My left arm hit the ground first, with a snapping sound, and when I got up I felt my left arm wasn't mine anymore, and I screamed in pain, drenched in sweat.

My brother and master heard the noise and rushed out. The Master lifted my arm to examine it, pressed on the joints, and then said to my brother, 'The forearm bone must be broken; hurry to town to find a doctor to set the bone.' Without saying a word, my brother squatted down to carry me to the orthopedic clinic in town, more than three miles away. Usually, when we were out together, and seeing me tired from walking, he would let me lie on his back or ride on his shoulder. But this time, because of the unbearable pain in my broken forearm, I couldn't grasp his shoulder or hand. After thinking it over, he stood up, bent down, and picked me up in his arms. The master said, 'This won't work; I'll get you something.' He then went back inside the room, came out with a bedsheet, tied a knot, and hung it around my brother's neck. Later, I was wrapped in a gray-white bedsheet, my head resting on my brother's arm, my whole body hanging on his neck, swinging all the way into town.

What a painful yet fascinating day it was. I felt excruciating pain with every pinch, every pressure, and every pull as the doctor set the bone. But thinking about how my brother had carried me all that way, enduring even greater hardship, I gritted my teeth and got through it, even keeping from crying out. So much so that both the doctor and the master later praised me as a strong and brave little girl.

After the bone was set and the cast applied, I wanted to walk on my own on our way home, but my brother insisted on carrying me. He said it was already dark, I was walking too slowly, and we needed to hurry home. Of course, I had no idea that the way he carried me is now known as the 'princess carry.' And I truly felt like a little princess being carried home by my brother. By then it had grown dark, and the moonlight spilled down like water, illuminating my brother's face. I gazed at his handsome, lean chin, the pearl-like sweat glistening on his face, and feeling the warm breath he exhaled, my heart was filled with joy. I wished for nothing more than to lie in my brother's arms like this forever. Although my forearm still throbbed with pain, my heart was floating in the white clouds and dancing in the moonlight of the forest. It was such a beautiful night that I felt all these sufferings were worth it, a generous blessing from the Buddha. Especially once I returned home, and, for nearly half a month, my brother took meticulous care of me, cooking for me, washing my clothes, washing my face, brushing my teeth, comforting me, sitting with me and telling me stories, and helping me to recover quickly. However—"

Tutu paused and turned her head to look out the window. This section of Highway 5, which originally had only three lanes, has now been expanded to four lanes, and in some places even five, widening the view considerably.

"However what?" said my wife, who had just faced forward to rest her neck after turning to listen to Tutu, but then twisted sideways again to look back.

"However, later, I didn't listen to him and even quarreled with him. Not only did I ruin him, but also Huaiyu, Fei Fei, and myself. I often think, if I had been firm in stopping Wu Huaiyu from smashing the Buddha statue, he might have listened to me. At least if I had told him that we would be through if he smashed the Buddha statue, he would have definitely thought about it. Also, I was saved by Buddha's followers; how could I not stand up and fight when the Buddha statue was about to be vandalized? Isn't that the same as biting the hand that feeds you? Moreover, seeing someone doing wrong without trying to stop them, isn't that harming them? Alas, how could I be so muddled? If I had decisively stopped him and spoken harsh words, he would have hesitated, he would have stopped, and then I would have saved him, my brother, and everyone else. However, when I thought this way, I wondered if I could really save someone. Buddha said that the power of Buddha is no greater than that of karma. My brother also told me that doing virtuous deeds generates good karma; doing bad deeds generates bad karma. Alas, how could I? The more I think about it, the more I am afraid to see my brother again. It was because of me, because of my momentary indulgence, momentary obsession, and my momentary confusion, that I produced such bitter fruits for everyone. Tell me, how do I have the nerve to see my brother again?"

As Tutu finished speaking, our car just happened to exit the highway. I couldn't overtake a few long container trucks ahead of us for a while and had to follow slowly behind them. I couldn't find the right words to alleviate Tutu's distress, so I remained silent.

"Why are you always so hard on yourself?" my wife said suddenly. "Why not think that you probably saved your brother and Wu Huaiyu?"

"How so?" I interjected.

"Isn't it obvious? The Khmer Rouge killed so many people in Cambodia. Who could guarantee that Miller would still be alive today if he hadn't escaped back then?"

"That's true. But how was Wu Huaiyu saved?" Tutu asked.

"He was doomed anyway, if not killed in battle, then by their internal strife. Wasn't his battalion commander executed by firing squad? In my opinion, dying the way he did spared him much suffering. Moreover, even if he had survived to this day, he would feel more tormented alive than dead."

I had seldom heard such insightful comments from my wife, so I spontaneously applauded her, saying, "Very well said! It's indeed 'seeing someone in a new light after a few days.'"

"What? Only men can be smart and wise, and we women can only be long-haired and short-sighted? Three cobblers together make a Zhuge Liang; aren't we two women better than you, a man?"

"Of course, of course." I immediately went with it.

Tutu, seemingly pondering my wife's words, appeared to agree. Nodding her head as a smile appeared on her face, it was as if the knot that had been troubling her heart was finally untied.

Just then, a ray of the morning sun shone through the window to our right, casting a red hue on her somewhat tired face. In that light, all her worries and unease were submerged in the joy of the upcoming reunion, and her face, which had started to show signs of aging, now bore a blush of shyness like that of a young girl.

CHAPTER 25

We arrived at the Cypress Flea Market a little before 7:30 in the morning.

After finding a place to park, we entered through the east entrance of the market, masks on, joining other early risers who were similarly cautious. The vendors were mostly in place at their stalls, but some were still setting up their sunshades and others were unloading goods from their vehicles and arranging merchandise on the tables.

Customers, mostly of Mexican descent, began to enter in small groups. Some came as families, holding hands; others were in pairs, arm in arm; some pushed small trolleys, others chewed bubblegum. They didn't look like they were there to shop but rather to visit a temple fair.

My wife has a poor sense of direction and always struggled to find Miller's stall every time we came, so I led the way with the two of them following closely behind me. After walking westward through more than a dozen rows along a relatively spacious walkway, I was the first to spot Miller, who had already set up his stall and was sitting in front of his deep blue Dodge van.

"Miller's already here," I said, turning back to them and pointing in his direction.

As soon as Tutu heard it, she stopped in her tracks, as if at the brink of an insurmountable chasm.

"What's wrong?" I asked.

"What should I call him? Brother? Jochen? Master Wu Lou? Miller?"

"Don't call him anything just yet. See if he recognizes you!" my wife immediately suggested.

"Alright." Tutu nodded at my wife, exchanged glances with me, and then continued to follow me.

"Hi, Terry!" Miller called out, raising a hand in greeting.

"How are you?" I said, moving forward to greet him. "We brought a friend along today."

"Ah, ah, welcome!" he said with a smile, glancing toward Tutu.

Tutu then appeared from behind me and took a step forward. Looking at him intently, she said, "Hello."

Perhaps sensing something unusual in Tutu's voice, her gaze, or the somewhat strange expressions of my wife and me, Miller gazed back at Tutu but said nothing. Turning to me, he asked, "So, what are you buying today? The yard should be all set, right?"

"We're not buying anything today. It was suffocating staying at home, so we just wanted to get some fresh air and accompany this friend," I said, nodding toward Tutu.

Miller's gaze once again fell on Tutu's face.

His expression betrayed nothing; his eyes were as tranquil as an emptied treasure vase in the hands of Guanyin Bodhisattva, silently drawing in the woman standing before him. Her eyes already moist and her hands trembling slightly, she fidgeted with the hem of her clothes.

Without a word, Tutu took off her light green mask and held it in her hand, but she still didn't speak, just silently held his gaze.

After a while, Miller removed his own mask, nodded to her, and spoke in a whisper, "I had a feeling you would come today."

The voice was so soft it was easy to miss if one was not paying attention. My wife, as stunned as I was, blurted out, "Who is she? Do you recognize her?"

"How could I not know who she is? I could tell by the scent alone. But I felt a bit unwell this morning and almost didn't make it," he said, looking back at Tutu, his eyes so serene, yet so empty.

Tutu immediately burst into tears. Her tightly pursed lips finally parted slightly, and in a hoarse voice she called out "Brother." She then knelt down, wrapped her arms around his legs, and buried her head between his knees, her body heaving with the force of her sobs.

Miller, still sitting upright in his original posture, continued to have no visible reaction. After a while, with a loving smile, he extended his hand and gently caressed her head, like stroking a baby or performing an empowerment in Buddhist Tantric rituals.

Some passersby stopped to watch, but Miller didn't seem to mind and continued to smile lovingly and stroke her head.

There was no need for further explanation. They had reunited.

I rubbed my eyes and took my wife's hand. Her eyes, like mine, were shimmering with tears. "Let's go," I said. "We'll come back later. Let them have some quiet time together."

But my wife had no interest in returning to the market to browse those familiar stalls anymore. She walked slowly, continuing to look back at Miller and Tutu as they receded in the distance. Later, we arrived at a roadside with a grassy slope from which we could still see their silhouettes. Refusing to go any further, my wife took out two thin plastic bags from her handbag, spread them on the ground, and then pulled me to sit down.

A gentle breeze blew from behind us, the sun shone from the right, and pedestrians passed before us in an endless stream, but nothing could distract us. Both of us held our breath and gazed into the distance at Miller's dark blue Dodge, and the brother and sister who had just reunited in front of it.

It was a reunion that spanned half a century and the vast Pacific Ocean, achieved after crossing the swamp of suffering, suffocating longing, and all the spiritual and material barriers of the world. Though somewhat cruel, it was deeply moving. For a moment, I even wished my life could freeze right then—in this moment both cruel and blissful—forever.

As if to fulfill my wish, the figures of Miller and Tutu remained frozen there for a long time. Despite the distance, I could still see his smile, both compassionate and forgiving, ordinary yet wise, seemingly apathetic yet full of love, emanating from the depths of the soul.

But after a quarter of an hour or so, I noticed Tutu looking at Miller in a nervous way and calling out something to him over and over, while Miller seemed unresponsive, still sitting like a clay statue, smiling.

Tutu then started looking around anxiously, as if searching for us.

I quickly pulled my wife, stood up, and said, "Quick, something's happened!" We trotted towards them.

As soon as Tutu saw us, she said, as if she had grasped a life-saving straw, "Look, he seems to be … not moving!"

I stepped forward and waved my hand in front of Miller's eyes. Seeing no response, I put my hand near his nose to detect any airflow; his breath seemed barely perceptible, so I pinched his philtrum. Still no effect.

"Quick, call 911!" I barked.

My wife's call went through first. "The ambulance will be here in ten minutes," she called to me.

I then asked them to clear off the CDs and records from the plastic table, then lifted Miller and laid him flat on it.

In a panic, Tutu kept recalling the scene. "His hand suddenly slipped from my head to my shoulder, and I knew something was wrong. What's going on? What's happening? What exactly is happening? Tell me! Tell me now!"

"I don't know either. Could it be a temporary shock? Or a stroke? He mentioned feeling a bit unwell this morning."

"What should we do?" she cried. As dozens of people began to gather around us, she shouted loudly, "Is there a doctor? Any nurse who knows first aid? Please! Please!" But not a single person responded.

"What can we do? Is there anything we can do? We can't just wait like this!" she said, looking at me again, distraught.

"Maybe artificial respiration," I said, although I was hesitant. Firstly, I had never done it before, and secondly, this was during the COVID-19 pandemic, and I wasn't sure if he was infected with the virus.

"Can you do it?" she asked, but immediately mumbled to herself, "Could it be COVID? I've heard of people collapsing suddenly." Then she anxiously asked me again, "Do you know how to perform CPR?"

"Yes. Roughly."

"How about this? You instruct, and I'll do it!" she said, bending down and pressing her ear against Miller's chest, then looking at me pleadingly.

"Take a deep breath, go mouth to mouth, blow in without letting any air escape to create inhalation, pinch his nostrils, then move away and press hard on his chest to create exhalation." I had learned artificial respiration during my military service and now I remembered it.

After a slight hesitation, she bent down, took a deep breath, and forcefully blew into Miller's mouth while tightly pinching his nose.

She did it so carefully, so earnestly, so anxiously, so selflessly, so devotedly, it was clear that she had completely forgotten the dreadful contagion that had changed life on earth so dramatically. She continued, her face streaming with tears and sweat. If I hadn't pulled her away later, she might have continued indefinitely, using her mouth in place of his, her breath for his, and her life to save his. This scene brought back something she had told me some days ago, about how Miller had fed her water mouth-to-mouth when she fainted, and her words began to roll across my mind as if crushed by a stone mill: You fed me water, I returned you breath; some things are destined to be repaid, whether good or bad, kind or evil.

Unfortunately, despite Tutu's persistence and how much she disregarded her own life and death, holding onto the slimmest hope, her brother still did not wake up.

However, he appeared quite content with the way he had parted with his newly reunited sister, his signature smile lingering at the corners of his slightly open mouth, curling up like a crescent, his eyes squinting, with deep laugh lines spreading from the corners. A long white eyebrow hair caught in one of these furrows looked like a white silk thread that had been sewn on haphazardly.

The ambulance finally arrived with sirens blaring.

As I felt again near Miller's nostrils and touched his rough hands and feet, I was alarmed to realize that not only had he stopped breathing, but his limbs were starting to get cold.

With tears in my eyes, I shook my head at Tutu, indicating that it was futile.

Tutu refused to believe it was true, and only after the paramedics made the same assessment did she cover her face with her hands, let out a loud cry, and threw herself onto her brother, sobbing uncontrollably.

My wife rushed over and gently stroked her trembling shoulders. "Don't do this," she said soothingly. "Tutu, please, you need to look after yourself."

Once Miller had been taken away by the ambulance, a paramedic informed us he would be transported to a nearby hospital for additional tests to determine the cause of death. She told us to go to the emergency room for testing, to minimize contact with others, and self-isolate for a week.

She gave in to our repeated requests and agreed to let Tutu ride in the ambulance to the hospital as a family member. Once the ambulance left, I checked my phone; it was five minutes past ten in the morning.

We were ready to head home, but then I saw the dozen potted plants on the ground, the CDs stacked on the metal table, the square green stool beside the table, and the dark blue Dodge with its passenger-side door still open. I asked the vendors neighboring Miller's stall if they knew Miller's address, but no one did. After thinking for a moment, one of them spoke up and said, "He doesn't seem to have a home; he's been living in that car."

This was tricky to handle. What should be done with his car? If left unattended, it would surely be towed away to a car junkyard. But if Miller's belongings were still in the car, they needed to be passed on to his relatives. After all, according to Tutu, he likely had relatives in Cambodia. If they couldn't be found immediately, there was still Tutu. Though they were not related by blood, karma had brought them closer than blood ever could.

I walked over to the driver's side of the Dodge, peeked inside, and saw that the key was still in the ignition. I then said to a middle-aged vendor who seemed familiar with Miller, "The lady who left with the ambulance is his sister. They had been separated for nearly fifty years and only reunited today. I'm going to drive this car to his sister's house. If anyone asks about this car in the future, please tell them to call his sister or me." I then asked my wife to find a pen and a piece of scrap paper from her bag, and I wrote down my name and phone number along with Tutu's and gave it to him.

My wife and I then started packing up the plants, moving them pot by pot into the Dodge's back seat. When we ran out of room for the pots, we used a ladder to place them on the roof and then secured them carefully with rope.

After everything was packed up, I looked at my wife, who was already sweating profusely, and said, "It looks like you'll have to drive our car back. Do you need me to walk you to the parking lot?"

My wife took a look at the dust-covered passenger seat and the back of the car filled with clutter, shook her head, and said, "It's OK; I'll walk over myself." As she turned to leave, she watched as I turned the key several times before the engine finally roared to life with a weak "clunk-clunk" sound. Looking concerned, she said, "Be careful. Drive slowly."

I nodded. "You be careful too."

Then, driving with great care, I guided the wheezy, ancient Dodge van through the bustling crowds of the Cypress Flea Market. As I reached the main road and the traffic light turned from yellow to red, I suddenly felt a headache coming on. Knowing the wait would be long, I rested my head on the steering wheel and briefly closed my eyes.

It all felt so unreal. I never would have thought that the beautiful, moving reunion I had so eagerly anticipated would be over so quickly—or so cruelly—or that I would be left deeply involved in the life of both the deceased and his car.

The driver's seat was too far forward for my legs to stretch. Feeling cramped, I fumbled around, trying to move the seat back, but in the end I gave up without success. However, the car was filled with a light, sweet scent, reminiscent of overripe fruits mixed with a unique fragrance. It reminded me of a monk I had visited in my hometown during my return to China. I had smelled a similar scent in his tiny room, put together atop a fourth-floor roof of only five or six square meters.

I suddenly began to doubt the routine my wife had pushed on me, her insistence that I take frequent showers and wash my face, hands, and feet.

Not everything in this world needs to be cleaned with detergent, nor can every scent be produced by cologne spray.

Some scents seem to emanate only from the soul.

Without my wife and Tutu in the car, everything felt deserted. With my hands gripping the steering wheel that Miller often held, my ears taking in the uneven roar of the engine that Miller often heard, and my nose smelling the fragrant sweetness filling the car, I found myself on the verge of tears.

"What is more cruel than parting is reunion, more cruel than parting is reunion, more cruel than parting is reunion…" In Miller's case, how was it not so?

I felt a deep sense of guilt and remorse, thinking that somehow I had inexorably orchestrated Miller's death. Without my intervention, albeit unintentional, the siblings would not have had such a bizarre reunion that ended in forever farewell. Even though Miller appeared as calm as still water, without a ripple of emotion, his heart might well have stirred up a huge wave the moment he saw Tutu. Perhaps he had a history of coronary heart disease and hypertension, and his very excitement took his life!

The sun suddenly disappeared, and the sky turned gloomy, as if it too was about to cry.

I pounded the steering wheel—how could I not have thought of this?

This relentless guilt tormented me for quite some time, only gradually subsiding as I was about to exit the highway. That was when it came to me—what Miller had mentioned earlier: that he knew Tutu was coming today and that he had come despite not feeling well.

If his words, or at least the gist of them, were true, then perhaps the divine or Buddha eye had been opened for him, enabling him to foresee the future... In that case, his departure might not be seen as death, but rather, as Buddhists often refer to it, "rebirth." Or perhaps it was a piece of performance art dealing with religious enlightenment that he deliberately arranged as both a reunion and a farewell. The words "Zuo Hua," or "entering Nirvana while seated," flashed before me like lightning. Yes, it was "Zuo Hua"! I had often read such stories in *Biographies of Eminent Monks*, where death was not viewed as the end. Enlightened monks harbored no concept of death, for they had perceived the non-dual truth of emptiness and existence, life and death, Buddha and demons: it's Nirvana.

As I pulled up to our house's iron-fenced gate, I saw that my wife's car was already parked in the garage, and she was standing at the front door waiting for me.

I parked Miller's van, got out, and was about to enter the house when my wife stopped me and asked, "What are we going to do with his car? Should we drive it to Tutu's?"

"Let's wait. We don't know when she'll be home," I said, heading inside. Feeling physically and mentally drained, I collapsed onto the living room sofa, let out a long sigh, and murmured, "Alas, it really felt like a dream…"

My wife quietly took a seat beside me, muttering, "Maybe, maybe, maybe…"

"Maybe what?" I asked wearily, without looking at her.

"Don't you also know fortune telling? Could Tutu really be a jinx, bringing misfortune to any man she meets?"

"What are you talking about!" I said, sitting up to glare at her.

CHAPTER 26

Later that day, in the early afternoon, Tutu called us from the hospital, saying that Miller had been tested by the hospital, which ruled out COVID but only classified his death as "sudden." The exact cause remained unclear at the moment. I then asked Tutu if she needed me to pick her up. She said her son was already on his way to the hospital.

Nevertheless, I still preferred to believe my judgement and speculation that he had entered Nirvana while seated. This belief aligned more closely with my personal impression of Miller and his identity. Moreover, regarding the ending, it was in line with my expectation that he had already achieved the leak-free body, which, of course, served only as a metaphor. I believe that, over time, he became less attached to the realm of Wu Lou, increasingly letting go of it.

Regardless of its truth, the knot in my heart gradually loosened. And later, through my guidance, Tutu also began to release her guilt; bit by bit, she learned to stop blaming herself, thinking she was indeed a jinx who brought misfortune to men.

I felt somewhat happy; the deceased had passed on, and I wished only for the living to transform grief into joy and achieve physical well-being and a peaceful mind.

I soon delivered Miller's car to Tutu's house. She had washed all of his belongings, wiped them clean, and arranged the potted plants in a row against the wall. The Dodge was parked in the backyard. She also told me that, at the hospital, she had been handed the outdated flip phone found in his pants pocket. It turned out that he had no more than ten contacts, and she called each number to ask about him. Most were temples where he often donated plants and money and would meditate in a corner of the main hall for half a day or even an entire day. There were also two or three numbers for nurseries where he had taken odd jobs and sometimes purchased plants on credit to sell outside.

We also learned that Miller had no relatives or friends in the United States; he was a person with nothing: no legal status, no family, and no savings. Thus, my wife and I assisted Tutu in handling his funeral arrangements.

He was cremated, and his ashes were placed in a beautiful porcelain bottle that resembled a treasure gourd. I had often heard that relics sometimes appear during the cremation of eminent monks after they had passed into Nirvana. These are typically white crystalline substances, said to appear in the ashes of monks who had cultivated a high state of Buddhism. Most were bone relics, but I had personally seen tongue relics, which were slightly greenish. These items were both substance and evidence representing the Dharma. It is said that after the passing of Shakyamuni Buddha, his relics were worshipped by Buddhists from the surrounding countries and regarded as the utmost treasure. I was eager to inspect the urn to see if it contained any relics that would confirm Miller had attained the leak-free body.

However, with Tutu so grief-stricken and exhausted, it felt wrong to ask her to tamper with the ashes of her beloved brother. Moreover, I found this thought overly obsessive, so I finally let it go.

Miller was buried in Rose Hill Memorial Park, in Whittier, with his grave facing west, yet symbolically also toward the east, given the Earth's roundness—towards the land of his birth. Surrounded by cypresses and roses, a small white marble stele stands in front of his grave. According to him, his ancestors also had Chinese heritage, so the epitaph and the regular script carved on the stele were written by me with a brush and then engraved:

Leakers leak, non-leakers won't.

Meet, yet not truly met; reunite, yet soon to part.

Maitreya Miller, Miller is not Maitreya.

Miller Maitreya, Miller is also Maitreya.

CHAPTER 27

At Miller's funeral, I met Wu Fei—Miller's nephew, Tutu's son. He was a middle-aged man with bulging cheeks, dark eyebrows, and a somewhat protruding forehead. He spoke gruffly, and his brows were constantly furrowed, giving off an impatient vibe. Throughout the funeral, he mechanically complied with his mother's wishes, kowtowing when it was time to kowtow, burning paper offerings when it was time to burn, all while barely uttering a single word. I got the impression that he viewed his absent uncle as something imposed upon him by his mother and was slightly relieved that the person he least wanted to face, who likely had no desire to see him either, had bizarrely parted the world, almost as if to avoid it.

One day, about a week after the funeral, I woke up in the morning with a fierce urge to visit the casino where I used to work.

"You're still in the mood to play cards?" my wife asked, sounding a little puzzled.

"No, I just wanted to go for a casual visit," I said. To convince her, I handed her my wallet, keeping only my driver's license, and added, "If you're worried, you can come with me."

She looked me up and down as if she didn't know me, handed the wallet back to me, and said, "If you want to play, go ahead, just don't come home too late."

But I shook my head and didn't take back the wallet.

In fact, I hadn't been back to the casino for a long time.

I was fired. Someone reported that I had been inattentive in dealing, making many mistakes and occasionally even tossing chips that should have gone in the jackpot box into my own chip tray. Indeed, there were times when I accidentally put my own tips in the collection box. To this day, I haven't figured out how I could misplace those chips in plain sight. All I knew was that I had become tired of the job by then and was determined to quit, so my mind often wandered and increased the likliehood of errors. Perhaps I also felt that the chips, always flowing like water, might as well flow into my tray instead of the casino owner's box. After all, this was nothing back in my country. Taking collective and public property, such as corn, peanuts, or melons in the fields, or paper and envelopes from the editorial, for personal use was common practice and didn't seem inappropriate; people felt justified to do these things.

Of course, there was also the possibility that God had seen me indulging in the waters of wealth, getting lost and having long forgotten my mission as a member of the literati. So he chose this way to help a prodigal son return to the right path.

After I left, the casino underwent significant changes, adding a new building of more than ten floors to serve as a hotel and transforming itself into a convenient one-stop destination for dining, accommodation, travel, and gambling. I wandered around the lavishly decorated hotel lobby, then walked through a long corridor carpeted in red, and in a few minutes I entered the bustling gaming area that was so familiar to me.

The God of Wealth was still there at the entrance to the Asian area. I stood in front of him for a good while, pondering what was different and distinct about his features and his seemingly eternal smile compared with the smile of Maitreya Buddha. But suddenly, in my mind, I saw these smiles wondrously unified and gradually tranformed into a vivid, lifelike Miller.

And then it dawned on me that Miller's visit to the casino to play cards and his selling of plants at the flea market might have been a continuation of the Southern Buddhism that predominated Southeast Asia in the early days. However, he evolved it, just as Pol Pot of the Khmer Rouge had evolved Marxism-Leninism and Mao Zedong thought, Miller had evolved Siddhartha Gautama's "alms gathering" into "card playing for alms" and "trading for alms."

The Buddha is in your mind, as is the God of Wealth.

Thus, I thought that the so-called Maitreya Buddha or God of Wealth was, in fact, just a kind of paranoid perception in our minds. They actually coexist.

In "Ode to Lotus," the Northern Song dynasty philosopher Zhou Dunyi highly praised the lotus flowers for "emerging from the mud unsullied." But now I had a pressing urge to write an "Ode to Mud," which must include the words, "The mud is the lotus, and the lotus is also the mud; both are merely manifestations of emptiness, appearing as different illusions as one's state of mind changes, and one should not cling to either."

Before I knew it, I had walked up to the counter in the middle of the corridor where the casino's manager was on duty.

Years had passed, things had changed, and many of the people working there were unfamiliar to me. But this location is relatively elevated, making me feel like I was standing on the shore of a lake, able to overlook the myraid of lives within the gambling pool. Look, it was in such a small casino that people of all colors, races, religions, and ideologies from all over the world gathered every day and engaged in frightening yet silent wars without gunfire, of all kinds and scales. It was also like the United Nations assembly hall, except here, each resolution was passed not by a show of hands but by the number of chips in one's hand.

I looked out across the dozen or so card tables in the corridor and saw two long-time dealers I recognized. I waved to them, but they seemed to barely remember me. My gaze lingered on the card table where I first met Miller. The green velvet cloth on the table looked brand new, probably just replaced, but the chips looked much faded, although that didn't affect their value.

Next, I walked around the casino aimlessly and found that the rules had remained largely unchanged except that dealers at each table now rotated every forty-five minutes instead of the original half-hour. This was a very clever design; it reduced the downtime of the casino machines, allowing for more hands to be dealt and more money to be raked in.

For a moment, I had the illusion that I was sinking to the bottom of a lake of wealth, and all I could see, aside from the vines and stems of lotus flowers, the fish, and shrimp darting around, was dark and foul-smelling mud.

I considered myself lucky to have worked here, not only having experienced the oppressive and even suffocating sense of living in the mud but also having had the opportunity to witness and experience the unique lotus flowers blossom on the waters of wealth.

However, at that moment, I caught a glimpse of a familiar figure on the large television screen hanging from the ceiling. It was Tutu's son, Wu Fei. I had just seen him a few days ago. He was among a group that had broken away from the main protest and was engaging in vandalism, setting police cars ablaze, and physically clashing with the police.

I quickly reached for my phone and called Tutu, saying, "I just saw your son on the local news."

"I'm watching too. I already know," Tutu said, suddenly starting to cry. "How did I end up with such a son?" she wailed.

Just as I was about to comfort her, she stopped crying and asked, "You have a son-in-law who is a lawyer, right?"

"Yes," I said. "My eldest son-in-law. Why do you ask?"

"Can you come over? Please, I'm breaking down ..."

From her tone, it was clear she was in a desperate situation. "Sure," I quickly responded. "I'm on my way!"

Tutu's house was on the hill behind ours. Having been there several times, most recently to deliver Miller's van and attend the funeral, I knew my way well. It wasn't far from the casino, so I arrived in about ten minutes.

I rang the doorbell and heard hurried footsteps from inside. The door opened and there was Tutu, her eyes as red as those of a rabbit.

She welcomed me inside, and we sat in the living room. I took a seat on the three-seater, while she sat on the single-seater.

Tea had already been poured and placed on the rectangular glass coffee table in front of us. Without waiting for her to offer me the cup, I picked mine up and took a sip. Then I turned to look at her, inquiring with my eyes, "What's the matter?"

She moved her lips but said nothing; instead, she turned her head toward the wall on the side of the hallway behind me—where a noticeable bowl-sized hole appeared.

"What happened?" I asked.

"He smashed it. With his fist," she said nonchalantly. I looked at her with astonishment, and she continued, "Do you remember my brother's photo that your wife sent me? After editing it, I made a black-and-white portrait for the funeral. After the funeral, I enlarged it, printed one in color, and framed it to hang there. I didn't expect Wu Fei to lose his temper when he came home and saw it. He yelled at me, 'He's dead! Why do you keep obsessing over him? Are you trying to keep stabbing me?' I was confused and said, 'He is my brother, your uncle; how does hanging his photo here bother you?' This made him even more furious. 'Yes, yes, he is your brother. But I've never admitted that he's my uncle! Understand?' He added, 'You might not hear or pretend to be deaf. Don't you know that I was always picked on as a child? Called a bastard, of unknown origin?'

" 'What? Is there such a thing? How come you never told me?' "

" 'How would I tell you? To ask my own mother if she had that thing with a monk? Plus, I heard from my aunt that you left me behind to marry an American in order to find your brother in America. It's clear that your brother has always been more important to you than I am. For him, you could even abandon your own son. Do you know what I heard the most when growing up? People calling me a "little bastard," and worse, a monk's "little bastard"? I hate this man, I hate your brother. Because of him, I lost my father and almost lost my mother…When I think of all the insults and discrimination I suffered back home, I hate this person on the wall intensely. He not only killed my father, but also mentally controlled you. Yes, he might look kind and benevolent, but I find him even more hypocritical, rendering me unable to hold my head high and keeping you forever in his shadow! Do you know what the locals used to say because both my father and grandfather were born fair-skinned?'"

"'What did they say?' I asked, almost afraid to hear the answer."

"'They said my grandfather was the seed left behind by a white missionary; that's the only reason he could be so fair. Well, it was one thing for them to talk about my grandfather, but when they went around saying that I was also the seed of a monk, I could no longer hold my head high. I even feared encountering monks in my dreams, and whenever I heard someone mention the word "monk," I thought they were deliberately using it to insult me. But you, my own mother, treat this man as your savior, always thinking about him, missing him. What could I do? I could only endure, enduring all the way to my forties when he finally disappeared, like a tumor on my heart gone. I had thought that I could finally forget him and turn the page. Yet now you bring out this photo and hang it in such a prominent place in the living room? Do you know how I feel when I walk past that photo? I'm not going to lie; I've thought about burning it along with this whole house! Since you're determined to be against me, to make me suffer, then I just don't care anymore! From now on, I'm no longer your son, and you're not my mother. I'm leaving this house, and we'll each go our separate ways!'

"He then took hold of the frame and ripped it down, slammed it on the floor, stomped on it, and punched a hole in the drywall before storming off—and he hasn't returned since.

"What's all this about! Only then did I realize that he harbored such deep resentment towards my brother. His mind must be messed up; he's sick. No wonder he had to remove my brother's van in the back-yard, because it was an eyesore to him. Alas, all these years, I always felt there was some unseen fury inside him. Without an outburst, without causing troubles, there wouldn't be peace. I didn't expect this to be the reason. Actually, considering his hatred towards my brother for killing his father, deep down he knew that he was still a Wu. He just couldn't bear that I missed my brother. Alas, I finally came around; I just let him be. It was my fault to have given birth to such a cursed, sinful child. He could go out and find whoever he wanted, join whatever groups he wanted, even if he didn't want to work and only wanted to play video games all day or wander the streets; I wasn't going to bother anymore.

But no matter how much of a jerk you are, you can't go out on the street to vandalize and loot. America is a nation of laws; you can march, protest, and openly say that you dislike this president or that president, but you can't break the law. Just before you called, the police had already called, saying he had been detained and that we needed to hire a lawyer. That's when I thought of your son-in-law. I'm really sorry, but please help me. I'll cover the lawyer's fee."

She said so much in one breath. But it was hard for me to help with her request, so I told her candidly, "My son-in-law specializes in economics and trade law; your son's case seems to be criminal. However, I have a college classmate who used to work as a criminal lawyer, and I can ask him for you."

"Thank you, so very much!" she said, nodding continuously in thanks, nearly on the verge of tears again.

CHAPTER 28

In the aftermath, Tutu drained nearly all her savings to cover the steep bail set by the court for Wu Fei. His lawyer had fought hard to secure his temporary release.

Upon returning home, Wu Fei spent most of his time locked in his room, emerging only to eat, and refused to speak a word. One day, Tutu knocked on his door, but it was locked and there was no response for a long time. She found the key and opened the door, only to discover that he had already vanished ...

Tutu knew he had fled out of fear of being sentenced to prison, but she still hoped he would have left her a note or a clue to his whereabouts. However, after searching every nook and cranny of his room, she found nothing. Afterward, Tutu suffered a heart attack and was seriously ill, spending four or five days in the hospital.

When she was discharged, my wife and I went to pick her up and noticed that she had aged significantly, looking worn and absent-minded, repeatedly saying, "Ah, I slept too soundly that day ... I'm usually not like that; I thought he was still there ..."

A few days later, we took her to the seaside to help her relax. My wife supported her as they walked ahead of me along the shore. Tutu's spirits lifted slightly, a touch of color returning to her cheeks. Later, as we sat on a dry, flat reef, she turned to me and said, "Thank you for bringing me out. Honestly, when my brother left, it felt like my heart was hollowed out, and with Fei Fei running away, it feels like my soul has been swept away too ... Where could he have fled to? Back to China? But he suffered so much ridicule and shame there as a child, and his beloved grandfather has long passed away, so it's unlikely. Where else could he go? To Cambodia? No way ..."

"Maybe ... possibly ... it's hard to say," I replied.

"Ah, from now on, all I can do is continue to wait and hope. Fortunately, I'm used to waiting ... But why does fate have to treat me this way? Is my life doomed to be a constant search for fugitive loved ones?

As we watched the vast and boundless Pacific Ocean, with its waves ceaselessly beating against the shoreline, whipping up bursts of white foam that rose and fell, I was struck by a thought, and I blurted out, "Heaven's net is vast and wide, but it lets nothing slip through; human nets are tight and tense, but they have leaks."

· · ·

After some time, a newly planted peach sapling in the yard died from too much exposure to the sun and needed replacement, so my wife and I took another trip to Cypress Flea Market.

As we passed Miller's former stall, we both instinctively stopped. Although the stall had long since changed hands, I felt as though I could still see his presence and hear his laughter.

We didn't find a peach sapling, but just before we headed home, at a corner we saw a bronze statue of two cranes standing with their necks crossed in an embrace, a rare find in the U.S. People say that cranes are elusive; indeed, in real life, we seldom see them or hear their calls because cranes often come and go without a trace.

I stopped and gazed at the pair of cranes as if facing two acquaintances I hadn't seen in a long time.

I turned to my wife and said, "Honey, look at this one, its left foot, the little toe is missing a piece…"

She squatted down and touched the crane's damaged toe.

I then persuaded my wife to buy it for three hundred and eighty dollars. Upon arriving home, I immediately placed it in the yard, in front of the fountain, behind the iron begonia.

CHAPTER 29

After another autumn rain, the iron begonias were covered with water droplets. When I carefully pushed aside the clusters of red flowers and dense green leaves, I could see the long thorns on the branches.

Now, every morning when I open the curtains, the iron begonias and the pair of cranes come into view first.

I often have the illusion that they are representations of Miller's dharmic body, manifestation, and reincarnation standing there.

Whenever I see them, I touch my chest, feeling as if something that had melted off was frozen again and become as hard as those thorns.

For a while, I wanted to capture the impression Miller left on me.

I think: If he were to be depicted as a geometric shape, he would be a circle.

If described in a physical state, he would be both soft and hard, just like the iron begonia.

If represented by the marks he left behind, he would be a crane, coming and going without leaving a trace.

If portrayed by his demeanor, he would be ever-smiling, just like Maitreya.

However, I must also admit, in what we think of as the real world, he is still a "murderer," a wanted "fugitive," or a "homeless person."

At the same time, he had a more important identity—that of a monk or a renunciate

However, in a broad sense, who among us is not?

* * *

One day, when I was out on an errand, I happened to pass by Tutu's house, so I made a special detour to her door. From a distance, I saw her watering plants in the yard, about ten potted plants, all iron begonias, lined up along the wall on one side of the gate, their bright red flowers looking radiant and delicate. I parked the car by the roadside and rolled down the window to greet her.

Tutu turned and saw me and was very pleased, immediately inviting me to come inside.

"Your iron begonias are really beautiful!" I said as I walked straight to the vibrant cluster of flowering, bending down to gently touch the petals of a particularly large begonia.

"These were all left by my brother. I planted all the others in the backyard, but these pots, which I particularly adore, I keep at the entrance. And, I won't lie, it's strange, but every time I see these begonias, it's like seeing my brother; his voice and smile seem to emerge from these flowers. It's as if he never left, but instead transferred his life to these iron begonias."

"Ah, well said. I deeply share the feeling," I responded, nodding vigorously before asking a sudden question. "That day you saw your brother—did he say anything to you?"

Furrowing her brow in thought, she said, "I asked him why that white jade Buddha statue in our small temple was covered with a layer of mud on the outside. He told me that according to the master, the original abbot was a Taoist from China who later converted to Buddhism. His favorite saying was from the *Tao Te Ching*: 'Temper all the glare to mix in the dust.' It means that the finest things, including people, are safest when they blend into the light and become one with the dust."

"Is that all?"

"I also asked him if he had achieved the state of no leaks."

"What did he say?" I asked eagerly.

"He just laughed and said, 'Why are you still thinking about that?' "

"I said, 'Because I want to practice it too!' "

"He laughed again, gently patted my head, and said, 'Don't ask, and I won't tell. Once you ask, it's wrong, and if I answer, it's also wrong.' "

"Is that all?"

"That's all," Tutu said with an affirmative nod, but then she added, "Lately, while tending to these plants, I noticed that every pot has at least one hole at the bottom. I couldn't help thinking, Doesn't that mean the water will leak out? But if they were made without any holes, then the plant's roots would rot. The more I thought about it, the more confused I became, unable to grasp what the dharma of non-leakage that my brother wanted to achieve really is.

Her words immediately sparked my own reflections.

"What are you thinking about?" she asked. "Do you have an answer?"

"Oh, no." I was taken aback and then murmured, both to her and to myself, "I was just thinking that maybe there's nothing in this world that doesn't leak. Like the tea in a teapot, or the water in a vase; even if they don't leak from the bottom, they still evaporate from the top. Take the ocean, for instance. Although its water can't leak downward, it all evaporates upward, into clouds, fog, rain, ice, and snow … But then again, who can really say which way is up and which way is down?"

"Yes, doesn't an old Chinese saying go, 'The net of Heaven is vast, with large meshes, yet lets nothing through'? But when I think about it, wasn't my brother just a fish that slipped through the net? If there were no leaks my brother couldn't have escaped. So, even the finest net has its holes. Some leaks are invisible to the naked eye and only seen clearly through the eyes of the enlightened or the Buddha."

"That—" I couldn't quite keep up with the leap in her thinking and found myself at a loss for words, but after a moment I managed to say, "Maybe the dharma of non-leakage is essentially about neither being nor non-being."

· · ·

The pond sprouted spring grass.

When spring arrived, during a midday nap, I dreamt about Miller again.

This time, he was no longer an ice sculpture standing in the clouds, but a snowman sitting atop a mound of grass. When the sun came out, he was moved to shed tears that swiftly melted into a puddle from which a cyan-hued fish emerged.

After I woke up from the dream, as if there was a spiritual connection, Tutu called to say she would be coming by my house.

She brought me several books wrapped neatly in cardboard paper, saying, "I found these in the storage box in my brother's car; all are scriptures, the last things my brother put in when I packed for him back then."

I started to flip through them. Many pages were crumpled, and some were missing corners. There were texts in Cambodian and traditional Chinese characters, including one titled *Master XX's Quotations*. I skimmed through it and noticed there was a section dedicated to the practice of the dharma of non-leakage, so I read it with keen interest. Sure enough, I saw a page in the book saying that if a man practiced this method, he would be in the highest state of non-leakage if he leaked not a single drop of semen. I closed the book and thought, According to this, Shakyamuni Buddha, who was married and had children, would be considered leaky? Then I smiled slightly.

"What are you smiling about?" Tutu asked.

I gently tapped my finger on the book and said, "This book of quotations reminds me of the Cultural Revolution, when everyone in China studied *Quotations from Chairman Mao* daily. But after all, quotations are just quotations; removed from context, they are often one-sided and fragmented. Therefore, one shouldn't be too obsessive and serious about the practice of 'Wu Lou.' Moreover, words can't always convey complex things. Shakyamuni preached and taught Dharma for forty-nine years but later said that all he ever preached was to hold the flower on the podium. He also said that 'The dharma that I have preached is as little as the dirt on my fingernails, while the dharma that I have not preached is as much as the dirt of the Earth.' There are things in the universe that cannot be expressed clearly in words, that can only be understood by mind and soul."

"No wonder my brother didn't seem to think much about the dharma of non-leakage anymore."

"Maybe that's what the sutra means by 'gaining and abandoning the raft.' "

"What is 'gaining the raft and abandoning it?' "

"After a person crosses a river with a raft, would he keep it on his shoulders out of gratitude and not put it down in time? Therefore, the Buddha said, 'The Dharma has to be abandoned, not to mention those that are not the Dharma.'"

"I feel at ease now after listening to you. It seems that my brother had already cultivated his leak-free body, so I should feel especially relieved. Oh, I forgot to tell you, I asked a friend who has a relative working at the Phnom Penh police station. She helped check the case. Jochen's case has not been dismissed, and he is still on the roster of 'murderers' and 'fugitives.' Also, his parents are long gone."

"Ah, I think — it's time for us to let go too."

"I don't understand what you mean." Tutu stared at me with a look of confusion.

I told her, "Before you came, I just had a nap and dreamed about your brother, and guess what he looks like now?"

"What does he look like?"

"First, he was a snowman, and then he turned into a puddle of water and became a fish."

"How could it be like that? He should have already attained enlightenment; even if he didn't become a Buddha, at least he should still be a human being! Why would he have been reincarnated into the animal realm?" She paused, then said abruptly, "Write about my brother. He is not a murderer, and the truth needs to be revealed."

"The truth? Is there such a thing in this world?" I asked, smiling faintly. Then, with a slight note of apology, I told her, "Yes, yes, I will write about it. Not only will I write about your brother but also about Wu Huaiyu, about you and your son, and also about…"

However, I was slow to pick up the pen.

Without warning, I began to suffer from severe memory loss. Miller and Wu Huaiyu and many others were rapidly fading from my life, thoughts, and memories, leaving only a few blurred shadows…yet, strangely, Wu Fei's image was becoming clearer.

I was unable to grasp any part of history, nor could I understand the emptiness and nothingness that reality seemed to be. Even if I jotted this down in words, it might still have ended up being nothing.

I have also seen that life often discards what it deems inappropriate, and history continually discards some things while picking up other things.

One night, I sat on the sofa in front of the TV and watched a group of climbers on the screen. A gust of wind suddenly blew across the ridge, and feathery snowflakes went flying. Bearing witness to this, I felt that it wasn't just snow I was watching, but also language and words, which, alas, could neither be appreciated nor understood.

Then I thought of Miller and my friends who were in exile or fugitives, and I realized that the pursuit of Wu Lou is actually common among humans. Not only do religious people like Miller pursue the state of non-leakage, but business people also seek non-leakage of fortune, dictators try to block the path of free speech, preferring to "wrongly kill all than let one escape," and war planners always aim for "complete victory."

I also realized that I was thinking too much.

The snow on the screen served as a warning to me: many words are spoken and written in vain.

Nevertheless, I stubbornly completed my story and sent it to my friends at the relevant magazines and publishers.

And then, one afternoon, as I sat quietly at my writing desk in my study, I stood up and gazed down through the window at the bamboo garden, orchard, flower garden, and meadow I had painstakingly built.

New bamboo shoots were sprouting in the grove, and the begonias still bloomed in front of the fountain pond.

My wife was weeding in the yard, and when she saw me, she
shouted, "Honey, the tree needs pruning."

I misheard her, thinking she meant my new book manuscript
needed pruning. My heart tightened. Then my cell phone rang—it
was the friend who had recommended that same manuscript. He told
me that the magazine had decided to publish it in its sixth issue this
year, but the chapters on the Khmer Rouge and the Cultural Revolution would have to be removed.

"If those chapters are removed, does the story still hold?" I asked.

"Well, maybe," he replied. "You know how it is these days. Very
strict, very top-down. It's good that it's even getting published."

I was speechless.

"Are you going to prune it or not? Come down!" my wife called
again.

"Ah, of course, it needs pruning. I'm coming right down!" I
responded, rising from the desk and heading downstairs. Yet, I couldn't
help but grumble to myself, "Prune it, remove it, whatever—it's all
written in vain anyway."

THE END

Milton Keynes UK
Ingram Content Group UK Ltd.
UKHW042059240924
448733UK00007B/410

9 781960 172082